Ocean of Guilt

A Murder on Maui Mystery

Robert W. Stephens

For
Felicia Dames

Chapter 1
Selfies & the Decline of Modern Civilization

I got poked in the eye with a selfie stick. Yes, I realize that's a weird way to start this story, but it needed to be said. How else am I supposed to explain the fact that I had a patch on my eye for this entire tale? It's embarrassing and humiliating, but what could I do about it?

I hate everything about selfies: from the ridiculous faces people make to the inexplicable obsession with promoting one's self to the world. Trust me, people, no one really cares that much about you.

Things only got worse when someone invented that horrible little pole people put on their phones to get better shots of themselves. They're a menace to society. Have you ever stopped to look at all the idiots walking around like brainless zombies as they talk on their phones and essentially ignore the people and the world around them? I could write another ten thousand words on the subject, but I don't want to bore you, and I'm sure you already agree with me anyway.

I apologize for my rant, as well as my failure to introduce myself. My name is Edgar Allan Rutherford. My parents, God rest their souls, named me after the legendary mystery writer. The name Edgar was not an easy name to bear. Children can be vicious, as we all know.

My best friend, Doug Foxx, started calling me Poe during high school. The nickname was an obvious one, and I wished he'd come up with it earlier. I wished I'd come up with it, too, and had made the suggestion to him. Fortunately, the nickname stuck. Most people call me Poe these days.

However, now that I'm in my thirties (the latter half of that decade, not the beginning or even middle), I'm no longer bothered by my birth name, so you may call me Edgar if you wish. It's purely your decision.

Foxx changed my fate a second time when he invited me to visit him on Maui. He'd moved to the island after his short and disappointing career with the Washington Redskins ended from a nasty knee injury. He fell in love with a wealthy artist shortly after arriving on the island. His invitation to me came several years later. Actually, he'd extended me several invites. I just never took him up on any of the offers. I don't know why that was. Maybe the timing just wasn't right. I sometimes like to think that there were bigger forces at play, and the universe simply knew I wasn't ready for the massive change that was about to befall me.

Foxx's invitation, the one that I finally accepted, was twofold in its mission. The first part was for me to meet his girlfriend and soon-to-be fiancée, at least that's what he'd hoped she'd become. If you know Foxx like I do, you'd recognize what a huge deal that is. The man put the word "confirmed" in confirmed bachelor.

His second goal was for me to attempt to get over my stalled architecture career, as well as my failed romantic relationship. I'd come to dislike them both – the career and the girl – but I was having trouble getting past them. I tend to overthink things, which often makes it difficult for me to let stuff go.

In hindsight, the job loss was no big deal. It probably should have been, especially after all the years of schooling. Architecture wasn't what I thought it would be, though. I thought of the iconic buildings I'd seen with my parents during our travels abroad. These structures had stood the test of time, but that's not what I found myself working on at the firm. Instead, I'd toil away designing schools or warehouses or other large rectangular structures that were more about function and fiscal restraint and less about style and wonder. Reality always come crashing down on our dreams, doesn't it?

The failed romantic relationship was an entirely different level of stress and regret. The woman had meant so much to me at one point, but I'd come to question what I'd ever seen in her. She was not a nice person, and that's really all I want to say about her now.

Foxx is my best friend, so he naturally recognized that I wasn't being honest when I told him I was fine. He also knew that Maui was just the place to rest my mind and try to put the past where it belonged, firmly in the past.

Unfortunately, my Hawaiian vacation didn't go as planned. Foxx was arrested on my first night there for murdering his artist girlfriend. Everyone thought he did the deed, everyone but me, and I set about proving his innocence. It wasn't an easy thing to do because he did appear guilty. I wouldn't be honest with you if I were to suggest otherwise. There was also the inconvenient fact that I'd never conducted any kind of criminal investigation before. I knew Foxx, and I felt in the deepest part of my gut that he could never do what he was accused of doing. One has to have faith in some things. I'd put mine in my friendship.

I discovered something quite interesting about myself during the case. I'm pretty good at reading people and figuring out when they're not being completely honest with me, as well as their motivations for trying to keep their secrets hidden. It's like a giant puzzle just screaming to be put together piece by little piece. I enjoyed the process, which I realize might not be the best way to describe my feelings considering that my success or failure would result in my friend spending or not spending the rest of his life in jail. It was not a game, yet it felt something like that to me. I was matching wits with a killer, only I had no idea who that killer might be.

I did manage to prove Foxx's innocence, but there was also something else that came from the investigation. It was a big something, too. I fell in love with the detective who'd arrested Foxx. Her name is Alana Hu, and she's the gorgeous half-Hawaiian and half-Japanese woman I took with me to Italy to celebrate our second wedding anniversary. How would I describe Alana? Physically, she's a ten. She has long black hair and dark eyes that see into the deepest parts of my being. Emotionally or psychologically, she's even more impressive. She's highly intelligent and insightful, which is probably why she's so good at her job. She's also caring and considerate. Can you tell how much I admire her? Perhaps adore is the better and more accurate word.

Alana and I flew from our home on Maui to Florence, where we spent four nights exploring the beautiful city famous as the birthplace of the Italian

Renaissance. Our hotel had a rooftop bar with an incredible view of the world-famous Duomo. We hit all the museums. The David was, of course, the highlight, and we ate so much pasta that I was sure I'd gained twenty pounds. We also took a wine tasting tour in Tuscany. One must drink something to help wash down all that food.

After Florence, we took a two-hour train ride to Venice. I don't think I've ever been to a city as gorgeous as Venice, but it's beauty is compromised by insane crowds on narrow streets, overpriced everything, and the plethora of people obsessed with taking pictures and videos of themselves with no apparent regard for anyone else. I'd never seen anything like it. Don't worry. I won't go on another bombast about selfies.

In addition to its architectural wonders, Venice offered the bonus of being the home of Harry's, a bar known as a popular hangout for the likes of Ernest Hemingway. I wanted to see it since it was apparently the inspiration for a bar I co-own with Foxx in the Lahaina section of Maui. The original owner of our Harry's, a guy named Bart, opened the restaurant a few years before Foxx and I bought it. We decided to keep the name since the place was doing well.

The Venice Harry's was a bit surprising since I found it almost nothing like our bar with the sole exception of the name on the door. It was tiny inside and had drinks that cost almost as much as our hotel room. It was nice to say that we'd been there, but I had no desire to visit the bar ever again. Don't get me wrong. The staff was pleasant, but I shouldn't have to take out a second mortgage to order a Bellini.

So, where was I when I caught the selfie stick with my face? I was turning the corner to go to Saint Mark's Square when I collided with a young man who was apparently hosting his personal YouTube show. His phone, extended on the end of one of those vile selfie sticks, jammed into my left eye. The pain was excruciating, and I was completely convinced I'd lost my eye.

I was in a doctor's office an hour after that having various medications squirted into my eye. They put a bandage over it and then the aforementioned patch on top of that to help hold everything in place. I'm sure I looked ridiculous, but I was far more worried about the condition of my eyesight.

The doctor suggested I let the medicine do its thing for a couple of days and then have a doctor in my hometown check me out. It was a terrible end to what had been a wonderful trip.

Our journey home to Maui was uneventful, despite my continued pain. If you've read my previous stories, then you'll know what a minor miracle our easy air travel was. I tend to have horrible experiences on planes. The one thing that stood out on the journey back was the boat ride from our Venice hotel to the airport. The hotel actually had a small dock attached to it. The porter places your bags in the back of a water taxi, and then you take a thirty minute ride to the airport. It makes perfect sense considering the city is surrounded by water, but how many of you have ever taken a boat to the airport? Pretty cool, if you ask me.

Alana and I were beyond exhausted by the time we landed at the Kahului airport. She drove my Lexus SUV home since I still had the eye patch on. We live in a house on the ocean in the Kaanapali section of Maui, so it's close to an hour drive to get to our part of the island.

Foxx lives just down the street, and we decided to swing by his place to pick up our dog, who is named Maui. He's a ten-pound mix from a Yorkshire terrier father and a Maltese mother. The mischievous pooch has personality to spare. I was excited about seeing him, but there was a small part of me that was a bit apprehensive. The dog has been known to throw me serious attitude for leaving him. I think he suffers from separation anxiety, and he has no problem with letting me know how disappointed he is that I would ever consider traveling somewhere without him.

We pulled into Foxx's driveway and saw his vehicle in the open garage. Alana turned off the ignition, and we both climbed out of the SUV. I heard laughter and splashing a second later. Foxx must have been in his swimming pool. We walked into the backyard and saw Foxx in the pool with his two-year-old daughter, Ava. Her mother is Alana's sister, Hani. Foxx and Hani aren't married, nor are they dating. They're barely even speaking to each other if the truth be told. It's an unfortunate situation, but neither Alana nor I have been able to do anything about it.

Foxx stood in the middle of the pool while Ava sat on a large raft beside him. Maui the dog barked at them as he raced around the pool. He hates being left out of the action.

"She sure likes that pool," Alana said.

Foxx turned to us. He was about to respond to Alana when he saw the patch on my eye.

"What in the world happened to you?"

"I'm not sure you'd believe me if I told you."

"I'd believe anything if you were involved," Foxx said.

Maui stopped barking and ran over to us. Ava is his best friend, so his good mood at having her near him must have caused him to temporarily forget that he was mad at me. He jumped up and down and ran circles around my legs.

"Good to see you, boy," I said, and I scratched him behind his ears.

Foxx pushed the raft to the side of the pool, and Alana picked up Ava.

"You're such a beautiful little girl and you're getting so big," she said.

She kissed the girl's nose, which made Ava burst into laughter again.

"Seriously, what happened to the eye?" Foxx asked again as he climbed out of the pool.

I told him about my one-sided fight with the selfie stick.

"Is there permanent damage?"

"I hope not. I'm supposed to go to the doctor tomorrow," I said.

"I hope you took that selfie stick and rammed it up his…"

"Foxx!" Alana yelled. "There are ladies present."

Foxx turned and looked at Alana and Ava.

"Sorry, Ava."

"Just Ava? What about me?" Alana asked.

"Sorry."

I scratched Maui again. He'd rolled onto his back to let me know he now preferred a chest rub.

"Thanks for watching this little beast," I said.

"He wasn't a problem. Ava enjoys him."

"Is she spending the night here? It's getting kind of late," Alana said.

I knew what was behind her question. Foxx saw Ava at least four days a week, but she always spent the night at her mother's house.

"Hani should be here soon," Foxx said.

"Would you like us to stay here until she arrives?" Alana asked.

I couldn't believe she'd made the suggestion as I was about to fall over since I was so tired. Who knew when Hani would actually make it over? Turns out, it was just seconds later.

"Poe, I'm so glad to see you."

I turned around at the sound of Hani's voice. She walked through the backyard gate and then held her hands up to her face once she caught sight of my stylish eyewear.

"Oh my God, what happened to you?"

I didn't have the heart to go through the selfie stick story again, so Alana briefed her on my accident.

"But you're going to the doctor tomorrow to get the patch off?" Hani asked.

"I don't know what the doctor will do. Hopefully, my eye will be okay."

"This is terrible. I can't believe this has happened."

Her concern for me was touching, but I was beginning to suspect there was something else behind it. Hani is not exactly the most caring person. Don't get me wrong. I liked her despite her many flaws. We're all flawed in some way or another, and one must be careful not to throw stones at glass houses, if that's how the saying goes.

I've always strived to make our relationship a positive one since she's my sister-in-law, but there are certain rules or guidelines you should keep in mind when dealing with her. For example, if you want something repeated, tell it to Hani. Another example, don't ever automatically assume what she tells you is the truth. It probably won't be an outright lie, but there's almost certainly much more to the story than she lets on.

I think that's the main reason she and Foxx didn't work out. As much as he found her physically attractive, he just didn't think he could trust her.

"Wait a minute. You just need one eye to look through the little hole on the back of the camera, don't you?" Hani asked.

"You mean the viewfinder?" I asked.

"Hani, what are you talking about?" Alana asked.

"Poe can still take photos even with the eye patch on."

"I don't think photography is his biggest concern right now," Foxx said.

Hani turned to me.

"What time is your appointment tomorrow?"

"Nine in the morning."

"Good. You'll have plenty of time before the yacht leaves."

"What yacht?" Alana asked.

"I'm sorry. This is all just so stressful," Hani said.

"For the love of God, would you tell us what's going on?" Alana asked.

"The Lockwood-Calloway wedding. I need help. The photographer backed out this morning, and I haven't been able to find a replacement."

"You want me to photograph a wedding?" I asked.

"Not just the wedding. The entire trip."

"What trip?"

"They land on Maui tomorrow afternoon, then they go directly to the yacht. I'll need you to meet me at the marina sometime in the early evening."

"They're getting married on a yacht?" Alana asked.

"No. They're doing a one-week trip to the major islands. We sail from Maui to the Big Island, then over to Oahu, and we finish on Kauai. That's where the wedding will take place, at a resort in the Princeville section."

"I'm sorry, Hani, but I'm not shooting someone's wedding. I don't do professional photography," I said.

"I've seen your work. It's way better than most of the pros I work with."

I am a pretty good photographer, but I've never even seriously considered trying to do it for a living. Money tends to ruin many of the things it touches, and I have no desire for my love of the art form to be ruined by working with clients. I'd much prefer to stick to shooting tropical flowers, waves, and other Maui wonders like sunsets and waterfalls. Weddings or families and couples on the beach? No chance and no thank you.

"You don't understand," Hani continued. "They're paying me to have a photographer stay with them on the entire trip. They want to capture everything."

"Why did your other photographer cancel?" Foxx asked.

Hani didn't reply, which in itself spoke volumes.

"Are you dealing with a bridezilla or something?" Alana asked.

"I wouldn't exactly call her that," Hani said.

"What would you call her then?" I asked.

"She knows what she wants and what she doesn't."

"You mean she's picky?" Alana asked.

"Something like that."

"That must be one hell of a bill. A week-long cruise on a yacht followed by a wedding on Kauai," Foxx said.

"It's costing well over a million dollars. This commission could really set me up for a long time. I can't risk screwing this job up by not having a photographer."

"Have you thought about calling photographers on some of the other islands? They could easily catch a flight over here by tomorrow evening," Alana suggested.

"I've called twelve photographers. None of them have that much availability at such short notice. I even offered to double their rates, but no one will take the job."

So I was number thirteen on her list? I wasn't sure whether I should be insulted or not.

"I'm sorry, Hani, but I'm in no condition to do this for you," I said.

"Please, Poe. This job is important."

"I'm sure it is, but I just can't. I'm sorry."

I looked at my watch. I tried to calculate how long we'd been awake since leaving the Venice hotel, but my brain wouldn't work from the exhaustion.

"I need to take off. I'm so tired from the long flights that I think I'm about to fall over."

I turned to Alana.

"You ready?"

"I'm going to hang out here for a few more minutes. Why don't you drive the car back to the house? I'll walk and bring the dog with me."

"Okay. I'll see you soon."

I turned to Foxx.

"Thanks again for watching Maui."

"No problem. Good to have you back. Call me tomorrow and let me know what the doc says about your eye."

"Will do."

I said goodbye to everyone and walked back to the driveway.

It took me all of twenty seconds to drive from Foxx's house to mine. It hadn't been my intention to buy a house so close to his, but I'd spotted it on one of my morning jogs around the neighborhood. I'd lived with Foxx for a couple of years after first moving to Maui. I fell in love with the views from his backyard. It was just a stroke of luck that a house went on the market that had the same spectacular view of the Pacific Ocean. Alana and I had just gotten engaged, so it made sense to buy the house for us both. It was way bigger than we needed, and it cost a small fortune, but you only live once.

I took the suitcases into my house. We'd each packed one bag, but Alana had suggested that we bring two empty bags for potential purchases while in Italy. I thought one empty bag would be enough. I was wrong. Way wrong. We'd barely been able to cram our purchases into those two bags, and we'd even shipped a few larger items we'd bought, like a hand-blown glass vase from the island of Murano, as well as a few paintings and a large case of olive oil.

I wheeled the bags into the living room and pushed them against one of the walls. I thought about watching television for a while to calm my mind. Instead, I went upstairs and took a long bath to try to loosen the stiff muscles in my back.

I'd been back at the house for at least forty-five minutes by the time I climbed out of the tub and slipped on a t-shirt and pair of shorts. I was starting to wonder if I needed to go looking for Alana when I heard the door open.

I left the master bedroom and walked over to the top of the stairs. I saw Maui race around the house and inspect every corner of the family room and kitchen. He does it every time he's been gone from the house for a while. I think he's convinced that some other dog might have invaded his territory while he'd been away.

I walked down the stairs to talk to Alana when the dog ran over to me and did a dramatic roll onto his back. I kneeled down to scratch his stomach. I looked up at Alana. She'd just opened the refrigerator and pulled out a bottle of water.

"Want one?" she asked.

"No. I'm fine."

I stood and walked to the kitchen to join her.

"Have you been at Foxx's house all his time?"

"Yeah. I was trying to calm Hani down. She's really upset about this wedding."

"All because of this photographer-thing?"

"I'm sure that has a lot to do with it. She's completely overwhelmed. This is the biggest wedding she's ever done."

Hani became a wedding planner a couple of years ago after organizing my wedding to Alana. I'd been against the idea – her doing our wedding, not becoming a planner for other people – but I had to admit that she'd done an excellent job, even if the wedding did cost me an arm and a leg. Nevertheless, everything on this island cost a ton, so I wasn't sure how much I could put on Hani and her ease of spending other people's money. Her career had really taken off since then, and Alana had mentioned a few months ago that she thought Hani had reached the point where she needed a full-time assistant.

"A week-long cruise and a wedding on Kauai. I wonder how she landed such a big one," I said.

"Apparently, these families come from serious money. One is an investment banker from New York and the other is a doctor."

"How did she get hooked up with them?"

"I'm not sure you want to know," Alana said.

"What do you mean?"

"The family called several wedding planners and ultimately decided on Hani because she told them she specialized in large-scale weddings. She dropped the name of an investment banker whose wedding she did."

"Really? I didn't know Hani had done a wedding for a banker."

"Technically, she hasn't."

"So she lied about it?"

"Sort of."

"You're not making sense," I said.

"You're not going to like it."

"Just tell me."

"She said she did a wedding for an Allerton."

"She didn't."

"I'm afraid so."

"How did she even know that name?" I asked.

"I might have told her."

Time for a little aside. Allerton was my mother's maiden name. Her father, my grandfather, had been a successful banker who'd left her millions. My father was not an investment banker. He was an orthodontist who did rather well for himself. Nevertheless, he didn't come anywhere close to earning the kind of income my grandfather had. I think you could best describe that as being rich versus being wealthy.

Money never mattered much to my mother, though, probably because she always had it. The point is that she never touched her inheritance. The funds continued to grow, and they eventually made their way to me upon my parents' passing.

My relationship with that money has always been a bit odd. I'm sure you're going to think I'm certifiably nuts for saying this, but I never felt good about having the funds because I knew I hadn't done anything to earn it. For the longest time, I insisted on living off the salary I made on my own, which was mainly what I earned from my career as an architect.

I didn't really do much with the inherited riches until I moved to Maui. Actually, it wasn't until I got engaged to Alana that I even dipped into those funds. As I mentioned before, I lived with Foxx for a while, and the rent he charged me was practically nothing. I'd been living off the money I made from selling my modest home in Virginia. Once I got engaged, I knew I wanted a nice house for Alana, so I used a very small portion of my inheritance to buy it. I then used more to purchase Harry's bar. That was more out of my friendship with Foxx and my realization that he needed something like the business to give him a sense of purpose.

Alana knew where my income came from. Hani did, too. I hadn't realized that Alana had dropped the name Allerton to her sister, though. I knew my maternal grandfather had been a well-known and successful New York banker. It didn't occur to me that he would still be that known after all these years. Of course, maybe Hani's clients had never heard the name before but just made the assumption that they should have since Hani dropped it.

"Are you mad?" Alana asked.

"At which part? You telling Hani my mother's maiden name or Hani using it to score a big client?"

"Either."

"It's not a big deal. If our wedding can help her make money, then I'm fine with it."

Alana took a long sip from the water bottle.

"I'm going to head upstairs and hit the bed."

"Thank you again for our anniversary trip. I'll never forget it," Alana said.

"You're welcome."

She walked over and hugged me. If I thought she could have held me up, I would have been content to fall asleep standing there in the kitchen.

Chapter 2
The Wedding Photographer

Alana took me to the eye doctor the next morning. We had an appointment, but we ended up in the waiting room for over an hour before he called me. He was a pleasant enough guy, at least that's what I thought at first. He was maybe sixty years old, a little round across the middle, and he had a mostly bald head that was rimmed with short white hair. It was kind of a Jean-Luc-Picard-from-Star-Trek look, but he didn't pull it off nearly as well.

The good doctor tried to crack a few jokes as I answered his questions on how I'd gotten hurt. I supposed it was a rather absurd story. How many people do you know who get themselves injured with a selfie stick in Venice? His laughter didn't do anything to reduce the anxiety I was feeling as I waited for him to remove the bandage.

He pulled the gauze away and then immediately shined a light into my eye. I heard him suck air through his teeth, which wasn't exactly the sound I'd been wanting.

"Yeah, he got you pretty good," the doctor said.

I thought that was an obvious observation, so I didn't bother with my own obvious response, such as "Yeah" or "He sure did" or "Why are you being so darn insensitive right now?"

He pulled the light away and held up a hand in front of my face.

"Cover your good eye with your hand and let me know how many fingers I'm holding up," he continued.

I did as he instructed. It wasn't the clearest image, nor was it exactly sharp, but I could still see, mostly.

"Three."

"Very good. How's the pain?"

"It feels like there's something in my eye, like an eyelash or something."

"Your cornea's been scratched, and it's still healing. You should be okay, though. So, how was Venice? Is it worth the long flight?"

"I think so."

"Did you stay near Saint Mark's Square?"

"Just around the corner."

"Did you guys do one of those gondola rides?"

"Yeah."

"Shopping's pretty good, I heard."

Did this guy think I was his travel consultant or something?

"How much longer until my eye's healed?" I asked, trying to change the subject back to why I was there in the first place.

"I think we should put on a fresh bandage. Give your eye more time to repair itself. Let's see you back here in a few days."

"Can I stop wearing the bandage after that?"

"Probably so."

The doctor asked me a few more questions about Italy while he applied more medicine to my eye. Then he covered it with another bandage.

"Should I put the eye patch back on?" I asked.

"Sure. It will help hold the bandage in place. Looks cool, too."

This was definitely one of the oddest doctors I'd ever met.

I walked back into the lobby and gave Alana an update on what the doctor had told me. I left out the part about his nonstop questions about Venice and whether or not it was worth the price to spring for first class airfare versus business class.

We left the office and walked out to my BMW Z3 convertible. Alana looked at the time on the car's clock as we climbed inside.

"You want to stop by Harry's for lunch?" she asked.

"Yeah, I'm actually pretty hungry. I haven't really eaten anything since that wonderful airplane food."

"I had an apple this morning, but that's been about it since our flight. I still don't know if that was chicken or pork they gave us."

"Really? I thought it was fish."

Alana laughed.

"Might have been. It tasted like rubber, either way."

It took us about half an hour to get to the bar. In case you ever find yourself on Maui, you might want to swing by and check out Harry's. It's a few blocks off Front Street, which is the main tourist strip in Lahaina. Front Street is populated with a fun collection of art galleries, restaurants, ice cream parlors, and clothing shops. Foxx and I can afford the rent, but we like being off the beaten path.

Harry's is probably a fifty-fifty mix of locals and tourists who want to escape the crowds. Our food is decent, and the drinks are about half the price of other places. We could easily charge more and get away with it, but we just don't feel like it.

So, what does Harry's look like? It's been described as a dive bar. I don't know if I'd call it that, though. It's definitely a bit classier. The place is clean, and the bathroom walls aren't covered in graffiti and other nasty sayings one finds in those types of establishments. We have a large bar that runs the length of one wall. A few large screen televisions are mounted above the mirror behind the bar. The opposite wall has several booths with wooden benches. The middle of the bar is populated with round tables that can sit anywhere from two to four people. Most of the walls are covered with various photographs I've taken of the island. I don't try to sell them like other places. They're purely for decoration.

Foxx and I share an office that's off the storage room behind the bar. That's where Alana and I found him when we went inside. Ava was with him. She was sitting on a blanket on the floor, playing with a toy convertible I'd bought her that matched my own. I'd even managed to find the same silver color.

Is it weird that Foxx often brings Ava to the bar during the day? I didn't think so. She definitely enjoyed hanging out with him, and many of our regular customers showered her with attention.

"Hello, Ava," Alana said, and she kissed her niece on the forehead.

"You still got that thing on?" Foxx asked me.

I told him it was just for a few more days.

"So your eye's going to be okay?"

"Seems so. I got lucky."

"What are you two up to today? I would have thought you'd go back to bed and try to get some rest."

"The thought crossed my mind," I said.

"We're trying to get back on Maui time," Alana said.

"We're starving, too. I was hoping to grab a burger."

"We'll get Kiana to ring it up. What would you like, Alana?" Foxx asked.

"I'll just go with a salad," she said.

"And we wonder how she stays thin. I wish I had your discipline," Foxx said.

We left the office and sat at the bar, which was mostly empty this early in the day. Alana lifted Ava onto the bar top and handed her a stuffed elephant, which was her favorite object in the world. Good luck getting her to go anywhere without that thing.

Kiana came over to us. She'd been an employee at Harry's since the first day the bar opened. We gave Kiana our order after telling her why I was wearing a black eye patch underneath black sunglasses. I'm pretty sure she didn't believe the story about the selfie stick. I was starting to doubt it myself the more I repeated the tale. Of course, that might be because I kept enhancing the details each time I told it. By the next day, I'd probably be telling people I was injured fighting off a terrorist attack.

"Would you like a Manhattan, Mr. Rutherford?" Kiana asked.

"Sure, why not? I'm not driving."

"Ms. Rutherford?" Kiana asked Alana.

Alana hadn't taken my last name, and we'd mentioned that to Kiana a few times since she kept calling her Ms. Rutherford. Nevertheless, that was still the way that she preferred to address Alana.

Alana hadn't offended me when she declined to take my name. Maybe that would have bothered some guys. I didn't blame her, either. Hu is a cooler name than Rutherford anyway, and it flowed with Alana much better.

"Just a water, Kiana. Thank you."

"I'll get the drinks," Foxx said.

Kiana walked over to the register and placed our order while Foxx gave Alana her water. He started mixing my Manhattan, which had been my cocktail of choice for as long as I could remember. Foxx had given me beers before, but he'd never offered to mix me a drink. Was something up?

"I was wondering if I could ask you something," he said.

Here we go. By the way, I've found that whenever someone asks you if they can ask you a question, it's almost never a question you want to hear. I had no idea what he was going to ask me, though. In retrospect, I should have guessed, but I'll blame my slow brain on the jetlag.

Foxx handed me the Manhattan.

"Hani's been working pretty hard with this wedding planner thing," he said.

I took a sip of the drink. It wasn't the best Manhattan I'd ever had, but it wasn't bad. I put the glass on the bar and waited for the question to come. It didn't.

"So what's the question?" I asked.

"I was hoping you might reconsider helping her with this wedding photo gig."

I happened to be looking at the mirror behind the bar when Foxx made his statement. I say this to explain why I got an excellent view of Alana. She was busy playing with Ava, but I expected her to have a reaction to Foxx's statement. She didn't. Was I about to get double-teamed? I thought so.

"Did Hani put you up to this?" I asked.

"No. She doesn't even know I'm asking."

I turned to Alana.

"This was your idea, wasn't it?"

"What idea?" she asked, and she smiled.

"You assumed I'd have a harder time saying no to Foxx than to you."

"I told her it was the other way around," Foxx said.

"Oh, so you're admitting there's a conspiracy?"

"No conspiracy, but we both agree that Hani's made a lot of progress in the last year. I've never seen her so dedicated to something in her life. She really wants to make this work," Alana said.

I turned to Foxx.

"Are you and Hani on better terms?"

"I'm hoping we're going in that general direction."

He looked over at Ava, who was distracted by her elephant.

"I want to see Ava's mother succeed," Foxx continued.

"I only have one issue," I said.

"What is it?" Alana asked.

"I have the gear to do this job, but it's a lot for me to handle by myself, especially with this injury to my eye."

I turned to Foxx.

"That's why your butt's going to be on that boat with me."

"I am?"

"You're my assistant, pal."

"Love to, but I can't."

"Why not?"

"Who's going to look after the bar if we're both gone?"

"Kiana can do it. Hell, she's worked here longer than either of us."

"I'd love to do it," Kiana said, as she placed our lunches in front of Alana and I.

"Have you been eavesdropping on us?" Foxx asked.

"Hard not to. I'm only standing four feet away," she said.

"I think it's a great idea," Alana added.

"I need one more favor from you, Kiana," I said.

"Name it."

"Can you stay at our house while we're gone? Someone needs to watch my dog. I think he'd feel more comfortable if he was staying in his own house."

"I'll be with him," Alana said.

"Oh, I saved the best for last. I spoke with Hani this morning, and she agreed that you'd be a wonderful assistant for her. She's got way too much to handle on her own."

"You spoke to her this morning? When?" Alana asked.

"When you were in the shower. I'm not going to let Ava's mother fail, so I called her to tell her I'd shoot the wedding and the trip. There is one thing I found interesting. I got the distinct impression she was expecting my call. I asked her about it, and she admitted that the three of you agreed to gang up on me. Apparently, all of this was discussed after I went home last night."

"That girl can't keep a secret to save her life," Foxx said.

"Unless it's about herself," Alana added. "Unfortunately, I've got to get back to work."

"I'm sure they can give you a few more days off, especially after everything you've been through in the last months," I said.

I was referring to a rather large scandal in the department that Alana had helped shut down a few months before our Italy trip. The Maui Police Department owed her big.

"Well, all that aside, I'm sure there's not enough room on the yacht for the four of us," Alana said.

"There is. I've already cleared it with Hani. She has two rooms for us. I'll bunk with Foxx and you and Hani can have the other room."

"Great," Foxx said, but it was clear from his tone that he thought it was anything but.

"What about Ava?" Alana asked.

"Hani's already arranged for your mother to watch her," I said.

"Sounds like you have everything planned out," Foxx said.

"Pack your bags. We're going sailing, buddy."

Chapter 3
The Epiphany

Alana and I drove back to the house, and I immediately went to bed to take a nap. In retrospect, it was a bad move. I woke up three hours later feeling way worse. I climbed down the stairs and walked outside to the pool. I stripped off my shirt and hopped into the water, careful not to get my eye patch wet. I walked the length of the pool several times and hoped the minor exertion would help wake me up. It didn't.

I got out of the pool and let the hot sun dry me off. I looked at my watch. It was two hours before we needed to be at the marina. What had I gotten myself into with this photography gig? I spent a grand total of ten seconds trying to figure out a graceful way to back out of the assignment, but I knew I'd never be able to do that without ruining my relationship with Hani.

Alana came outside and told me she'd packed a small bag for me. I found that a bit odd. She'd never done it for me before, nor did I need her to. I was more than capable of packing my own suitcase. Then I realized she more than likely knew I'd pack t-shirts and shorts, and she probably thought I needed to be in something nicer to impress the wedding party. That meant I was probably doomed to wear white linen and khakis for the next week.

Kiana came over about an hour later. Alana showed her around the house and told her where all of Maui's treats, toys, and food were. The dog had never met Kiana before, and I was worried he wouldn't be too friendly with her and that he'd lunge for her lower legs. Fortunately, that didn't happen. It might have been the handful of treats she gave him that won him over. He gobbled them up and then flopped onto his back so she could rub his round belly. He always acted like he was doing you a favor by letting you scratch him. Ah, to come back in your next life as a well-cared-for dog.

We thanked Kiana multiple times for watching Maui. Then I walked outside after hearing Foxx honk the horn of his SUV. I'd already taken my photography gear and the two small suitcases out to the garage. Foxx helped me load them into the back of the vehicle.

"Is this going to be the nightmare trip that I think it's going to be?" Foxx asked.

"It's a cruise around the islands," Alana said, and we turned to see her exit the house. "Think of it as a free vacation," she continued.

"No. A vacation is when you get to lie in the sun and someone serves you Mai Tais while another person rubs your feet. I get to carry around a tripod for Poe."

"You should feel honored," I said.

"Really? That's how I should feel? What if I faked a medical emergency or something?"

"And what would that be?" Alana asked.

"I don't know what would sound believable. That's the problem."

"I'm not rubbing your feet by the way. Just so we're all clear on that," I said.

"Think of it this way. You're helping out the mother of your child," Alana said.

"Did Hani already drop Ava off at her grandmother's?" I asked Foxx.

"Yeah. Hani called me few hours ago. She should already be at the marina by now," Foxx said.

Normally, I would have made some crack about Foxx being able to count his blessing by not having had to go to see Ms. Hu himself, but Alana hadn't spoken to her mother in a long time. The topic of her mother had become a sore subject. They'd had a falling out after I'd been falsely arrested some months ago. My mother-in-law automatically assumed I was guilty as hell. Was I surprised by that? Not really. The lady had taken an instant disliking to me as if I'd belched in her face on our initial greeting.

I didn't know why she disliked me for the longest time, but I'd come up with a working theory. I reminded her of her ex-husband. He'd been a wealthy man who'd come to Maui and had swept her off her feet. Then he'd left her with two young children. I still didn't know what the source of the break-up was, nor had I summoned up the courage to ask anyone in the Hu family.

Nevertheless, Luana Hu had lumped me in with the rest of men and had assumed it was only a matter of time before I betrayed Alana in some way. My incarceration – even though I'd been completely innocent of the charges – had been her prophecy coming true. I'd obviously gotten out of jail, but the damage between Alana and her mother had already been done. I hoped it wouldn't be permanent, but I simply didn't know what to do to repair or bridge the chasm that had grown between the two women.

"It does sound like things are improving between you and my sister," Alana said.

"Maybe," Foxx said, and then he paused if as he were trying to recall their last few interactions. "I certainly hope so."

We got into the SUV and drove to the marina. It wasn't hard to locate the yacht. It was the biggest thing there. I'm not sure there are adequate words to describe it. It was truly magnificent.

Foxx parked the vehicle and we all climbed out.

"Have you ever seen anything so gorgeous?" Foxx asked.

"Nothing," I said.

Then I caught Alana's surprised expression out of the corner of my eye.

"Nothing except Alana, that is."

"I would think that goes without saying," Alana remarked.

Apparently not, especially after that look she threw my way.

"How big do you think that is, two hundred feet?" I asked.

"Maybe two-twenty," Foxx said.

"What do you think something like that costs?" Alana asked.

"To charter or to buy?" I asked.

"Either."

"I can't even begin to guess. Maybe two hundred thousand to charter."

"Certainly nine figures to buy," Foxx added.

We grabbed our bags out of the SUV and walked down to the dock. The yacht was even more impressive the closer we got. The hull was black and the topside was white. There were at least three levels above the hull. We saw a few people on the deck. They were busy washing windows. I kept waiting for a deckhand to appear and help us with our bags. Then I remembered we were the hired help.

Foxx grabbed three of the bags and I took the other two as we made our way up the gangway.

"I'm calling Hani and letting her know we're here," Alana said.

A woman in her early twenties appeared at the top of the gangway. She had long blonde hair that was pulled back in a ponytail. She was wearing a white skirt that showed off her deeply tanned legs and a dark blue polo shirt with the name of the yacht on the upper left corner: Epiphany. It was one of my favorite words. Why? Because how can you not like a word that means, "The sudden realization of truth"?

"Hello, you must be Hani's team," the woman said.

At least she hadn't called us Hani's employees, I thought.

"That's right," Alana said.

"I'm Kimi Lange, the second stew."

Kimi? Dear God, really?

"Hani's inside going over the itinerary with Angela, our chief stewardess."

"Is there somewhere we should put our things?" Alana asked.

"Just leave them here. I'll have one of the deckhands take them down to your cabin."

I wasn't sure, but I thought she said "cabin" not "cabins." I hoped that didn't mean they were cramming the three of us, maybe the four of us, into one room.

"If you'll follow me, I'll take you to Hani," she continued.

Kimi led us into the main room of the yacht. We saw Hani seated beside a woman who was dressed in the same outfit as Kimi. She had short gray hair. She stood to greet us, and I got a better look at her. Despite the gray, this woman couldn't be more than twenty-eight or twenty-nine years old. The more I studied her hair color, the more I realized it wasn't quite a natural color. It was almost a charcoal gray with a faint metallic look to it. Maybe it was some new stylish thing inspired by an actor or pop singer. Regardless of that, the look worked for her, and the metallic gray contrasted with her dark brown eyes. The woman had an intriguing look. I'd give her that.

"Good afternoon. Welcome to the Epiphany. I'm Angela Toppliff."

Hani stood as well.

"This is Alana. She'll be assisting me," Hani said.

"Hello," Alana said, as she shook Angela's hand.

I didn't have a good enough angle on Alana to catch her facial expression after Hani had introduced her as her assistant. I assumed Hani didn't want to mention that they were sisters, although that was obvious just by looking at the two women standing beside each other. Nevertheless, Hani was obviously trying to pass off her business as being bigger than it currently was. We all have to start off somewhere, and I was impressed with what she'd accomplished in two short years. Here we were on a super yacht, catering to clients who apparently represented the one percent.

"This is Poe. He'll be the photographer, and this is his assistant, Doug Foxx."

"Nice to meet you," Foxx grumbled.

I caught Angela staring at me and it wasn't hard to figure out why.

"I guess you're wondering about the eye patch," I said.

Angela didn't respond. Maybe she was too polite, or maybe the sight of a one-eyed photographer was too much to comprehend. I knew I was going to feel ridiculous explaining the eye patch thing, but now I realized the word ridiculous didn't even begin to capture how uncomfortable I felt. It was like I was living one of those dreams where you suddenly realize you're completely naked in a room full of people who all have their clothes on.

"I'll be fine," I continued.

"I'm sure," Angela said, but it was clear she wasn't even remotely sure.

She turned to Kimi.

"Could you give these three a tour? They're going to need to know their way around if they're going to be documenting this cruise."

"Of course."

We spent the next forty-five minutes making our way through the yacht. Kimi started our tour on the main level where we met Angela.

"This is the main lounge we're currently standing in. It has a bar area there in the back. On the deck on the opposite side of the lounge is where the guests have their meals. Let's head over to the galley and say hello to the chef."

Kimi led us through the lounge and down a short hallway that opened to the galley. Before we got there, though, we ran into another young woman who was dressed identically to Kimi and Angela. At around five-foot-five and one hundred and twenty pounds, she was about the same height and weight as Angela Toppliff, but she had black hair that was pulled into a ponytail that ran almost the length of her back. At the risk of sounding like I was objectifying these ladies, it was obvious the owner of the yacht had hired three very attractive women to cater to his guests. Did I expect anything different? Of course, not.

"This is Angela Banks, our third stew," Kimi said.

"Another Angela," Foxx said.

"Yes. Most people just call me Banks. Less confusing that way."

"Nice to meet you, Banks," Alana said.

We said goodbye to Banks and continued to the galley. It was much smaller than I expected. We saw a forty-something-year-old man wearing a white chef's jacket and black pants. He was average height and on the skinny side, which I found pretty rare for a chef. He had jet black hair like Banks and dark eyes. He looked like he was from India. He was busy chopping vegetables.

"This is Baakir Rajan. He's our chef," Kimi said.

Chef Rajan looked up at us and smiled, but he continued to chop away. I didn't know how he managed not to slice off one of his fingers.

"Please, call me Bucky," he said through a thick Indian accent.

Bucky? Was he serious?

"Can I ask how you got that nickname?" Alana said.

"Kurt could never pronounce my name, so he started calling me Bucky. The guests seem to like it."

"Kurt's our bosun," Kimi clarified.

"But Baakir is such a beautiful name. Do you mind if we call you that?" Alana asked.

"I would be honored. And your name is?"

"I'm Alana. This is Poe and Foxx."

"Nice to meet you," Bucky, or Baakir, said.

As a side note, he didn't seem to notice my eye patch or maybe he had enough manners not to mention it. Maybe he was just busy with prepping the dinner.

We spoke with the chef for a few more minutes. He told us some of the meals he planned on serving. It all sounded delicious. I assumed we wouldn't be dining with the guests, so I had no idea what kind of meals we'd be having. Maybe we'd get their leftovers. Perhaps we'd be forced to fend for ourselves.

"Let's make our way to the next deck," Kimi said.

The level above the main deck had a small swimming pool and an attached whirlpool near the stern. I could picture Alana and me relaxing in it and looking out at the deep blue waters of the Pacific. Unfortunately, the only thing I was going to be really looking at was the viewfinder of my Canon camera.

We walked inside and found another lounge with another bar and a small reading area with two bookcases filled with hardback and paperback books. There was a workout room behind the lounge that consisted of a recumbent exercise bike, an elliptical machine, and one of those weight machines that can be converted for different exercises. The small gym had floor-to-ceiling windows on three sides so you could get great views while doing your military presses.

"There's a tanning deck on the opposite side of the lounge near the bow. It's also a great place to take a nap," Kimi said.

"How long have you worked on this yacht?" I asked.

"A few years now. I started out as third stew but moved my way up after the second stew went to culinary school."

"How do you like it?" Foxx asked.

"It's hard work, but the tips are worth it. You can't beat the views either. Would you like to meet the captain?"

"Sure," Alana said.

Kimi took us to the top level, which was the bridge. There was only one man inside. He was maybe sixty-years-old. He was my height at around six-two, but he was about thirty pounds lighter, which made him rail thin.

"This is Captain Piadelia. Captain, this is the team that came on board with the wedding planner."

Piadelia turned to us, and his eyes instantly bypassed Foxx and me and landed squarely on Alana.

"Vincenzo Piadelia at your service," he said, and he kissed Alana's hand.

I couldn't tell whether the Italian accent was authentic or just an attempt to impress the ladies. What did I think of him kissing Alana's hand? Was it a smooth move? Not really, especially since I caught him checking out Alana's body later in the conversation while she was looking out the window of the bridge.

I'm sure it didn't occur to him that she was married to the one-eyed wedding photographer or maybe he simply didn't care. Italian men have a reputation for being rather obvious when it comes to their admiration of the female form. I was tempted to say something to him, but I didn't want the cruise to get off to a rough start. Instead, I kept a fake smile plastered on my face and listened to him recount all the years he'd spent yachting. I wish I could say it made for fascinating listening, but it didn't.

I faked getting a text message and took a quick look at the blank display on my phone.

"It's Hani. She wants us to come back to the main deck," I said.

Kimi thanked the captain for his time. Piadelia ended the conversation by inviting Alana to join him on the bridge whenever she liked so he could show her how the controls worked. Yeah, I'm sure that's exactly what he wanted he do.

There were others we met on our tour of the yacht, including a first mate, an engineer, and a couple of deck hands, but those people played minor roles in this mystery tale to come. I have no wish to overwhelm you with names and descriptions.

As we made our way down the narrow staircase that would lead us back to the main lounge, Angela's voice came over Kimi's walkie-talkie.

"The guests have landed in Kahului. They'll be here in an hour."

Kimi grabbed her radio and held it up to her mouth.

"Copy," she said.

She turned to us.

"I better show you to your cabin now. I need to change into my whites for the guests."

"Your whites?" Foxx asked.

"Dress uniform. We wear it to greet the guests. It's part of the VIP treatment."

"When you say cabin, do you mean we each get our own?" I asked.

"Oh no, there's not enough room with all the guests. Don't worry, though. We have a couple of air mattresses we've brought into your room."

"Air mattress?" Foxx asked.

"It's not as uncomfortable as it sounds. Besides, Hani never told us she was bringing so many people with her."

Foxx turned to me.

"Maybe I should disembark now and give you guys more space in the cabin."

"Not a chance, pal. You're my assistant. Don't you remember?"

Chapter 4
Cher, Madonna, Prince, Poe

Kimi took us to our cabin and it was as small as I feared. There was a full-size bed that took up ninety percent of the room. Two deflated air mattresses sat on top of the bed. It would have been a tight fit, even if it was just Alana and I, but I knew that Foxx and I would be gentlemen and give the Hu sisters the bed. The worst part of it all? There was just one small bathroom.

Someone, presumably Kurt the bosun, had placed our small suitcases on the bed beside the air mattresses. Alana grabbed the bag and placed it near the foot of the bed since she hates putting bags on the bed. She unzipped my bag and, sure enough, I saw a white linen shirt and khaki pants on top. Alana grabbed them and handed them to me.

"You should put these on if we're going to be meeting Hani's clients."

"What's wrong with what I'm already wearing?" I asked, but let's be real. I already knew the answer to that question.

"You're wearing a black surf t-shirt that says 'Pirates Bar and Grill.' That's what's wrong."

"I thought it went with the eye patch."

"I thought so, too," Foxx laughed.

I looked around the room. Then I turned to Foxx.

"Which part of the floor do you want?" I asked.

"The side closest to the bathroom. I don't feel like tripping over anyone in the middle of the night."

"I don't see how you're going to avoid that," Alana said.

She zipped my bag back up and opened hers. She rooted through it and removed a white dress. I'd seen her in it before. It hugged her body in all the right places, if I may use that old expression.

"You're wearing that?" I asked.

"What's wrong with it?"

"Nothing, it's just that…"

"Just what?"

"I think what Poe's trying to get at is he doesn't want you to tempt the captain any more than you have already," Foxx said.

"What does that mean?"

"Come on, Alana. You didn't see how that dude was ogling you? I thought I was going to have to step in front of him before Poe broke his jaw."

"He wasn't ogling me," she protested.

"If you say so," Foxx said.

Alana turned to me.

"Do you think he was looking at me funny?"

"There was nothing funny about it," I said.

Alana looked at the dress in her hand.

"Well, Hani specifically asked me to wear dresses on the cruise."

"We wouldn't want to disappoint Hani, now would we?" I asked.

"Look, I understand this isn't the ideal circumstance."

"You can say that again," Foxx remarked.

"Just remember what we're here for," Alana said.

"Oh, I won't forget," I said.

The door opened, and Hani entered. Her eyes immediately went to the dress in Alana's hand.

"You're wearing that?" she asked.

"God, not this again," Foxx said.

"What?" Hani asked.

"Is there something wrong with this dress?" Alana asked.

"No. I think it looks good. I have a black one that's a similar style. They'll look good together."

Hani turned to Foxx and me.

"What are you two wearing?"

"I have Poe in a linen shirt and khaki pants," Alana answered for me.

Apparently, I now had a stylist.

"And you?" Hani asked Foxx.

"Do you guys even need me tonight? We're not taking photos tonight, are we?"

"Tiffany wants shots of her and Reese on the front of the boat as we make our way to the Big Island."

Hani turned back to me.

"Is there any way you can lose the eye patch and just wear dark sunglasses?"

"It's the health of his eye, Hani. He needs the patch for a few more days. They're just going to have to accept it," Alana said.

"All right. Sorry for asking."

Hani looked around the room.

"God, this place is really tight."

"You haven't been down here before?" I asked.

"Just for a second, but I was the only person then. It's a bit cramped now that we're all in here."

I thought that was an understatement, but it was pointless to debate just how jammed we were in this place. It was going to make for a miserable week. I made a mental note to stay on the deck as much as possible.

"Do you know what time they want to do the photos?" I asked.

"We didn't talk about it. What time do you suggest?"

"Probably just before sunset. We can put the sun behind them. Should look really nice."

"Sounds good. I'll mention that to her."

"Just how difficult is Tiffany?" Alana asked.

Hani rolled her eyes.

"I don't think I've ever encountered anyone like her before."

"Have you guys met in person yet?" Alana asked.

"No. Just phone calls and emails. I'm pretty nervous. I don't mind telling you that."

"I'll go with you if you want when they come aboard. That will give Poe time to set up his gear."

"Thanks. I appreciate it."

Hani went into the bathroom to change. I took the opportunity to slip out of my shorts and into the khakis. Hani came out after a few minutes, and then Alana went in to change into her white dress.

Something interesting happened while I waited for Alana to come out. I caught Foxx checking out Hani. She had her back to him while she was doing her makeup in a tiny mirror she removed from her purse. He clearly looked at her backside and then I watched as his eyes moved up her body. They paused when they got to the top. Then they moved back down and stopped at the same place they'd started. The whole thing had lasted a good four or five seconds, and I assumed Hani had been oblivious to it all.

Foxx snapped out of his trance when he heard the bathroom door open. Alana stepped out.

"Don't you look nice," Hani said.

"Yes, indeed," I said.

"Thank you."

Hani checked the time on her cell phone.

"They should be here any minute. We should go greet them."

"Okay," Alana said.

"Shoot me a text when you find out if they're good with the sunset photos," I said.

Hani nodded.

"See you in a little while," Alana said.

The sisters left the cabin. Foxx shut the door behind them and then plopped on the bed. I feared his massive physique might break the frame.

"I think I'm going to try to get an hour or so of sleep," he said.

Foxx closed his eyes as I started pulling lenses out of my camera bag.

"You weren't kidding when you said you and Hani were getting along better," I said.

"What do you mean?" he asked without opening his eyes.

"I think you know."

"No. I don't. That's why I asked."

"I saw you checking her out. You reminded me a bit of our good Italian yacht captain."

"That's ridiculous. I didn't check her out."

"If you say so."

Foxx opened his eyes.

"What exactly do you think you saw?"

"There's no uncertainty about it. Your eyes burned a hole in that dress of hers."

"You're crazy, man."

"I'm not judging. Hani's a good looking woman. I get it."

"No. You don't get it. There's nothing going on between us."

"I didn't say there was, but you're thinking about it."

Foxx closed his eyes again.

"I'm going to sleep. Wake me if you need my help later."

"You got it."

It had been a fascinating conversation. Foxx is an honest guy and I didn't think he ever lied to me. That left me with one conclusion. He was lying to himself, or better yet, maybe his conscious mind hadn't registered what his subconscious mind already knew. His feelings for her were changing again. I didn't know why, but it sure seemed like they were. Of course, I could have been getting it all wrong, and what I saw was nothing more than a man admiring the very admirable figure of a beautiful women.

I blew up the air mattresses while Foxx slept. How did I know he was asleep? Because he snored so loudly that the walls were shaking. I placed one air mattress on the floor between the bed and the bathroom. I placed the other mattress at the foot of the bed. You couldn't see one square inch of floor between the regular bed, the air mattresses, and the luggage.

I spent the next thirty minutes scanning through fashion photos I'd downloaded onto my phone. I studied the camera framing and poses so I could do my best to fake that I was a professional photographer.

Alana eventually texted me and told me to come to the main deck. I grabbed my camera and was about to leave the room when a second text from her came through: This lady is crazy.

"Great."

"What? What did you say?"

I turned around and saw Foxx starting to wake.

"Nothing. Go back to sleep."

Foxx closed his eyes and was asleep again within a few seconds. I didn't know how he did it, and I envied the ability.

I walked back to the main level and spotted Alana and Hani in the lounge. They were talking to a woman who was at least five or six inches taller than them, which would put her close to six feet. She had long dark hair that hung below her shoulders. She wore a white dress shirt that had several of the top buttons open to reveal a tan tank top underneath. She also had on black shorts that might have doubled as a bikini bottom if they'd been any shorter. Had she been wearing that on the plane ride? It's amazing what people wear on flights these days. We'd definitely moved beyond the golden days of air travel.

There was a guy beside her who looked to be about six-foot-four. He had short blonde hair and was deeply tanned as if he'd spent a lifetime on the beach or a fortune in the tanning salon. He had on a light blue polo shirt that was the same color as his eyes, tan shorts, and leather sandals.

There were no others guests in the lounge, so I assumed everyone else had gone down to their cabins, which were in a different section of the yacht to ours.

I subconsciously lifted my hand to my eye patch as I got closer to them. I don't know why I did it. It was clearly still there. I walked over to the group and stood beside Alana. My Canon 5D camera was in one hand and my smaller camera bag was slung over one shoulder.

Hani looked over to me. I assumed she was about to introduce me, but she didn't. She looked terrified.

"This is Poe. He's going to be your photographer for the week," Alana said.

"Are you wearing an eye patch?" the woman who I assumed was Tiffany asked me.

I guessed the question was a rhetorical one since I wasn't sure what else could have been covering my eye.

"I had a little accident in Venice, Italy, but I'll be fine to take your photographs," I said.

Tiffany turned to Hani.

"You're not serious, are you? What happened to the other guy?"

"He couldn't make it," Hani said.

"He couldn't make it," Tiffany repeated. "What's that supposed to mean?"

"He had something come up," Hani said.

"So he cancelled on us. Who does that? Why didn't you say anything?"

"I didn't want to mention it until I had a replacement. Poe agreed to the shoot just this morning. By then you were on the plane."

"So this guy is the fourth-string photographer?" she asked.

"Now wait a minute," Alana said.

"Who asked for your opinion? This is my wedding. It's the most important time of my life, and you're bringing me a one-eyed photographer."

I thought about pointing out to her that it was technically not just "her" wedding since the groom had some role to play even if she deemed it an insignificant one. I glanced out the window and saw the yacht was already underway, so it wasn't like I could walk off the boat and head home. I assumed this trip had the potential to be a disaster, but I didn't expect it to get off to such a rough start. In retrospect, I'd been naïve.

"What was your name again?" Tiffany asked.

"Poe."

"Poe what?"

"Just Poe," I said.

I don't know why I didn't want this obscene woman to know my last name or my real first name for that matter. Maybe I'd subconsciously thought I needed to protect some part of myself from her insults.

"What's with the one name? Are you supposed to be like Cher or Madonna?" Tiffany asked.

"No. More like Prince, except taller."

"So you're a smart ass, too?"

In full disclosure to you readers, this wasn't the first time I'd been called that, and it had been a very snarky reply I'd made. Still, I thought I was more than justified given the woman's poor behavior.

"Why don't we do this? Let me take your photograph in a few minutes. The light is just about perfect. If you don't like them, I'll be off this boat tomorrow when we reach the Big Island. I'll personally find you another photographer. But if you do like the photographs, I'll stay with you for this trip."

Tiffany didn't answer immediately. I kept waiting for her fiancée to say something, but he never did. Maybe he knew when to keep his mouth shut.

She finally said something after several long and excruciating seconds.

"Fine. We'll meet you in ten minutes."

"Not we. Just you. I'll take photos of you and your fiancée tomorrow. Tonight I want to concentrate on you."

Tiffany couldn't help herself, and I spotted a very small smile on her face.

"What would you like me to wear?" she asked.

"Something dark to contrast with the colors of the setting sun. There's a nice breeze outside so wear something flowy."

I didn't wait for a reply. Instead, I left the lounge and headed for the area I'd scouted earlier, and I began to go over my equipment a second time.

Alana joined me a few minutes later.

"You have a gift," she said.

"A gift?"

"For knowing how to manipulate people."

"That's a strong word, and it doesn't sound like a compliment."

"I meant it as one."

"She's a narcissist of the highest order. All she really wants is someone to kiss her ass. You just can't act like you're trying to do it. You have to push back some but not too hard."

"I'm sorry you're having to go through this."

"It's not just me. What about you?" I asked.

"You have no idea how much I wanted to slap handcuffs on that woman."

"Handcuffs? Did you bring yours?"

"No, but now I'm regretting that decision."

"Do you think anyone here has any idea you're a cop?"

"I don't see how."

Alana looked past me at the sky. It was just starting to turn a mixture of red and orange.

"Do you think you can impress her with these shots?" Alana asked.

"God's providing the light and the scenery. All I have to do is make sure the shots are in focus."

"I think you have to do more than that."

"What's to worry about? It's not like someone is pointing a gun at us."

"That's a nice change, isn't it?"

"It is. It is indeed."

Chapter 5
The Photoshoot

So, how did the photoshoot go? About as well as I could have possibly hoped. Tiffany was a few minutes later than she said she would be, actually several minutes later, but the light was still good. She took my advice and wore a long dark dress, a black one to be precise. It caught the soft ocean breeze as I thought it would. The billowing movement of the garment made for some dynamic compositions. I didn't need to coach her much in regards to posing. She seemed a natural at it. She was probably used to having her photograph taken, or maybe she was used to taking it herself. God, more selfies.

I know I gave a brief description of her earlier, but perhaps now is a better time to fill in some of the other details. She was an attractive woman with dark eyes. They weren't quite as dark as Alana's, but they were close. Her lips were thin, almost too thin, but her nose was perfect to the point that I thought it might have been cosmetically shaped. That, of course, made me question why she hadn't done the lips, too, and it was at that moment that I realized I might have been overthinking things. That's a bad habit of mine by the way.

She was a beautiful girl, and the camera loved her. You may be wondering why I used the word "girl" to describe someone in their late twenties. Well, simply put, I thought her looks were fleeting. There are two types of beauty in people. I tend to notice this more in women, but that's probably just because I'm a man. Granted, this is just my opinion, and you may think I'm being completely idiotic and probably even sexist.

Type one is a girlish beauty, or maybe I'd use the term cute, although that's certainly not the right word. This beauty will not last, and eventually the person will start to look rather ordinary.

The second type is a more mature beauty. People who possess this quality tend to not get noticed as early as the others, but their beauty is a lasting one. It never fades, despite how old the person gets.

Tiffany fit into the first category. Alana is firmly entrenched in the second. I'm sure you'll accuse me of being biased since Alana is my wife, and Tiffany spent our first several minutes together insulting me. It would be a fair argument, but it doesn't betray the truth of my theory. Come back to Maui in another twenty years, and I promise you Alana will be just as beautiful as she is today.

After the photoshoot, I asked Tiffany to join me in the main lounge. I pulled the card out of my camera and inserted it into my card reader, which was already plugged into my laptop. It took a few minutes to copy the files over since I'd shot everything in the raw format, and I'd taken over five hundred photos. Five hundred photos at sunset, you might ask? Trust me. It's not that hard to do.

Tiffany sat beside me on the sofa, and we looked at all of the shots. I did my best to glance at her out of the corner of my eye as I described what I was going for with each composition. It was complete B.S. on my part, but I can sell just as good as the best of them when I need to. She didn't respond to any of my comments. That didn't make me nervous because her body language gave it all away. She started to lean closer to the laptop screen as we got farther into the photographs.

"I think these look fantastic. The light really catches you perfectly, but they'll look even better once I run them through Photoshop and enhance everything," I said.

Tiffany stared at the laptop screen for a few more moments. I'd intentionally stopped it on a head-to-toe shot of her where the setting sun behind her was the most dynamic. Her hair and the black dress were blowing in the wind. It looked like something out of a high-fashion magazine, if I do say so myself. Annie Leibowitz eat your heart out.

She finally turned to me and said, "You can be my wedding photographer, Poe-with-no-last name."

I nodded as she stood and departed the lounge. I closed my laptop and packed everything back into my small bag.

Alana appeared a moment later.

"How did it go?" she asked.

"I think I passed the test."

"I didn't doubt you would."

"How's Hani?" I asked.

"She's in the cabin having a nervous breakdown."

"Over the photo session?"

"Over everything."

"Is there anything I can do to help?"

"Maybe go down there and let her know your session went well. That should help a little."

"I'll show her some of the shots. They turned out really well."

"Good idea."

Alana and I went back to the cabin, but Hani didn't really look at any of the photographs. She kept saying that she was convinced the trip would be a disaster and ruin her business. Nothing we said made any difference.

Foxx did his best to console her as well. He probably spoke to her more that hour than he'd said to her in the last several months.

I looked at my watch and saw it was almost time for the guests' dinner. I knew they wanted me to document the trip, so I grabbed my camera and made my way to the kitchen. I shot several beauty shots of their food. Baakir, or Bucky, did an amazing job with this wonderful lamb dish. I say wonderful, but I should emphasize that I didn't get to taste any of it, at least not then. The food was for the wedding party, and my growling stomach made me wonder if we were going to have to forage for ourselves.

I walked onto the back deck where the dinner table was located, and I snapped a few shots of the guests. No one really looks good when they're eating, so I only hung out for about ten minutes. It was the first time I'd seen the group together. There were eight of them in total: the bride and groom, the bride's father and the groom's parents, the best man, the maid of honor, and a bridesmaid.

Hani had given me a small packet with the names and photographs of the guests so I would know who was who. The photographs were an odd assortment of shots, and I guessed Hani had probably downloaded them from Facebook or some other social media website.

I've already told you about the bride and groom, Tiffany Calloway and Reese Lockwood, so here's a basic breakdown of the others.

Tiffany's father was Raymond Calloway. According to the bio in Hani's packet, Raymond worked as an investment banker of some kind. His age was listed as fifty-eight, which would have put him around thirty years old when Tiffany was born. He had dark hair that was a similar shade as Tiffany's. It had to be the result of a salon dye job given his age. Nevertheless, it was a good one, and it almost looked completely natural on him given his youthful face and lack of wrinkles. He was about the same height as Reese, at least he looked that way when I saw the two of them from a distance, which would explain where Tiffany got her height from.

There was no mention of Tiffany's mother in the packet. I didn't know if the woman was no longer living or if her absence was the result of an ugly divorce or some other familial disagreement.

Tiffany had brought two female friends with her. The first was Zelda Cameron, who was listed as the maid of honor. Zelda was the same age as Tiffany at twenty-eight years old. Also like Tiffany, she worked as a lawyer in New York. She had dark red hair that barely reached her shoulders. She had pale skin and brown eyes.

The bridesmaid was Sinclair Dewey. She was the blonde of the group and she was several inches shorter than the statuesque Tiffany and Zelda. What she didn't have in height, she made up for it with a body that was decidedly more curvaceous than her friends. It had more twists and turns than a rollercoaster. Sinclair also differed from her two friends in another way. She wasn't a lawyer. Instead, she worked in advertising in Chicago.

The best man was Trenholme Lockwood, who I'm sure you can guess was the groom's brother based on him having the same last name. His age was listed as twenty-six. He was tall and blonde like his brother. There was no mention of his job. I didn't know if Hani couldn't find out what he did or if she just didn't deem it important.

Reese's parents were named Dr. Artemis Lockwood and Catherine Lockwood. They were both listed as sixty-four years old, which made them several years older than Tiffany's father. I didn't know what kind of doctor Artemis was. Catherine's career or former career was not listed. Artemis was about six-foot-three, while Catherine was closer to Sinclair's height, maybe five-foot-two or three.

Clearly, Reese and Trenholme had inherited their father's stature. Both Artemis and Catherine had gray hair, so I couldn't tell who the boys got their blonde hair from. Dr. Lockwood's hair was certainly worth describing. It was so full and carefully styled that at first I assumed he was wearing some high-end toupee. Once I got a closer look at it, though, I realized it was his own. The man had clearly hit the hair jackpot. Catherine's hair was also immaculate. They both must have spent a small fortune at the salon. You may wonder why I'm so obsessed with hair. I don't know, but apparently I am.

So that's everyone in the wedding party. Did they all possess Tiffany's nasty demeanor? I didn't know at that moment, but I knew it was only a matter of time before I figured it out.

They completely ignored my presence at dinner, which somewhat surprised me since I assumed someone would have felt compelled to make a wisecrack about my eye patch. I did notice something, but I wasn't sure if it had any significance or not. Tiffany kept complaining to Angela, the head stewardess, about everything. The drinks didn't taste right. The food was too cold. The flavors weren't bold enough. The bread was too hard.

At first, I wasn't surprised by any of this since Tiffany had treated me in much the same way, but she kept emphasizing the name "Angela" whenever she said it. It was a hard emphasis, too. There was absolutely nothing subtle about it.

I studied Angela's reaction. She was taking it really well, and I was sure this wasn't the first time she'd been belittled working on a yacht. Many wealthy people have learned highly effective ways to insult people they view as beneath them.

I left the wedding group and decided to explore the yacht again. The lighting was incredible, both on the inside and outside of the vessel. It was a true work of art in its own way. I decided to grab several shots since I saw it as another way to document the experience. I put my wide angle lens on and snapped away.

I made my way through several rooms before running into someone in the smaller lounge that was just below the bridge. The guy I met looked like he could have been Laird Hamilton's younger brother. I don't know if you're familiar with Mr. Hamilton, but he's a legendary surfer who lives on the islands. Like Hamilton, this person had short blonde hair and a lean muscular physique that looked like it was the result of hard work versus spending hours in the gym.

He was sitting on a chair in the corner and seemed preoccupied with a magazine that had a yacht on the cover. He didn't notice me at all.

"Sorry to disturb you," I said.

He looked up at me quickly. Yeah, I'd startled him. I watched as his eyes scanned from my face to the camera in my hand.

"You're the photographer," he said.

"That's right."

"I saw you taking shots of Ms. Calloway."

"I'm Poe."

I walked over to him and held out my hand.

He stood and shook my hand.

"I'm Kurt Parrot."

"I think I heard your name mentioned earlier. You're the bosun, is that correct?"

"Yeah. That's me."

I looked around the room.

"Seems like a nice place to get away at night," I said.

"No one comes up here at night. They all stay on the main deck."

He looked at my camera again.

"You doing another photoshoot tonight?"

"Not really. I thought I'd get a few random shots. Nothing more."

I looked at my watch. It was approaching ten o'clock. It wasn't that late, but my body clock was still on Italy time.

"Do you know if there's anything else planned for the evening?" I asked.

"Not that I know of. There's a party planned for later in the week. Tonight the guests will probably just have a few drinks and then go to bed. Usually they're kind of tired after the long flight out here. Did they fly you out here?"

"Do people actually do that?"

"All the time for these big weddings. They bring their own photographers, their own hair and makeup people. Money can get you whatever you want."

"I actually live on Maui. I'm friends with the wedding planner."

"Good looking lady. I'd like to get to know her better," Kurt said.

I ignored his comment and looked at my watch again.

"Well, I better get back to my cabin. I'm pretty beat."

"Nice meeting you. You going ashore with them tomorrow?"

"Yeah. They want everything captured."

"Sounds good, man. I'll catch you tomorrow."

I nodded and left the lounge.

I walked down to the main deck and headed for the galley to see if I could grab a bottle of water. I had to cut though the main lounge to get to it. I saw most of the guests were still seated around the dining table. The plates had been cleared, but there was still several glasses and a pitcher filled with some kind of mixed drink. I guessed these were probably the third round of drinks judging from the volume of the laughter and conversation.

I noticed Reese, our groom-to-be, standing at the bar. Angela was on the opposite side. She was mixing him a drink that looked like a martini. That's not what got my attention, though. Reese had his body pressed against the bar and he was almost leaning toward Angela. They weren't talking loudly, so I couldn't make out what they were saying. Angela was facing in my direction and she saw me before Reese did.

"Good evening. Is there anything I can get you?" she asked.

I didn't think she meant that since there was no reason for her to wait on the hired help. Rather, I believe it was her way of letting Reese know there was someone else in the room.

"Actually, I could really use a bottle of water."

Angela reached under the bar and removed one. I walked over to the bar, and she handed it to me.

"Thank you very much," I said.

She gave me a rehearsed smile and headed toward the galley.

Reese took a sip of the drink she'd made him. He turned to me just as I was about to walk away myself.

"Tiffany is thrilled with those photographs."

"I'm glad."

He held his glass up to me as if in a toast.

"My compliments to the way you handled her."

"I'm not sure what you mean."

"Oh, I suspect you know exactly what I mean. She can be a lot to deal with sometimes."

"Is that right?"

"It is. Are you married?" he asked.

"Yes."

"For how long?"

"Two years."

"Glad you did it?"

"Very much so."

"You're the first guy I've heard give that answer, and I've been asking a lot of guys lately."

"Are you taking a poll or something?" I asked.

"Just an informal one."

"It's perfectly normal to get nervous before the big day. It's a lot to take in."

"I'm not nervous about the ceremony."

"You're worried about committing yourself to one girl?" I asked.

He laughed.

"Why in the world would I have to do that?"

I didn't like where the conversation was headed, so I took a long gulp of my water.

"What's your secret?" he asked.

"To what?"

"You just said you're happily married, so what's the trick?"

"No trick. Just pick the right woman. That's really all there is to it."

"How do you know she's the right one?"

"People make it sound more difficult than it really is. You can't overanalyze it. It's a feeling in your gut. You just know whether she's the right one."

"That sounds ridiculous," Reese said.

I wasn't sure how to respond to that, so I said nothing.

"How did you hurt your eye?" he asked.

"A photo shoot in Venice, Italy. I was working with a fashion model. I'm sure you've heard of her, Aurora Affini. "

"Yeah. I've heard of her."

"We finished the shoot and afterward we went out for a drink. Some guys got to bothering her, and it got kind of rough."

"This is where you tell me you fought them off?"

"I didn't. My crew did, but I got hit with a bar glass in the process. Anyway, you should mention the model's name to Tiffany. Let her know her photographs turned out even better."

"Still working the angles? I like that," he laughed.

"Have a good night," I said.

Reese didn't say goodnight or any other thing people say when they end a conversation. He didn't even nod to me. He just turned and walked toward the dining area to rejoin his family.

So what possessed me to make up the photo shoot in Venice, and who was this Aurora Affini model? Well, I just made the girl's name up, and I knew Reese Lockwood was too unsure of himself to admit he didn't know who she was. Yeah, it was a petty move on my part and it served no useful purpose other than me getting a small amount of pleasure out of bullshitting the guy. There was one other reason. No one wants to say they got pegged in the eye with a selfie stick.

Alana and Hani were asleep in the bed by the time I got back to the cabin. Foxx was on the air mattress that I'd placed between the side of the bed and the wall by the bathroom. He was tossing and turning, which made a squeaking noise as his body moved across the rubber mattress.

I lowered myself gently onto my mattress which was at the foot of the bed. It was uncomfortable as hell, and I almost immediately slid off it as I tried to find a sweet spot on the thing. I'll let you in on a little secret about air mattresses. There is no sweet spot.

I was so exhausted, though, that I fell asleep in ten minutes or so. I hadn't looked at my watch when I went to bed, so I didn't know how much sleep I'd actually gotten when Foxx woke me up in the middle of the night. He didn't do it on purpose, but he inadvertently kicked my air mattress on his way to the bathroom.

I tried to go back to sleep, but it was of no use. I don't want to offend sensitive readers, so I'll try to put this next part as delicately as possible. There was a foul odor that permeated the cabin after Foxx went inside the lavatory. I'm sure we've all encountered those fragrances before and one doesn't need to describe them in detail for you to get the point. I will say for the sake of explaining my next actions that this was the worst I'd ever been around. I began to gag and my eyes started to water. I hoped it would pass in a few minutes, but it didn't. It only got worse.

I sat up on the air mattress and looked at Alana and Hani. I was convinced they'd have to be awake by now, but they were both sleeping. I climbed off the air mattress and walked a few steps to the door. I took another look at Alana. She was still asleep.

I opened the cabin door and slipped into the hallway. I decided to head to the deck that had the area near the bow where guests could sunbathe. It was nearly three in the morning, and I doubted anyone would be up there at this hour.

I had to pass the crew cabins on my way to the main deck. Something unexpected happened as I neared the last door. It opened and a woman walked out. At first, I thought it might be one of the stewardesses. She turned toward me, though, and I recognized her as Tiffany's maid of honor, Zelda Cameron.

Her hair was a mess, her shirt was untucked, and she was carrying her shoes. I instinctively looked inside the cabin and saw Kurt Parrot, the bosun, sitting on the edge of his bunk. He wasn't wearing anything but his underwear. He did something that I found both tacky and ungentlemanly. He winked at me.

I certainly didn't wink back. Instead, I turned my head and did the polite thing of pretending I didn't see anything. Unfortunately, there was still the woman in the hallway. She was still standing a few feet from me, and she didn't appear anxious to get moving.

"Good evening," I said.

What else am I going to say given the circumstances?

"Ah, hi there."

She then turned from me and quickly walked away.

I was about to leave myself when I saw Kurt out of the corner of my eye. He was now standing in the doorway of his cabin.

"Listen, about that. You're not going to say anything, are you?" he asked.

"No. Why would I do that?"

"We're not supposed to be…"

His words trailed off, but I got the picture.

"Have a good evening, Kurt."

"Oh, I already did," he laughed.

The man had no manners. I thought briefly about returning to my cabin since I was now thoroughly embarrassed, but then I assumed those odors had probably not escaped in my short time away. I went back to my original plan and headed for the upstairs lounge. I found the area easily enough, and I looked around the room for something to read since I was wide awake by now.

I walked over to the bookcase and selected a book on sailing. It was about the history of ships and listed all sorts of nautical terms like bobstay, cathead, flagstaff, and gangway. You get the point. The book also offered a pretty nice selection of paintings and photographs of historic ships, both sailing vessels and those powered by engines.

I looked through the book for about ten minutes when I started getting tired again. I slipped the book back onto the shelf and exited the lounge for the tanning area just a few feet beyond the lounge's sliding glass door. I plopped down on the white cushions. They were about a hundred times more comfortable than the air mattress back in the cabin. I leaned back on them and was about to try to go to sleep when my cell phone pinged.

I looked at the display and saw a message from Alana: Where are you?

I texted her back and invited her to join me. She appeared several minutes later.

"I got lost. I thought this place was on the other deck," she said as she sat down beside me on one of the other cushions.

"Why did you get out of bed?" I asked.

"Probably for the same reason you did."

"Foxx."

"I hope that was Foxx and not you," she said.

"No. It wasn't me."

"Thank God. I was hoping someone I married was incapable of such a smell."

"You're not going to believe what happened to me on the way up here."

"What?"

I told her about my encounter with the horny bosun and the maid of honor. That sounds like a bad romance novel, doesn't it?

"He works fast. On the first night even," she said.

"He made a comment about Hani, earlier. I was going to warn her, but you guys were already asleep by the time I got to the cabin."

"He'd have no chance with her. He's not her type."

By that, I assumed she was referring to the point that the guy probably didn't have a lot of money, at least not enough to attract Hani. I don't mean to infer she's materialistic. Okay, that is what I'm saying.

Alana looked around the sunbathing section.

"Nice and peaceful up here. Maybe we should make this our sleeping area for the trip," she suggested.

"Maybe so."

"Wait a minute. What about Foxx and Hani? We can't leave them in the cabin alone. They'll be at each other's throats."

"I don't know about that. Foxx seems to be letting his guard down a little, and Hani is too obsessed with this gig to worry about Foxx."

"I'm really proud of what's she accomplished with her business. It hasn't been that long since she started it."

"I know. From planning our little wedding to chartering this week-long cruise. That's a pretty big jump."

"Little wedding? I didn't think it was."

"Well, maybe not little, but certainly not booking a super yacht for a cruise around the islands."

"I can't believe it's been two years since we got married. Feels like only a few months."

"It does, doesn't it? Time seems to really fly by."

"Do you remember the first time we met?" she asked.

"Of course. How could I forget that? But are you referring to the time we bumped into each other at the art show, or the time you showed up on Foxx's doorstep?"

My first real conversation with Alana was when she came by Foxx's house to arrest him for murder, just in case you haven't read that story. I was the one who opened the door that night. It was Halloween, and I'd seen her earlier in the night dressed as the little mermaid. She was a sight to behold, and I'd instantly fallen in love even though I didn't think I had a chance. I still don't know how I ended up marrying her. Part of me thought I'd been bonked on the head that night and the last few years had been some elaborate dream of mine.

"I still can't believe what you said to me when I asked if you were his lawyer," she said.

She'd asked me that question when I'd tried to defend him. I'd come across like a bad TV lawyer, which was my only experience with knowing how lawyers sound. I'd answered her question by saying that I was Foxx's architect. I still don't know what in the world possessed me to say something so dumb. I could always blame it on the jet lag. That was a convenient excuse.

"Well, it worked, didn't it?" I asked.

"What do you mean?"

"You married me, after all. Who knew you had a thing for unemployed architects."

"I guess you're right. I do have a thing for unemployed architects."

"They're unbelievably sexy."

"How could I ever deny that?" she asked.

I leaned forward and kissed her.

"I know what you're thinking, and it's not going to happen, mister."

"What am I thinking?" I asked.

"We're not going to have sex here. Not happening."

"But I'm Poe, the famous photographer."

"Then we're definitely not doing it. I'm not falling for some smooth-talking photographer."

I was about to protest and maybe even start to beg when we heard the door to the lounge slide open behind us. We both immediately went silent. It was doubtful they'd be able to see us since there was a small wall between the sunbathing area and the lounge. We were also lying down.

"I've given your son my blessing. I'm paying for this damn trip. What more do you want from me?"

I hadn't been around the guests long enough to recognize any of their voices, but I guessed it was Tiffany's father talking since he'd referenced giving "your son" his blessing. That meant the second voice I heard was Reese's father, Dr. Artemis Lockwood.

"How can you possibly ask me that? You know exactly what I want."

"I wouldn't even be on this God-forsaken boat if it weren't for my daughter."

"You think I want to be here anymore than you do?"

"You can always get off at the next port."

"Maybe I should."

"Please, don't do me any favors by sticking around."

There was a brief pause in the conversation, and we heard footsteps walking away from us.

Then Tiffany's father, at least the voice I thought belonged to him, said "And stop following me around. I'm done with you. I just want to get through this week and then we never have to see or speak to each other again."

Reese's father didn't respond. We heard the lounge door open and slam shut. I was about to say something when a loud crash rang out. It sounded like Reese's father had thrown his glass onto the deck. The door opened and slammed shut a second time.

We stayed silent for several long seconds. I turned to Alana.

"What the hell was that about?"

"Sounds like the families aren't exactly the best of friends."

"Did Hani mention anything about that?"

"No, nothing," Alana said.

"We should ask her about it."

"Maybe we shouldn't say anything. She's already stressed enough."

"Good point."

"They're on a yacht like this. How can they possibly be in a bad mood?" she asked.

"You heard what the one guy said. He's paying for the whole thing. Maybe he's pissed off because the other family isn't paying for anything."

"Maybe one person is paying for the cruise and the other picks up the wedding tab."

"Rich people and their problems," I said.

"Look who's talking."

"What's that supposed to mean?"

"You probably have more money than either of those guys."

"There's money and then there's money."

"I guess so. It's not a world I'm familiar with."

Alana looked at her phone.

"It's already four in the morning. What time did Hani want us to be ready to go?" she asked.

"She said seven, but I bet these guys won't be ready by then. They had an awful lot to drink tonight. I'm sure they're going to want to completely change the itinerary."

"I hope not. That might push Hani over the edge."

I looked up at the sky. It was a clear night and there were a million stars.

"What an incredible view," I said.

"It is, isn't it?"

"We certainly weren't planning this when we flew back from Venice."

"You can say that again."

I closed my eyes and tried to go to sleep.

Chapter 6
All Is Not As It Seems

We both woke when the sun started to creep over the horizon. Neither of us had slept well. For me, it was that thing that happens when you know you have to get up in a few hours. You know you're going to be dead tired, so that makes you feel a little anxious about how you're going to get through the day. There's also the fear that you're going to sleep through your alarm. I was on a yacht in the Pacific. I couldn't believe I was feeling anything but relaxed.

We walked to our cabin. Hani wasn't there, and I was surprised we didn't bump into her on the way down. Foxx was on the air mattress. He opened one eye as we walked into the room. His hair was a mess, and I had to suppress a laugh at how bad he looked. Alana didn't.

"What's so funny?" Foxx asked.

"You look like you've had a rough night," Alana said.

"I did. I spent the whole night running to the toilet."

"Oh, we're well aware. Why do you think we left the cabin?" I asked.

"Sorry, but blame Bucky the chef. It had to be something I ate. How did you guys not get sick?"

"I skipped dinner and just had a few snacks we brought with us," I said.

"Same here. By the time I finished with Hani, it was too late to eat," Alana said.

"Count yourself lucky," Foxx said.

Alana turned to me.

"I'm going to take a shower and then see if I can find Hani."

I waited for Alana to finish in the bathroom. It took her all of five minutes to brush her teeth, shower, and change into fresh clothes. She's probably the fastest person I know when it comes to getting ready in the morning. Granted, I haven't really observed that many people.

Alana emerged wearing a white tank top and tan shorts. She looked like a million bucks in such a simple outfit and having gotten so little sleep. Foxx and I on the other hand...

"I'll see you up there in a little while," Alana said.

Then she left the cabin.

I turned back to Foxx, who was still flat on his back on the air mattress.

"Can I go in now or do you need it?"

"I'm fine, at least I think I am. I'm going to kill that chef when I see him."

I took a shower and changed into new clothes. Foxx was asleep by the time I got out of the bathroom. He certainly wasn't the on-the-ball assistant I'd assigned him to be.

I left the cabin as quietly as I could so he could get some rest. As I made my way down the hallway, I was greeted by another surprise at Kurt's room.

"Thanks a lot, asshole."

Asshole?

I turned to see Kurt who was sitting on his bunk.

"You just had to open your mouth, didn't you?"

"What are you talking about?" I asked.

"You blabbed about what you saw last night."

"First of all, I'm not a blabber. Secondly, who was I going to tell?"

"Well, somebody told the captain, and he fired me this morning."

"Fired you?"

"We're not allowed to mess around with the guests. He's already lined up my replacement."

I didn't think Mr. Parrot had anyone to blame but himself, especially if he already knew the rules.

"Someone else must have said something because I sure as hell didn't. What do I care who you fool around with?"

"If you didn't, then who?"

"How should I know? Your cabin is surrounded by your co-workers. I'm sure they heard you fumbling around in the sheets. Maybe you should figure out who has a grudge against you."

"They wouldn't do that. They all have my back."

"I hate to break it to you, but not everyone is as they seem."

It was a lesson I'd learned a long time ago, only to have it reinforced many times on my investigations.

I left Kurt to finish packing his bags. A part of me felt bad for the guy. This seemed like it would be a pretty fun job, especially for a guy in his twenties. On the other hand, it shouldn't have been that difficult to keep his horny hands off the guests.

A thought then occurred to me. Maybe the attractive Zelda was romantically linked to one of the other guests. Perhaps it was the best man, and he'd been the one to rat out the bosun when his girl didn't come back to the cabin until halfway through the night. Maybe I'd unwittingly walked into a soap opera. Was this about to get good?

I was almost to the main lounge when I heard yelling. I hadn't been around the guests for that long, but I recognized this voice without a problem. It was Tiffany Calloway.

"Every single one of us were up sick last night. What else could it have been but the dinner that idiot cooked?"

I turned the corner to see Tiffany and her father, as well as Reese and his father. They were all on one side of the lounge. Facing them a few feet away was Captain Piadelia, Baakir, our lovable chef, and Angela.

"There was nothing wrong with the lamb. I assure you," Baakir said.

"Then how do you suppose we all got sick?" Raymond asked.

"Maybe you caught something on the plane," Captain Piadelia suggested.

"All of us, and we all came down with it at the exact same time?" Tiffany asked.

I looked past the group and saw Alana and Hani standing in the back of the lounge. Hani looked like she was in the throes of another nervous breakdown. Alana rolled her eyes, which surprised me because she's not that much of an eye roller. This cruise was certainly changing that.

"I apologize, Ms. Calloway. It won't happen again. We're here to give you an once-in-a-lifetime experience," Captain Piadelia said.

"By spending the night on the toilet?" Tiffany yelled.

"It wasn't the food," Baakir protested.

"Enough," Piadelia said.

"I demand that he be fired immediately and a new chef brought onboard," Tiffany said.

Captain Piadelia hesitated.

"Is there a problem?" Tiffany asked.

"Ms. Calloway, I can't simply find a new chef in a matter of hours. Chefs of this caliber are usually booked on other jobs."

"Of his caliber? Did you not just hear what we've been saying? He made us all sick," Tiffany said.

"It may take me a day or two to get someone new."

"I don't care, but we're not eating his food again. I'd rather have something out of a vending machine."

"I've never been spoken to like this before," Baakir said.

"Captain Piadelia, please tell your ex-chef that no one is speaking to him," Tiffany said.

Yeah, it was a childish thing for her to say, but there was a part of me that appreciated a clever tongue.

Baakir stormed off after Tiffany's last biting comment. Captain Piadelia watched him go. He turned back to the wedding party.

"My apologies. We'll make this right. You have my word."

Tiffany didn't reply. She just stared back at them. Piadelia hesitated a few more moments. Then he nodded and exited the lounge. Tiffany then turned her attack on Angela.

"This is just as much your fault, you know."

"How is it my fault, Ms. Calloway?"

There was something in the way she pronounced Tiffany's last name. She hit the words hard, as if it were a curse word.

"You can start calling me Mrs. Lockwood," Tiffany said.

"Oh, my apologies. I didn't realize you'd already gotten married. It was my understanding the ceremony wasn't until the end of our trip."

"What difference does a few days make? I will be Mrs. Lockwood, whether you like it or not."

Okay, that's a sure sign that all is not as it seems. What was I just saying to Kurt Parrot a few minutes ago?

"My feelings on the matter are completely irrelevant," Angela said.

"You're right. They are."

Angela turned from Tiffany and was about to walk away when Raymond Calloway called out to her.

"You can't talk to my daughter that way."

Angela looked back at Raymond.

"My apologies, Mr. Calloway. I was just going to see the captain and inquire if there's anything I can do to help him find a replacement chef. Is there anything I can do for anyone before I leave?"

No one responded.

"It's my understanding that Ms. Hu has a full day of activities planned for you. So I will see everyone in the evening," she continued.

Hani took that as her cue to walk up to the group.

As soon as Tiffany turned to Hani, Angela used the distraction to make her escape.

"The tour guide should be here any minute," Hani said.

"I don't want to do the tour anymore. Cancel it," Tiffany said.

"Okay, what would you like to do?" Hani asked.

"I'd like to spend the day on the beach."

"I'll get with Angela and arrange rides for everyone. What time would you like to leave?" Hani asked.

"In an hour, and don't forget you recommended this yacht. Everything has been a disaster so far. It better start improving soon, or I'll find another wedding planner."

Tiffany and her father left the lounge.

Reese walked over to Hani.

"Don't worry. I think you're doing fine, and it's not like she can replace you at this stage of the game."

It was a kind thing to say, but I was more than a bit surprised to see him contradict his fiancée so completely.

"See if you can help Angela find a new chef. That was a lousy dinner. I hate to think what Tiffany will do if that guy's still here when we get back," Reese continued.

"I'll do whatever I can," Hani said.

"Thank you," Artemis Lockwood said.

It was the first thing I'd heard him say, at least when I'd been looking at him. On a side note, I did feel like I had confirmation that Artemis and Raymond had been the two men arguing on the deck last night.

Reese and Artemis left, presumably to go back to their cabins to change for a day on the beach.

Hani walked up to Alana and me.

"I guess I better go see Angela," Hani said, but she made no move to leave the lounge.

"Are you okay? How can I help?" Alana said.

"Can you call the tour guide and cancel?"

"Of course."

"Maybe you shouldn't do that just yet. You have to pay the tour guide since you're canceling so late. Why not ask him or her to instead act as a driver to the beach. I'm sure they have a large vehicle since they'd already planned on driving them around the island," I said.

"That's a good idea. Would you like me to see if they can do that?" Alana asked.

Hani nodded.

"I'll get with the lovely Tiffany. I'm guessing she won't want to do any photos today, especially since they all feel sick, but I can help you two with whatever else you need," I said.

"After we get them to the beach, I was thinking of looking into a flight to Kauai. There's a lot I need to do in preparation for the wedding. Do you think you two could handle the rest of this cruise without me?" Hani asked.

At first, I thought she was joking, and I was expecting a smile to appear on her face. It didn't.

"Are you kidding? You're actually going to suggest that?" Alana asked.

I knew Alana's question was more a statement of exasperation and not an actual inquiry. It was a classic Hani Hu move. Think of yourself first, others second, even when they've gone out of their way to help you.

"I'm sorry. That was a horrible thing for me to say," she admitted.

"Look, Hani. I know this is hard, but you're going to get through it. It's just a week of your life and think what it's going to do for your business. This is elevating you to another level," Alana said.

"It's not going to happen. You've seen this woman. She's going to destroy my company's reputation. No one will ever hire me after this wedding."

I hated to admit it, and I certainly wasn't going to say anything there in that lounge, but I thought Hani had a valid concern. I could easily see Tiffany Calloway badmouthing Hani on whatever online wedding forum she could find, even if the rest of the trip did go off without a hitch.

"We won't let that happen. We're going to turn this thing around," Alana said.

"That's easy for you to say, but we can't control anything that happens on this yacht. I couldn't stop that crew member from screwing the maid of honor. I sure as hell couldn't predict Bucky or Baakir or whatever the hell his name is would poison the entire wedding party. What in the hell kind of surprise are they going to spring on me next? Will they run the ship aground? Will they push the bride and groom overboard? This thing is costing hundreds of thousands of dollars, and they apparently don't have any kind of back-up plan if something goes wrong."

Neither Alana nor I had a response, mainly because everything Hani had said was true. Kurt had bedded the maid of honor, and he'd done it on the very first night of the cruise. Baakir had made several people sick with his rotten lamb, and Captain Piadelia did seem at a complete loss as to how to repair the perception that he was running a two-bit operation. The crew should have been at the top of their game in an industry known for its excessive luxury but they were fumbling around like a bunch of clueless high school students working at your local fast food restaurant.

Hani left the lounge, seemingly in search of Angela.

"I can't believe this is happening," Alana said.

"Look at it this way. So far the worst that's happened is a bad dinner," I said, even though I knew that was just part of the problem. "It's just some stomach pains. It's not like anyone died."

Oh, Poe, you had to go and open your big mouth.

Chapter 7
The Black Bikini

Hani and Alana took my advice and asked the tour guide to drive the group to a local beach. He didn't take it particularly well, and I heard him mutter something about being a guide and not a taxi service. I thought he was overreacting, but apparently this was the day for letting one's emotions get out of control.

I slipped the guy a hundred bucks and told him we were sorry for changing the plans at the last minute. I'm sure it was the money and not my apology that made his mood change somewhat. I use the word "somewhat" because it wasn't like his reaction immediately altered. He just shoved the cash into his pocket and told Hani there was a nice beach several miles away.

Angela, Kimi, and Banks brought out several beach chairs and blankets and loaded them into the back of the van. Speaking of the van, I was surprised the thing actually made it to the marina. It looked like it had been parked on the beach for several years without ever having been washed. It wasn't exactly a strong recovery from the chaos of the morning.

I wasn't sure how he could have thought it was okay to pick up guests from a mega yacht in something that looked like a van from the 1960s. The paint was badly faded, and all the windows were rolled down. The window thing wouldn't have bothered me, but it was a hot day. I didn't know if he'd rolled them down because his Scooby Doo van didn't have a working air conditioner.

"Are you guys okay?" Alana asked the three stewardesses after they finished loading the beach gear.

On a side note, I thought one of the deckhands should have been the one to bring the beach gear down to the van, but maybe they were busy getting their butts handed to them by the captain in his attempt to keep any more male crew members from hitting on the ladies.

Angela looked back at the yacht. I assumed she did this to see if the guests were within earshot.

"I will be. It's been a rough morning."

"How's Baakir?" Hani asked.

"He's upset. I don't blame him."

"What's the captain going to do?" I asked.

"He's already told Baakir he's done."

"Is he kicking him off the yacht?" Alana asked.

"Probably not. He'll stay below in his cabin until we get back to Maui."

"I thought we were going to Oahu after this," Hani said.

"We were, but it's highly doubtful we'll find a replacement chef on this island. The two other chefs we work with are on Maui."

"Can they fly out here today?" I asked.

"Maybe. It just depends on how fast the captain can reach them. They may already be booked on other jobs. The best ones always are."

Angela told Hani that she planned to make snacks for everyone and bring them out to the beach in an hour or so. I wasn't sure how she was going to do that since the chef had just been fired, which made me wonder if Baakir was going to secretly make them and intentionally spit in the appetizers. As a general rule of life, I do my best to never piss off the person who makes my meals.

Hani was clearly thinking the same thing for she had this look of concern plastered on her face. Angela interpreted it easily enough, and she assured Hani that she was more than capable of making the food herself. She also suggested that she would find a nice local restaurant near the beach and would make reservations for the group for lunch. It was a good idea and probably an outstanding one if the restaurant she found had plenty of alcohol.

The wedding party eventually made their way off the yacht and came down to the tour guide's van. I think Reese was the only one to acknowledge his presence. Everyone else walked right past him and climbed into the van. I watched the guide closely and wondered if he would go off again. Fortunately, he didn't.

He closed the door and turned back to Hani, Alana, and me.

"I'm taking them to Hapuna Beach. Do you want me to come back for you three?"

"No, thanks. We'll grab a taxi and meet you out there," Hani said.

The guide turned away without saying anything else. He climbed into his van and drove off.

"What are the chances they make it to the beach without Tiffany criticizing him for something," Hani said.

"It wasn't exactly the nicest van," Alana admitted.

"I'm sure Tiffany was expecting a limo or something," Hani said.

"Did you promise her that?" Alana asked.

"No, but does that make a difference?" Hani asked. "That thing was a piece of junk. Could this day possibly get any worse?"

Alana didn't answer her. I didn't either. I'd gotten the impression that Tiffany was the type of person who'd complain if the weather was sunny and warm. Nothing seemed to be to her standards. Of course, you didn't need to be a picky person to expect a better van than the one this guide had brought.

It took almost thirty minutes for a taxi to arrive to drive us to Hapuna Beach. It was a beautiful ride down the coast. This was my first trip to the Big Island, and I realized along the way that I knew almost nothing about it beyond it obviously being the largest in the Hawaiian island chain. I would have enjoyed it much more if I hadn't been so concerned about Hani's state of mind. There was also mine and Alana's as well. None of us wanted to be on this little adventure. I, for one, wanted desperately to be home lounging by my pool and patting my dog on his head while I enjoyed an ice old Negra Modelo.

I tried to push that vision of contentment out of my mind and concentrate on the task at hand. I needed to figure out a way to help Hani turn this disaster around.

The taxi drove us past a sign that said Hapuna Beach Recreation Area, and

I immediately got nervous that the beach would be crowded. We were bound to find a furious Tiffany screaming at the tour guide. There was a small crowd, though, and most of them seemed to be gathered on one side of the half-mile beach.

It took just a few moments to find the Lockwood-Calloway group. They were about as far away from the other tourists as possible without actually going into the ocean. We sat down about twenty yards from them, close enough for them to easily see us, but not too close as to make them feel that we were eavesdropping on their conversations.

After about five minutes, I suggested to the Hu sisters that they take a stroll down the beach and try to unwind since the wedding party seemed content at the moment to lounge in the sun. I told them that I would do my best to address any needs our clients might have while they were away. They took me up my offer and walked in the opposite direction of the Lockwoods and Calloways.

One of the bridesmaids, Sinclair Dewey, walked over to me a few moments after Alana and Hani left. I hadn't talked to Sinclair much, nothing beyond a simple hello or good evening.

I was busy looking through some of the photos I'd taken the day before when she stopped in front of me. I hadn't seen her until the last second since she'd approached my position from the side where my eye was covered. I looked up and was greeted by two tanned and oiled legs that ran to a skimpy black bikini bottom and matching top that did little to cover her ample cleavage.

I almost dropped my camera in the sand and was glad, or at least hopeful, that my dark sunglasses hid my one eye from popping out at this seductive vision just a few feet from me. Fortunately, I managed to keep my mouth closed and not proclaim "Yowza."

Good Lord, what would you have thought of me if I'd actually uttered that old phrase?

"Hello," I said.

The words came out in a normal tone, and I was grateful I hadn't stuttered.

"I was wondering if you could take some shots of me on the beach. Tiffany said she was really happy with her photo shoot last night."

"Sure. When would you like to do it?"

"How about now?"

"Okay."

I stood and looked around the beach.

"Why don't we go over there by that black lava rock? That might make for an interesting background," I said.

"Whatever you suggest. You're the expert."

I looked for Alana and Hani, but they were on the opposite side of the beach by this point.

As I stood beside Sinclair, I realized just how attractive she was. I feel pretty confident in saying that most men would look at least twice, maybe even three times if they'd seen Ms. Dewey walk by in this tiny black bikini. Somehow I felt like I was cheating on Alana just being a few feet from this woman. She exuded sexuality, and I felt like it was reaching out to me and trying to pull me closer. It probably wasn't, and my hormones were just getting the better of me.

We walked over to the lava rock, and I snapped a few practice frames. The lighting was nice, and the combination of the black rock and the blue water made for an exceptional background.

Sinclair didn't have the natural posing ability that Tiffany did, so I suggested a few poses for her. I shot a ton of photographs, not as much as during Tiffany's session, but more than enough to get a lot of great images.

We sat on the sand, and I scanned through the photos with her.

"These are great. How can I get a copy?"

"I'll post everything online once we're done with the trip," I said.

"Where's Foxx? I thought he would have come out here with you."

I was a little surprised since I didn't realize he'd spoken to her or any of the guests for that matter.

"He got sick from dinner last night."

"Everyone did. Foxx said you and he own a bar in Lahaina. Is that right?"

"Yeah, it's called Harry's."

"He said it was the top bar on the island."

"I don't know about that, but it is popular."

"Foxx said he used to play football for the Washington Redskins."

"He certainly told you a lot about himself, didn't he?"

"He didn't tell me how he ended up on Maui," Sinclair said.

"He blew his knee out and came to the island after his football career ended."

I naturally left out the part about him falling in love with a famous artist since it was now obvious Foxx had set his sights on this young lady. I wasn't sure how Foxx had found the opportunity to tell Sinclair so much about himself, especially since I hadn't even noticed him around any of the guests. The yacht was huge, though, and Foxx had a way of quickly targeting the ladies.

"Is he seeing anyone right now?" she asked.

"I don't think so."

"Good."

"Are you seeing anyone?" I asked.

"He's assured me it was never going anywhere, but one can always hope they'll change their mind."

She stood.

"Thanks again for the photo session. I guess I'll talk to you later," Sinclair continued.

She left, and I stayed seated on the sand and stared out at the water for a few minutes before making my way back to Alana and Hani.

Even though I currently had only one working eye, it wasn't hard to see the scowl on Alana's face as I got closer. I had no idea why she was upset, which in hindsight was pretty ignorant of me.

"Now I see why you suggested we take a walk on the beach," Alana said.

"What do you mean?" I asked, and I sat beside her on a towel.

"Could that bikini have gotten any smaller? It looked like it was made of dental floss," Alana said.

"I think I'm going to see if Angela is here yet," Hani said.

She stood and walked toward the parking lot. I was tempted to chase after her and tell her that I would help bring the food to our guests, but I knew I had to resolve this issue with Alana before it turned into a full-blown battle.

"I'm not sure why you're apparently mad at me. I'm not the one who picked out her swimsuit."

"You couldn't take your eyes off her body."

There were multiple counterpoints I could have made to that statement.

Point one: How could she have seen where my eyes were since my back had been to her?

Point two: The only reason I was even here was as a favor to her sister.

Point three: I was working as a photographer. How am I supposed to take photos of the guests if I don't look at them?

Point four: I couldn't have had my "eyes" all over her since I technically only had one eye working at the moment. Granted, that's a smartass response, and there's no chance I would have ever said that.

Point five: I didn't ask Sinclair to do the photoshoot. She'd asked me, and she'd approached me after Alana and Hani had left for their walk, not before when I'd been the one to suggest it.

Point six: If you've read any of my previous tales, then you'll know I'm a complete dimwit when it comes to women. Nevertheless, I have learned some things as I've gotten older. Logic seldom works when one is engaged in an emotional argument. Therefore, points one through five should be dismissed by me, and I should concentrate just on point six and the soon-to-be-mentioned points seven and eight.

Point seven: Regardless of whether or not you're on the side of righteousness and honesty in your debate with a woman, you should still immediately admit defeat and apologize at once for your insensitivity, ignorance, lack of manners, and anything else that emphasizes just how wrong you are.

Point eight. If at all possible, blame someone else or at least come up with some other topic to deflect the blame. It usually works, and this is a technique I've relied upon many times.

"She asked me to do the photoshoot. I didn't want to do it, but I didn't see how I could say no."

"I'm sure you just hated having to look at that body through your little viewfinder," Alana said.

Little? Was that a jab at my you-know-what?

Time for point eight.

"The whole shoot was just her way of asking me if Foxx is dating anyone right now."

"What are you talking about?" she asked.

"Foxx told her about Harry's and his career with the Redskins."

"When did he do that?"

"I assume last night. He didn't say anything to me about it."

"So he was putting the moves on her?" Alana asked.

"I guess so. It must have worked because she's clearly interested."

"Is this your way of deflecting blame?"

That's one of the challenges of being married to someone who is smarter than you. You can never fool them.

"First of all, there's nothing to deflect. I didn't do anything wrong. Second, you're way sexier than her."

"I don't feel sexy."

"That's because you spent the night sleeping on a boat deck, but trust me, you're still sexier than her."

"It's not working. You're still in trouble, and so is Foxx. He's supposed to be your photography assistant. Instead, he's hitting on Hani's clients and then spending the day in bed. Wait till I get back to that boat."

What did I tell you? Point eight. It's a lifesaver.

Chapter 8
The Argument

Angela, Kimi, and Banks arrived a little after my impromptu photo shoot with Sinclair. They had simple snacks and some cold drinks, which the group quickly devoured. Angela walked over to us after dropping off the food and told us she'd made lunch reservations at a nearby restaurant that she'd been to before. It was one of her favorites on the Big Island.

Our trusty and testy tour guide drove them over. The restaurant didn't look much better than the guide's van, which didn't necessarily mean it didn't serve fantastic food. Sometimes the best adventures in cuisine can be found at hole in the walls. Of course, sometimes exploding diarrhea can be achieved at those places, too.

The restaurant was painted in a faded and chipped blue and red. The sign at the top read Makani. I was proud of myself because I recognized that the word meant breeze or wind. It was an appropriate name as there was a cool wind coming off the ocean.

As we arrived, we saw the hostess waiting for us, and she led the wedding party to a long table inside the restaurant. There were several large fans that did a pretty good job of cooling the place down, especially with the aforementioned Hawaiian breezes. It was a welcome change from the hot beach where the white sand seemed to reflect all of the sun's rays directly into our faces.

Alana, Hani, and I grabbed a table outside since we still wanted to maintain a respectable distance from our favorite wedding guests. The outside dining area was covered, though, and it was still fairly pleasant despite the absence of fans out there. We waited a long time as the waiters spent all of their energy on our clients. That was fine by me, for the first fifteen minutes, that is. My stomach pains started getting the better of me as I smelled the food being prepared in the kitchen.

"I'm so hungry I think I could eat my flip-flops," I said.

"That's disgusting," Alana said.

"I didn't mean that literally."

"I know, but I couldn't stop myself from picturing it in my mind."

"Do you think they're having a good time?" Hani asked.

"How could they not? It was a gorgeous beach, not too crowded, and I heard a lot of laughter," I said.

"Maybe things are starting to turn your way," Alana said.

"Don't jinx me," Hani said, and she tapped twice on the wooden table.

"I'm three seconds from going inside and placing my own order," I said.

"I'm so thirsty, it feels like I swallowed a bucket of sand from that beach," Alana said.

"Okay, I'm going in there," I said.

I don't know if the waitress overheard our complaints, but she emerged from the inside just as I pushed my chair back.

She walked over to our table, and we ordered the same lunch as the Lockwoods and Calloways. Fortunately, the food came out fairly quickly. The meal was a seafood lover's delight with a scrumptious mix of lobster, shrimp, scallops, and mussels. It smelled like a little corner of heaven, and we attacked the food as if we were a raiding party of Vikings who hadn't eaten in days.

I'm sure it wasn't the best meal I'd had in my life, but it sure felt like it at that moment. I washed it all down with a couple of cold beers, while Alana and Hani opted for iced teas.

"Too bad Foxx isn't here. I know he'd love this food," I said. "Do you think we should order anything to go for him?"

"I'm sure he's gotten something to eat on the yacht," Alana said.

"Maybe I should call him," I said.

"If you want," Hani said, and there was no mistaking the attitude in her voice.

Alana must have mentioned our conversation about Sinclair to Hani. I thought Hani was mostly over Foxx and had given up the notion of ever having a romantic relationship with him again, but I might have been wrong.

I pulled my phone out of my pocket and called Foxx. It rang several times before going to voicemail. I left him a quick message and placed the phone on the table so I wouldn't miss a possible return call.

I asked Angela as she was leaving the restaurant if she'd seen Foxx at all, and she said she'd been too busy in the galley to have noticed him. I checked my phone again but didn't see any text messages or missed calls from him.

I was tempted to order a third beer but didn't. I felt like I needed to be sharp around this group. At some point after their empty plates had been removed, I heard Reese's brother, Trenholme, order tequila shots for everyone, at least everyone at their table. I thought it a terrible idea, especially after a day of lying in the hot sun, which can drain all the energy out of you. Of course, I generally felt that way about that particular liquor regardless of what I've done throughout the day. Fortunately, the waitress didn't ask us if we wanted any shots, not that I would have accepted anyway.

The wedding party was fairly buzzed if that's the word to use these days by the time they were driven back to the marina. I wasn't sure if that was a good thing or not.

By the way, what do you think of the name Trenholme? I'm not sure if I like it. It kind of sounded like a name that might belong to someone with a very punchable face. This Trenholme didn't have one, though. He had a face like a male model you'd undoubtedly see on the cover of some men's fashion magazine. Some guys just get all the breaks, don't they? I think that might actually be the lyric to a song if memory serves.

Alana, Hani, and I took a cab back to the marina. Angela, Kimi, and Banks had left the restaurant well before since they needed to start the preparation for dinner. I'd assumed they would have suggested another meal on the island since The Epiphany was missing a chef, but the itinerary called for the yacht to depart before dinner, at least that's the excuse Angela gave us. It was another questionable move by Captain Piadelia, but that was just my opinion.

The taxi dropped us off at the entrance to the marina, and we were almost to the yacht when we heard Foxx call out to us. We turned and saw him jogging our way.

"How did the beach go?" he asked.

"Looks like you're feeling a lot better," I said.

"Yeah. The stomach cramps finally subsided a couple of hours ago. I didn't want to bother the chef for lunch so I just walked a mile down the road until I found this little café."

"You didn't want to bother the chef or you didn't trust him?" I asked.

"Both. We should probably hit a grocery store before we leave tonight and stock up on food."

"You don't want to join the guests tonight for dinner?" Hani asked.

"We can do that?" Foxx asked.

"We're not supposed to, but I just assumed you'd want to spend more time with Sinclair," Hani said.

"What are you talking about?"

Time for a little side note. This was the one drawback to point number eight that I mentioned in the last chapter. You can certainly throw someone else under the bus to help take the heat off you, but there's always the danger that the bus is going to turn around and run you over if the other person comes gunning for you.

"Poe had a photo session with the lovely Ms. Sinclair Dewey. She told him all about your little conversation last night where you mentioned you were a retired NFL player who now owned a highly successful bar in Lahaina," Hani said.

Foxx didn't respond. He just turned my way and shot me a look that could have easily knocked me off the dock and into the water.

"You're supposed to be disguising yourself as a photographer's assistant," Alana said.

"I never said I didn't do that. I just mentioned some other things I did," Foxx protested.

"Why were you even talking to that girl?" Alana asked.

"I think we all know the answer to that," Hani said before Foxx could even answer. "He can't keep it in his pants if his life depended on it."

"Now hold on," I said. "Give the guy a break. He was just making small talk."

"You stay out of this," Alana said.

Suddenly, I felt like this was a battle of the sexes.

"I can't believe this. I sacrifice a week of my life to help you, and you're going to attack me because I had a conversation with one of your clients. She approached me last night. Would you have rather me said nothing to her and walked away?" Foxx asked.

"Do you know how hard this is for me? I don't need you making it more difficult," Hani said.

"So that's what I'm doing? I spend all night and most of today sick as a dog because of your job, and somehow that translates into me making this harder for you. Well, what about me? Where's everyone's appreciation for me offering to help on this B.S. trip?"

He didn't exactly use the letters B.S. but I always try to keep the cursing at a minimum in these tales for the sensitive readers.

"I'm out of here," Foxx continued.

He turned from us and headed down the dock toward the marina office.

"Where's he going?" Hani asked.

"I think Poe is right. I think we were a little hard on him," Alana said.

"It's my fault. I never should have mentioned he even spoke with Sinclair," I said.

"Maybe we should go after him," Alana suggested.

"I'd give him a little time. It's never a good idea to approach him when he's this angry," I said.

"Do you think he'll come back?" Hani asked.

"When does the yacht leave?" Alana asked.

"In a few hours," Hani said.

"I'll call him in a couple of hours if he's not back by then," I said.

Alana and I went back to the cabin while Hani went looking for Angela. I set the alarm on my cell phone to go off in exactly two hours. I plopped down on my air mattress and almost immediately fell asleep. I woke up in what felt like three minutes. I was absolutely sure I'd made a mistake when I set the alarm time on my phone. I hadn't, though. Those two hours had simply passed in the blink of my one eye.

I sat up and looked at the bed. Alana wasn't there. Neither was Hani. I looked over to the bathroom and saw the door was open and the light out. I stood and walked into the bathroom and brushed my teeth. I slipped a fresh shirt on and grabbed my phone. I called Foxx and heard his phone ring a second later. He'd left it on his air mattress.

I left the cabin and eventually found Hani and Alana in the main lounge.

"Have either of you seen Foxx? He left his phone in the cabin, so I can't call him."

"No, but I haven't really been looking for him," Alana said.

I walked outside the lounge and looked down to the dock. He wasn't there. I disembarked and made the short walk to the marina office. They had a small restaurant and bar there as well. I assumed I'd find him sitting at the bar and watching television. He wasn't there, though. I asked the bartender if she'd seen a six-foot-four-inch guy that outweighed me by at least fifty to sixty pounds. She told me that she'd served him a couple of beers but that he'd left at least an hour ago.

I took a slow walk around the marina but didn't see him anywhere. I finally gave up and walked back to the yacht. I searched that as well, but Foxx was nowhere to be found. I knew he didn't have his cell phone since I'd seen it in the cabin. However, he did have his wallet since he'd bought at least two beers at the marina bar. He could have easily called a cab and headed for the airport since he just needed a credit card and ID to buy an airline ticket.

I didn't think he'd have wanted to leave his phone on the yacht, but Foxx had been mad as hell. Maybe he didn't even realize he'd left his phone there, or maybe he was so mad he didn't want to come back and risk running into one of us.

I felt like a total jerk and a terrible friend since I was the one who'd started this mess by ratting him out to Alana. I needed to find a way to make this up to him.

Chapter 9
A Difficult Question

The sun was setting, and the yacht was minutes from leaving when I spotted Tiffany at the bow. The light was beautiful. She was still wearing her swimsuit from the earlier trip to the beach, but she had a flowing sarong that fell just a few inches shy of the deck.

I walked as quickly as I could to my cabin and grabbed my camera. Fortunately, she was still there when I got back. I snapped several shots of her before she noticed my presence.

"Did you enjoy your day on the beach?" she asked.

"I did. I liked the seafood lunch even more."

"It was good, wasn't it?"

I walked up to her and showed her a couple of the photos I'd just taken.

"They're nice. Thank you. Are you looking forward to this wedding or are you dreading it?"

"I'm sure it will be great. Plenty of opportunities to get some nice photographs," I said.

"That's not what I was talking about."

"Then I'm not sure what you mean."

"I imagine your group hates me by now."

I didn't want to hesitate in giving my answer. Unfortunately, I did.

"Why would you ask that?"

"I'm very aware of how I can be, as is Reese," she said.

I wasn't sure I could possibly respond to that, so I said nothing.

"Every time I look at Hani, I think she's about to have a coronary," Tiffany continued.

"Would you believe me if I said she always looks like that?"

"No."

"Okay, then. I won't say that."

Tiffany turned from me and looked out to the setting sun.

"Do you think I'm a bitch?" she asked without looking back at me.

"What does it matter what I think?"

She turned back to me.

"I guess that means yes."

"No. That's not what it means at all. I don't think you're a bitch. I do think you can be rather forceful in your expressions."

Tiffany laughed.

"I've never heard it described like that."

The light had begun to get even more beautiful, so I took a couple of quick shots of the sun setting into the ocean.

"You're not a professional photographer, are you?" she asked.

"I'm not sure how to take that."

"I don't mean to sound like I'm criticizing your work. I think it's rather good, but your friend, what's his name?"

"Foxx."

"He mentioned to Sinclair last night that you and he own a bar in Lahaina."

"Maybe I'm a bar owner and a photographer."

"I don't think so."

"Why is that?"

"Because you act like you don't give a damn," she said.

"I'm not sure how to take that," I repeated an earlier statement of mine.

"I meant it as a compliment."

"How could that possibly be construed that way?"

"You have the confidence of someone who can tell anyone to take a leap."

She didn't use the particular phrase "take a leap," but again, I like to protect the more sensitive readers.

"You only get that confidence from one thing," she continued.

"And what is that?"

"By being rich, and you sure as hell didn't get rich by being a wedding photographer."

"Are you happy with my work?" I asked.

"So far."

"Then I'll admit to you that I'm not a professional, at least in terms of seeking out paying assignments in this field. I do have a ton of experience, probably much more than many of the photographers posing as wedding specialists on these islands."

"Posing? Interesting choice of words. Isn't that what you're doing?"

"I suppose I'm guilty as charged."

"Was I right about the money?"

"About me being rich?"

"Yes."

"A gentleman doesn't disclose what he's worth."

"Ah, so you're not just rich. You're wealthy."

She looked at the ring on my finger.

"How long have you been married?" she asked.

"I just had my second wedding anniversary a few days ago."

"Congratulations. Your wife is Hani's sister."

"Did Hani tell you that?"

"Not at all, but it wasn't difficult to figure out."

"I find that intriguing. May I ask what gave us away?"

"Body language."

"Anything more specific?"

"You invade each other's personal space. Nothing major, but I noticed a few times. There was something else that was even more telling."

"What was it?" I asked.

"The way you look at her."

"How do I look at her?"

"With admiration and awe."

"I'm going to steal that line for my next Valentine's Day card to her."

"You have my permission."

Now it was my time to laugh.

"How many photographs of my family have you taken so far?" she asked.

"It's only been a couple of days."

"Take a guess."

"I don't need to guess. I have it right here on my camera."

I looked at the menu display.

"I've taken over a thousand shots so far," I continued.

"It must be interesting to study people through the viewfinder of your camera."

"You definitely notice things you wouldn't ordinarily notice."

"I want to ask you another question, and I want absolute honesty."

"I've been completely honest with you so far."

We both knew that wasn't technically true since I'd dodged the "Am I a bitch?" question with a question of my own.

"How does Reese look at me when you study him through the camera? Is it the same way you look at your wife?"

I hadn't had the time to process possible questions in my mind after she'd told me that she wanted to ask me another question. It wouldn't have mattered. I'd never have come up with that one, even if I'd had several hours to guess.

I certainly had no way to answer it, mainly because it wasn't something I'd considered while shooting photographs over the last two days. I'd not really seen them interact one-on-one. So far, everything had been in a group setting, yet she hadn't seen Alana and me one-on-one, either. I didn't know if that meant Tiffany Calloway was more observant than me, or maybe I'd done a poor job of truly watching the group.

A photographer's mission is to try to find the truth of his or her subject. I hadn't been doing that. Instead, I'd just been looking for good shots and paying attention to the technical details such as lighting, composition, exposure, you get the point. Her question had jarred me into realizing that I was really here for something else. I needed to find the essence of their relationship, one that was about to take another step forward and transform them into the next phase of their lives.

Unfortunately, that realization did nothing to bring me closer to finding an answer to her question. I assumed Reese Lockwood loved her. Why else would he marry her? Nevertheless, I hadn't really seen any display of that love that I could point to. The only real interaction I'd had with Reese was at the bar in the main lounge where he somewhat criticized Tiffany.

"I have no doubt he loves you," I said.

Yeah, it was fairly lame, but she'd hit me with that whopper of a question with no warning. What else did she expect?

"Why do you say that?" she asked.

"Because I was talking to him last night and he told me how excited he was to be marrying you. We were standing at the bar while Angela was making him a martini."

"He said this to you in front of Angela?"

"Yes, Angela, the chief stewardess."

"I know exactly who she is, and now I know you're lying."

"Why do you think that?" I asked.

"Because he would never say that in front of Angela."

"I don't understand."

"Let's change the subject to something more pleasant. How did you and your wife meet?"

"It was my first trip to Maui. I saw her in a Halloween parade."

"Was she in a costume?"

"Yes. The Little Mermaid."

"Oh, so it was the skimpy bathing suit that got your attention," she said more than asked.

"Among other things."

"What were the other things?"

"I guess there was nothing else, at least not at first. Of course, one's feelings develop as you really get to know someone else."

"Do you have children?"

"A dog, but he's very attached to us, as we are to him. Does that count?"

"Maybe so, depends if you ask a dog lover or not?"

"Are you a dog lover?" I asked.

"Of course."

That was a bit of a surprise to hear, especially since Tiffany had been rather cruel to everyone since I'd come into contact with her. I always had a hard time believing that someone who could become attached to a dog could also be a jerk. Granted, that was a terrible theory, and it was one that would fall apart after just a few seconds of critical analysis. I'm sure Hitler liked his dog, too, not that I was comparing Ms. Calloway to Adolph.

"How did you and Reese meet?" I asked.

"In college. We met at a fraternity party."

"Really?"

"I know. It's a terrible cliché, but it's the truth."

"What was it that attracted you to him?"

"Maybe it was the other way around. Might he have been the one who spotted me from across the room like you did seeing your wife walk down that street?"

"Of course he was the one who pursued you, but you must have been attracted to him in return. Why else would you have given him your phone number?"

"He was in the backyard talking to a few of his friends. It's not hard to notice Reese in a crowd. His height alone guarantees that. He had a confidence about him, though. That was probably the second thing I noticed. We didn't talk long before his girlfriend came back."

"A girlfriend? Really?"

"It didn't last long, not after he and I started talking."

"So you stole him away?" I asked.

"Stole him? No, he came willingly."

I laughed.

"I'm sure he did," I said.

"Why is that funny?"

"It's not. I could just picture you at that party, determining that you were going to get Reese Lockwood for yourself."

"I usually get what I want," she said.

"Has it always been that way?"

"No. The only way to always get what you want is when you have money, but I'm sure you already know that."

I didn't agree with that assessment at all. Money certainly increases your chances, but it doesn't guarantee anything, most of all making someone truly care about you.

"My father didn't always have money," she continued. "That came when I was older. Everyone always wants what you have. That's something I've learned."

"Is someone trying to take something from you?" I asked.

"Every day."

It had gotten dark by now, and the ocean had faded to a sea of black. We could still hear the waves against the yacht as we made our journey back to Maui and then along to Oahu.

"I should get changed for dinner. Hopefully, it will be better than last night's," she said.

She got ready to leave but then turned back to me.

"Oh, I almost forgot. Reese's parents wanted me to ask you to photograph them tonight before dinner. What time works for you?"

"Please ask them to come to the lounge about half an hour before dinner. I'll walk the yacht now and find an appropriate place for the photo shoot."

"I'll tell them."

She turned from me and went toward the lounge. I watched her as she left. The breeze off the water had picked up, and the white sarong flowed as she moved across the deck. The boat light above the door was shining directly at her, so it created this glow around the form of her body. It would have made for a stunning photograph. I was too slow on the camera, though, and she vanished into the lounge by the time I raised the camera to my eye. I'd been distracted by our conversation. I'd seen a side of Tiffany Calloway that I'd doubted I'd ever get to see. Up until now, she was a one-dimensional figure that seemed more intent on making everyone's life a misery if they didn't give her what she wanted.

I couldn't stop thinking about my last question to her and her response.

"Is someone trying to take something from you?"

"Every day."

Was she referring to something or someone specific, or was she speaking in a more general sense? I didn't know, and I doubted I'd ever know. It wasn't a grand mystery on any kind of level, but I was still intrigued by it. Tiffany was apparently a woman with secrets, but we all have those, don't we?

Chapter 10
Under the Bus

I stayed topside, hoping that Foxx would magically appear, but he didn't. I was convinced that he'd either checked himself into a hotel on the Big Island or else he'd made his way to the airport for the first available flight back to Maui.

I decided to head back to the cabin and do the photography scout later so that I could get an hour or so of rest before the evening activities, mainly the photo shoot and dinner and drinks. I doubted there'd be any chance to take photographs at the dinner, nor did they probably want me to, but there was likely going to be some fireworks to witness, either Tiffany being mad at the staff or Hani or all of the above.

As I made my way past the crew cabins to get to my own, I noticed Kurt and Baakir inside theirs. Apparently, they were roommates, and Baakir must have agreed to vacate the room the previous night, at least for the time, so Kurt could have his playtime with the lovely Zelda.

"How did the beach go? Did everyone have a grand time?" Kurt asked.

If you're reading this versus listening to the audio version, then I know you didn't catch the sarcasm and bitterness in his voice.

"I hope me seeing you both still here means the captain has changed his mind and allowed you to stay as part of the crew."

"No. He's just too cheap to book us a flight back to Maui," Kurt said.

"We're to stay below until we get there in the morning," Baakir added.

"Did they ever find a chef for tonight?" I asked.

"Angela's doing it," Baakir added. "She'll be fine. She's helped me in the galley many times."

I didn't think that was the issue. Tiffany clearly had a thing against her. I doubted there was any five-star meal Angela could prepare that would meet Tiffany's standards.

"Hey, if you see Zelda, can you let her know I'm down here?" Kurt asked.

Kurt must have noticed the surprised look on my face for he followed up that question with another.

"What are they going to do? Fire me a second time?"

"No, but I would have thought you'd planned to ask the captain for a second chance after these guests departed."

Baakir laughed and then turned to his roommate.

"This cruise was the second chance, or was it the third?"

"Maybe the fourth," Kurt said, and they both laughed.

"Goodnight, gentlemen," I said, and I immediately regretted using the word gentlemen. It clearly didn't apply to either one of them.

I walked the rest of the way to the cabin and found Alana inside lying on the bed. Her hair was wet from what I guessed was a recent shower, and she'd changed into fresh clothes. I walked over to the bed and was about to plop down when she held up a hand.

"Don't drop that sweaty, sandy butt on this bed. Go jump in the shower."

"Where's Hani?"

"She went to the smaller lounge just below the bridge. She said she needed some quiet place to work on the itinerary for the rest of the trip. She's probably trying to come up with some back-up plans should Tiffany change her mind again like she did this morning."

"That's probably a smart move," I said.

"Did you see Foxx anywhere?"

"No. He never came back, at least not that I saw."

"It's my fault," she said.

"No, it's not. It's this whole situation. Everyone's in a rotten mood."

"We'll have to figure out a way to make it up to him when we see him on Maui."

I nodded.

"I'm gonna take a quick shower and then see if there's anything I can do to help. Maybe I can make the drinks tonight. I'll put my Harry's experience to good use."

"You never mix drinks at Harry's. Foxx and the other bartenders do that."

"Yeah, but how hard can it be?"

She didn't answer me, which made me think she doubted my bartending skills.

I took a hot shower, which was a challenge considering how small the shower stall was. It was difficult to turn around without my naked butt hitting something off the tiny shelf. I was pretty sure I got all of the sand off despite being unable to bend over or lift my leg more than a few inches before my knee went into the side of the shower stall. I climbed out of the shower, dried off with a lush white towel, at least the towels were good in the crew cabins, and changed into some nice clothes for my expected evening making cocktails.

"You're really going to play bartender tonight?" Alana asked as I slipped on my shoes.

"Sure. Why not? I'm just trying to help your sister."

"I get that, but dinner's not our responsibility. Captain Piadelia should have picked up additional staff members. He had all day to find someone."

"He didn't, though, at least I didn't see anyone earlier this evening."

"I think you're setting a dangerous precedent. Now they're going to expect this out of you every night. Next thing you know, the captain's going to want you to pilot the yacht."

"Won't that be fun?"

"I'm not kidding."

"Look, I can either stay down here all night and be bored, or I can mingle and be entertained."

"Entertained? By that vicious group?" Alana asked.

"You're right. They're not exactly the nicest bunch, but I'm trying to take a different perspective on all of this."

"Which is?"

"I'm looking at this like a reality TV show. Yeah, they're train wrecks, but something tells me Tiffany is going to pop tonight. I want to be there when it happens."

"Why do you think she's going to pop?"

I told Alana about my long conversation with Tiffany and how I suspected there was something much deeper going on.

"That doesn't sound like someone who's going to pop. It just sounds like she's having second thoughts about getting married. Everyone does right before the ceremony."

"Everyone?"

"Sure."

"So you had doubts?" I asked.

"It's only natural, Poe. It's a big commitment, a lifelong commitment."

"I don't know how I should be feeling right now."

"You're overreacting. I married you, didn't I?"

"Yes, but apparently only after you were wracked with indecision and doubt."

"That's not at all what I said. You're putting words in my mouth."

"How am I doing that? You just said twenty seconds ago that everyone has doubts. Did you not just say that?"

"I did, but having general doubts is a far cry from being wracked with indecision. You act like I was in some kind of dark room, sobbing and panicked because I didn't know what to do," she said.

"Dark room? Strange that your imagination took you there. Is that how you felt?"

"No. Now you've gone way past ridiculous. I'm sure you felt some degree of doubt."

"Not one bit and not for one second."

"I don't believe that."

"Believe what you want. You were perfect, and I knew how lucky I was to have you."

"Now I know you're lying."

"I'm not. I gave you a compliment."

"Are we really going to have this argument? All I was trying to say was that I thought Tiffany's feelings of uncertainty are completely normal. I'm not sure how that translates to you thinking she's about to pop."

"It's just a feeling I have. I can't explain it."

I turned to walk to the door.

"So are we still fighting about this?" she asked.

"About what?"

"About whether or not I had doubts before the wedding."

"We were never fighting. I was just playing with you."

She grabbed one of the pillows from the bed and tossed it at me.

"You enjoy messing with people too much."

"It's just a game."

"To you, maybe, but others won't appreciate your wit."

"Other people? Does that mean you don't?" I asked.

"I'll say it again. I married you, didn't I?"

"And I appreciate that."

"You better get up there and start practicing your drink-mixing skills. You don't want to make a bad martini with this bunch of characters."

"Are you coming up?"

"Eventually. I want to try to nap for half an hour or so."

"Okay. I'll see you in the main lounge."

The door to Kurt and Baakir's cabin was closed as I walked by. Either they'd decided to go to bed already for an anticipated early departure on Maui before the guests awoke, or Kurt had somehow gotten a message to Zelda and they were having round two. So, where would that have left Baakir? I shuddered to think, so I did my best to close my ears as I walked past.

I climbed the short staircase to the main lounge and sat on the sofa while I waited for Reese's parents to arrive for their photo session. They showed up just a few minutes later. Artemis was dressed in a sharp navy blue suit with a pale yellow tie, while Catherine was dressed in a black dress that hugged her body a bit too tightly around the midsection. It was low-cut, much lower than I would have thought it should be.

I suspected she was trying to match the glamour of Tiffany, Sinclair, and

Zelda, but she no longer had the figure to pull it off. I know that's judgmental of me, and I apologize for it, but I want to give you an accurate image of what she looked like. I will give her this compliment. Her hair still looked good, despite the long day outside with that strong island breeze.

Both of them seemed impressively sober, especially after the tequila shots at the Makani restaurant. How did they do it? I had no idea. Maybe they were experienced drinkers, or maybe they'd chugged a gallon of strong coffee before coming to meet me.

I asked them to follow me to the tanning area where Alana and I had spent the previous night. I'd discovered a light switch on the inside of the lounge that did a fairly good job of illuminating the outside deck. It would make for an adequate fill light, while the star-filled sky behind them would hopefully provide a dynamic background. I also thought the V-shape of the bow created a powerful composition, especially since I positioned Artemis' and Catherine's bodies to complement the lines of the yacht.

The Lockwood couple was about as stiff as I expected them to be. Actually, I should say that Catherine looked a bit uncomfortable. Artemis was fine, more than fine if the truth be told. The man had a natural love of the camera, and I began to wonder if he'd modeled before going to medical school. He just knew how to angle his face to get the best results. Catherine? Not so much.

I did my best to coach her and offer tips on posing. It took a while, but she eventually relaxed a bit, and I was able to get some nice shots of the two of them. I made a combination of wide shots and close-ups that deemphasized Catherine's body. The black dress helped hide her weight in the wide shots, whereas the close-ups didn't show her midsection at all. I didn't think she'd notice the lack of medium shots. Ah, how cameras lie.

After the shoot, we walked into the upstairs lounge, and I showed them the results. They seemed happy, or at least happy enough.

"Hani mentioned that she's worked with you several times," Catherine said.

I wasn't sure when Hani might have told them that, but I assumed it was part of her story to make me more presentable to them as a last-minute substitute photographer.

"Yes. I've known her for a while."

"I'm still not sure I trust that she knows what she's doing," Catherine said.

Was she talking about Hani having hired me, or was that more of an overall judgement on Hani's performance as a wedding planner? Either way, it wasn't just a rude thing to say, but it was also the way she said it. The lady seemed to be disgusted by Hani. I had no idea what she could have possibly done to deserve that attitude. Of course, Catherine Lockwood just might be a nasty person.

"I have every confidence in Hani. She'll deliver your son and his fiancée a fabulous wedding," I said.

"She only got the job because she did the Allerton wedding. I should have called them to verify she actually did it. I wouldn't be surprised if she lied about it."

"She didn't lie about it," I said, and then I instantly regretted it.

"How do you know? Did you photograph that wedding?" she asked.

"Not exactly, but I was there."

"What does that mean?"

I thought about making up a story, but I was too exhausted from the lack of sleep the night before, the long day in the hot sun, and now having to listen to this vile woman's mouth.

"It was my wedding. I hired Hani, and she did a remarkable job."

"You're an Allerton?" she asked.

"No. My last name is Rutherford, but my mother's maiden name was Allerton. And yes, they are the Allertons of New York."

"You're an Allerton, and you're working as a wedding photographer?"

"Yes, in a manner of speaking."

"My, how the Allertons have fallen," she said, and she turned to Artemis. "Wait until I tell Carol."

I had no idea who Carol was, nor did I even care. I found the woman deplorable, and I was tempted to hit her over the head with my Canon camera. I waited a moment to see if Artemis would tell his wife to settle down. Perhaps he'd even apologize for her. Unfortunately, he did neither. I guess we know who wears the pants in the Lockwood household.

I should have kept my mouth shut and just swallowed my pride. Instead, I threw her some shade.

"Please let dear Carol know that the Allertons are still doing fine."

"I'm not sure I like your tone," she said.

My tone? The lady certainly had nerve.

I stood.

"I better get downstairs. I'm glad you're happy with your photo session. Maybe we can do another on Oahu. There's some beautiful scenery there, as I'm sure you're aware."

I left before either of them could respond. I expected Catherine to hurl an insult at me before I exited the lounge. She didn't. Maybe she just wasn't smart or quick enough to come up with something clever.

I went downstairs to the galley and was about to say hello to Angela, Banks, and Kimi when I saw just how chaotic things were. Pots and pans were everywhere, and there was a general feeling of panic in the air. I realized that Alana was probably correct in her advice to me to stay below that evening. Nevertheless, I'm often a sucker for punishment. I decided not to bother the ladies, and I went to the lounge where I got behind the bar to practice a few popular mixed drinks.

I decided to start with a Manhattan since that was my drink of choice, and I assumed I could use a cocktail to help dull the tension of the evening after my verbal sparring with Mrs. Lockwood. One would think that I'd be an expert at making the drink since I've had more of them in my life than I care to admit.

The only alcohol I consume at home is beer or the occasional scotch. It's not that complicated to pop the top on a beer bottle or pour a small amount of Yamazaki into a glass. A Manhattan isn't the world's most complex cocktail by any means, but I'd never had one that wasn't made by a professional bartender.

I say all this to explain how my first attempt was not exactly good. I wouldn't even place it at the level of okay. It tasted somewhat like a Manhattan, but the portions were off, and I would have undoubtedly sent it back if I were served this at Harry's or any other bar for that matter.

I poured the drink down the sink and tried to figure out how I'd managed to screw it up so badly. I also tried to find a way to quickly back out of my volunteer role as the night's bartender. I'd clearly overestimated my talents.

"That bad, huh?"

I looked up and saw Foxx standing in front of the bar.

"Foxx, where have you been?"

"I was hanging out in this bar at the marina. I ran into Kimi on the way back to the yacht."

"Kimi?"

"We got to talking about what a disaster this whole thing has been. She was heading back to her cabin. I was heading to ours. We kept the conversation going and one thing led to another."

"Are you serious? You hooked up with Kimi?"

"Why is that so hard to believe?"

"I thought you were interested in Sinclair?"

"I was just talking to her last night. It was nothing more than that."

"So that's where you've been all this time? In Kimi's cabin?"

"Yeah. She told me I could stay there for a while. I was still pretty pissed at you guys, so I decided to take a long nap."

"About that. I'm sorry I brought up the thing with you and Sinclair. It was a huge mistake on my part."

"You threw me under the bus, pal."

"I did. I was trying to cover my own butt, and my behavior was deplorable. I hope you can forgive me."

Foxx hesitated.

Then he said, "On one condition."

"Name it."

"You promise not to make me one of those."

He laughed and pointed to the empty glass in my hand.

"Not a word about me and Kimi to Alana and Hani," Foxx continued. "I know she's not one of the guests, but I'm sure those two will still be pissed."

"Not a word. Does this mean I'm forgiven?" I asked.

"Yeah. I can't stay mad at you. Besides, I would have done the same thing if I were in your shoes."

Foxx joined me behind the bar.

"What were you trying to make anyway?"

"A Manhattan. I opened my big mouth and volunteered to make drinks for the night since Angela is bogged down with dinner. I wasn't sure if Kimi and Banks could serve the food and mix all the drinks I'm sure that group is going to consume tonight."

"I hate to break it to you, but you're a lousy bartender."

"You should have told me that before I volunteered."

"Don't worry. I'll help with the drinks. You do what you do best and stick to the photography."

"Thanks, man."

"You're welcome," Foxx said.

So, why was I seemingly okay with Foxx fooling around with Kimi while I thought Kurt was a jerk for messing around with Zelda? Was I employing a double standard? Of course I was, but Foxx is a friend. Don't most of us usually look the other way for our friends?

Chapter 11
I Know What You Did

The evening started off much smoother than I could have expected. Our wedding party arrived for dinner around eight. Angela had prepared a fairly simple yet classic meal. The first course was a salad with a light vinaigrette dressing. It seemed to be a success for I noticed most of the plates were completely empty as Kimi and Banks brought the dishes back to the galley.

This course was followed by filet mignons with side dishes of asparagus with minced garlic, mashed potatoes, and sautéed mushrooms in a butter sauce. All of the sides were served family style in large bowls placed in the center of the table.

The group opted for red wine, so there really wasn't much for Foxx to do in terms of bartending duties. We were close enough to the dinner table to eavesdrop on the conversation, which grew louder as the wine was consumed. There weren't any major revelations during the conversation. Most of it predictably centered on the upcoming wedding on Kauai and how beautiful the beach had been that day.

There was brief mention of my photography session with Sinclair. Trenholme seemed to take delight in teasing her about it. I wasn't sure why he did that. Perhaps he had a thing for her, and this was his indirect way of expressing it.

At one point in the dinner, Raymond Calloway, Tiffany's father, reflected on his wedding to her mother years ago. Apparently, they were married at the famous Hotel del Coronado. I'd visited there before on a business trip to San Diego.

It wasn't hard to tell how much he missed his wife. He spoke of the dress she'd worn that day, how her hair had looked, how he'd felt as he watched her walk down the aisle. It was all quite touching, and I felt terrible for him that she'd been taken away. I wasn't close enough to the table to see if Raymond's eyes had teared up during the story, but I did hear his voice crack once or twice.

The table had gone silent during his story. Then Artemis suddenly changed the subject back to the upcoming wedding. I thought it was a rather rude thing to do, especially since he hadn't waited for a natural end in the story. He'd basically cut the man off mid-sentence. I didn't think he'd thought Raymond had been getting uncomfortable and he'd jumped in to try to spare the man. If he had, he certainly wouldn't have started his sentence with the two words, "Well, now."

Raymond, for his part, seemed content to let the incident pass. I halfway expected Tiffany to speak up and point out Artemis' lack of manners. She seemed to have no issue with doing so for everyone else, but she said nothing. Maybe she was trying to stay on her future father-in-law's good side.

The final course of the meal was dessert, which consisted of cheesecake topped with fresh fruit from the Big Island. All in all, I would say that Angela outdid herself. It also served to highlight just how weak of a chef Baakir seemed to be. I would pick Angela over him any day of the week.

After dinner, Zelda, Sinclair, and Trenholme walked back into the lounge and headed over to the bar where Foxx and I were. Trenholme asked for a bourbon, which Foxx poured for him.

Foxx turned to the two women.

"Can I get you ladies anything?"

"So you're not just a photographer's assistant? You bartend, too?" Sinclair asked.

"I like to think of myself as multi-talented," Foxx said.

"I'm sure you are," Trenholme said somewhat under his breath, and he took a sip of his bourbon.

On any other night, Foxx would have told Trenholme what he could do with his muttering self. Tonight, though, Foxx swallowed his pride like the rest of us had been doing since stepping foot on this yacht.

"Did you enjoy dinner?" a female voice asked.

We turned to see Angela emerge from the galley. She was dressed in a chef's white jacket and black pants.

"It was delicious," Zelda said.

"I would hope so, after last night's debacle," Tiffany said.

I looked to my left and saw Tiffany and Reese walk up to the bar.

"The steaks were cooked perfectly," Sinclair added, and she dragged out the word perfectly to emphasize it.

Was that more a compliment to Angela or a dig at Tiffany? I didn't know.

"I thought mine was a bit on the raw side," Tiffany said.

"Raw? You should have sent it back. I would have gladly cooked it longer for you," Angela said.

"I thought about it, but I didn't want to be a bother."

Really?

"It wouldn't have been a bother," Angela said.

"What is the status of your search for a new chef? Will we have one tomorrow night?" Tiffany asked.

"I believe so. I think he's supposed to join us at our next port of call," Angela said.

"I'm glad. I'd hate for you to be so overworked," Tiffany said.

"Why do you always have to give her such a hard time?" Sinclair asked.

And this was the moment I'd been waiting for.

"Pardon me?" Tiffany asked.

Why do people always ask that when we all know they heard exactly what everyone else heard?

"You're always riding her. She's doing her best," Sinclair said.

"This is my cruise. What I do or don't do is none of your concern."

"How is it not my concern? We're all friends here," Sinclair said.

"Are we?" Tiffany asked.

"Sure, Tiff. You know we are," Zelda said.

"I'm not so sure about that," Tiffany said to Zelda. Then she turned back to Sinclair. "I know what you did," she continued.

Normally, one would expect Sinclair to respond with a question such as, "No, what did I do?" She didn't do that, though, and I could only surmise that it was because she did, in fact, know exactly what Tiffany was accusing her of doing. Did I know? Of course not, but that didn't stop my imagination from kicking into overdrive.

No one said anything after the "I know what you did" statement. I waited for someone else, such as Zelda or Reese, to pipe up and try to diffuse the situation. They didn't.

Sinclair continued to look at Tiffany, who by now had this smirk on her face, and neither woman seemed willing to break eye contact.

I felt a nudge on my arm. I looked down and saw Foxx holding out a shot of bourbon. He had another one in his other hand. I took one of the glasses from him, and we quietly touched them together as if toasting to this gladiator smack down that we were witnessing. Tacky on our part? Absolutely. It's what we did, though, and I want to as honest as possible in the telling of this tale.

"Maybe it was a mistake to ask you to be my bridesmaid," Tiffany finally said after several seconds of silence.

"You don't mean that," Reese said.

"Why don't I?" Tiffany asked.

"Sinclair is a good friend, and she came all this way to help us celebrate," he said.

Tiffany laughed.

"It's amazing what people are willing to do when someone else is footing the bill."

"Screw you, Tiffany," Sinclair said, although she actually used a more colorful word than "screw." "You don't want me to be in your wedding? Fine."

"Calm down, both of you. It's been a long day, and we've all had too much to drink," Reese said.

"You're not the boss of me, Reese," Tiffany said.

I sipped my bourbon and turned to Foxx. He didn't notice me looking at him because he was too busy watching the fight between Tiffany and everyone else. I looked past Foxx and saw Alana and Hani standing at the entrance of the hallway that led back to the galley. They were just as caught up in the moment as the rest of us.

"You can be a real bitch," Reese said.

He turned from the group and walked back toward the dinner table where Mr. Calloway and Mr. and Mrs. Lockwood were also watching the disagreement. Sinclair must have taken that as her cue to exit as well. She walked in the opposite direction and presumably headed back toward her cabin.

"I think I'd like another drink," Trenholme said, and he put his empty glass on the bar.

"Sure thing," Foxx said.

He quickly poured him another bourbon.

Zelda walked over to Tiffany and put her hand on her shoulder.

"Why don't we go outside and get some air," she suggested.

Tiffany nodded, and the two women left the lounge.

Alana and Hani walked over to us while Trenholme went back to the dinner table to join his brother and parents. I don't know if Raymond said anything else or not, especially after Reese had called his daughter a bitch, but he eventually stood and headed in the direction Tiffany and Zelda had gone just a few minutes earlier.

"How did that all start?" Alana asked.

"Sinclair made the mistake of complimenting Angela on her dinner," Foxx said.

"Let me guess. Tiffany wasn't having any of that," Hani added.

Foxx nodded.

"You got it."

"I think that's enough drama for me for the night. I'm going to try to get some sleep," I said.

"Are you sleeping on the air mattress or the deck like last night?" Alana asked.

"Probably the deck. That cabin is just too small."

Then I realized that Foxx might be joining Kimi later, which would leave more room for the rest of us. I didn't say anything since I vowed to keep my mouth shut, something that's often difficult for me to do.

"I'll meet you up there. I need to grab a sweatshirt," Alana said.

It was after midnight by the time Alana and I lay down on the sunning deck. The air was cool, a little too cool, but Alana also had the foresight to grab a blanket when she'd gone back to the cabin.

"What do you think Tiffany was referring to when she said 'I know what you did'?" I asked.

"Sinclair slept with someone she shouldn't have, had to be."

"Really?"

"I don't know what else could possibly make Tiffany that mad."

"So who do you think she slept with?"

"Good question. Maybe Reese."

"Reese? I doubt that. There's no way she'd ask Sinclair to be her bridesmaid if she'd had sex with her fiancée," I said.

"Maybe she just found out."

"I don't know. Something tells me Tiffany would have physically attacked Sinclair if that was the case."

"You're probably right. So if it wasn't something to do with sex, then what was it?" Alana asked.

"Maybe it's money. Isn't that usually the two big things in a relationship fight, sex and money?"

"I'd add power. It's always been the big three in my experience."

"How many more days are we stuck with these people?" I asked.

"Three more days of sightseeing and then the wedding on the fourth day."

"Four more days. I'm not sure if I can make it or not."

I don't know how long it took us to fall asleep, but it was around two in the morning when Foxx woke us up.

"I've been looking all over for you two. You didn't hear me yelling?" he asked.

"We must have both been sleeping pretty hard."

"What's going on? Why are you here?" Alana asked.

"Tiffany's been attacked. You need to come below," Foxx said.

"Attacked? By who?" Alana asked.

"I have no idea what happened. You better see for yourself."

We followed Foxx back to the lounge on the main deck. As soon as we entered the lounge, we saw a crowd standing near the dining table in the back. Zelda and Sinclair were crying. Artemis had his arm wrapped around his wife. Reese was standing away from the group. Trenholme walked over to him and put his hand on his shoulder. Reese didn't seem to even notice his brother. He looked like he was in a state of shock.

Most of the crew, including Angela, Kimi, Banks, Baakir, Kurt, and Captain Piadelia were there as well. As we pushed our way through the crowd, we saw Raymond sitting on the floor near the dinner table. Tiffany's body was also on the floor, and her head was in her father's lap. There was a massive amount of blood all over the deck boards and down the front of her dress.

Alana stepped up to Tiffany and pulled her long hair away from her face and neck. I saw what looked like a stab wound to her throat.

Tiffany Calloway was dead.

Chapter 12
Raymond Calloway

Alana checked for a pulse in Tiffany's neck. It seemed like more of a formality than anything else. It was obvious she was no longer with us.

Alana turned back to me and subtly shook her head. She then turned to Raymond.

"What happened, Mr. Calloway?"

He didn't respond. He just kept looking at his daughter's lifeless face. He hadn't even responded when Alana had moved Tiffany's hair away from her neck.

"Mr. Calloway, did you see who did this to her?" Alana asked.

He still didn't say anything.

"Mr. Calloway," Alana said louder.

He finally looked over to her.

"What happened?" she asked again.

"I found her on the floor. She wouldn't wake up."

"Was there anyone else here?"

"No. I looked, but there was no one."

Alana turned to the group.

"Who was the first person here after Mr. Calloway?"

"I was," Kimi said. "I was on my way to the galley to get something to drink when I heard him scream. I ran in here and saw him just like he is now."

"We came up after that," Sinclair said.

"We?" Alana asked.

"Zelda and I."

"Yes. We both rushed up here," Zelda confirmed.

Alana turned to me. I was just a couple of feet from her at this point.

"Do me a favor. Look for the murder weapon," she whispered.

I nodded.

"Captain Piadelia, how long until we make it back to Maui?" Alana asked.

"Six to seven hours."

"Can I speak to you in private for a moment?" she asked.

I saw Alana and the captain walk away from the group.

While they were talking, I examined the area under and around the dining table. Blood had pooled on the deck directly in front of the table, but there was nothing that even remotely resembled a murder weapon.

I looked around the area. It was only about fifteen to twenty feet from the table where Tiffany's body was to the railings that ran along the outer edges of the yacht. It would have been easy to simply toss the knife or whatever had been used to kill her over the railing and into the ocean below.

I pulled my cell phone out of my front pocket and activated the flashlight app. It took me less than ten seconds to find several blood drops leading from the table to the railing, which confirmed my theory.

Alana finished talking to the captain, and they both walked back to the group.

I looked over to Reese. He still seemed to be frozen in place as if someone had simply deactivated him. He didn't look distressed, nor did he seem sad or even panicked. He just had this neutral look about him that defied logic.

"We'd like everyone to leave the main lounge area. Please either return to your cabins or go to the lounge area on the deck above us," Captain Piadelia said.

"I'm going to be talking with each of you in the next few hours," Alana said.

"Why? Who made you boss?" Catherine asked.

"I happen to be a detective with the Maui Police Department."

"A detective?" Artemis asked, and he turned to Hani. "I thought she was your assistant."

"My sister's a detective," Hani said. "I asked her to help me with this wedding since it was such a big job."

"This is ridiculous. We're not going to be interrogated like common criminals," Catherine said.

"Your daughter-in-law has just been murdered. I would think you'd want to help catch whoever did this," Alana said.

"Of course, we'll help, detective. Please forgive us. This is all just so much to process," Artemis said.

"Yes, we want to help," Reese said, somewhat out of his trance.

He'd made the statement like some sort of zombie, though, as if he'd said something that he assumed he needed to say out of sheer politeness. There was no passion or determination behind it. It was beyond strange, and I'd never experienced anything like it before.

I watched as his father looked at him. It was clear from the look on Artemis' face that he was just as confused by his son's demeanor as I was. Was this odd behavior indicative of guilt, meaning had Reese been the one to knife his fiancée to death and now he was in a state of utter shock and confusion as his brain tried to process the horrific act he'd committed? Maybe, probably, and I only thought that because I couldn't come up with another explanation.

Alana turned to Hani, whose hands were visibly shaking by now.

"Hani, please go below and grab a bedsheet out of our cabin."

Hani left the lounge without saying a word and headed for the stairway.

"Did you find anything?" Alana asked me.

I told Alana about the blood drops leading to the railing and my suspicion that the killer had tossed the weapon overboard.

"I assumed as much," she said.

"How can I help?" I asked.

"In a moment."

Alana turned back to Captain Piadelia.

"Captain, please radio the authorities and let them know there's been an incident onboard. I want law enforcement to meet us at the marina."

Piadelia nodded, and he left the main lounge.

"Everyone, please return to your cabins," Alana said, since no one seemed to have taken the captain's earlier request seriously. "We'll be with you as soon as we can," she continued.

No one wanted to be the first to exit. Then Angela, Kimi, and Banks headed out and one by one, the group slowly left the lounge.

"Let me know if you need anything," Foxx said.

"Thank you," Alana said.

Foxx looked at me a second. Then he walked away.

The only people left at this point were myself, Alana, and Raymond, who was still cradling his daughter.

Hani reappeared a moment later with the bedsheet, which she handed to Alana. "Thank you."

"Do you need anything else?" Hani asked.

"No. You should go back to your cabin."

Hani left again, and Alana walked over to Raymond.

"Mr. Calloway, we need to talk to you. Can you come over here and sit with me?"

He didn't respond.

"Mr. Calloway, please. I need to talk to you. We need to find out what happened."

Raymond said nothing, but he gently lifted his daughter's head off his lap as he got to his knees. He rested her head on the deck boards.

Alana handed me the white sheet, and I laid it over Tiffany's body. The blood immediately soaked into the sheet and turned it red.

Raymond watched me the entire time. He slowly turned away from the table, and Alana led him to the large sofa at the opposite side of the lounge.

I wasn't sure what Alana wanted me to do. I'd interviewed people with her several times, but she was the cop. I wasn't. I didn't want to cross the line and interfere with her investigation, even though she'd already asked me to search for a murder weapon.

She and Raymond sat on the sofa. Alana looked over to me and motioned to the chair beside the sofa. I walked into the lounge and sat down.

"We're going to find out who did this, Mr. Calloway, but we need your help. Tell us what you saw," Alana said.

"It was him. It had to be him."

"Who? Who did it have to be?" Alana asked.

"Her fiancée. Who else could it be?"

"Did you see him doing something?" she asked.

"No, but you saw how they were after dinner. I'm sure you heard him call her a bitch. He never treated her the way she deserved to be treated. She was such a wonderful person. She didn't deserve this. No one does."

"How did Reese treat her? Had he physically hurt her before?" Alana asked.

"No, not that Tiffany ever talked about, but I didn't like the way he talked to her. He'd yell at her, treat her with disrespect."

"What would they fight about?" I asked.

"She thought he was unfaithful," Raymond said.

"She told you that?" Alana asked.

"Not exactly, but I knew that's what was bothering her."

"I'm not sure I understand. If Tiffany didn't say he'd been cheating on her, then what made you suspect that?" Alana asked.

"She said she had doubts about him. She wasn't sure she wanted to marry him. What else would it be?"

There were plenty of things, I thought, but I assumed there must have been something else Raymond wasn't telling us, either intentionally or not.

"When was the last time you spoke with Tiffany?" I asked.

"Around midnight. We were all here in the lounge."

"Who exactly was here?" Alana asked.

"Everyone. Reese, his brother and parents, Sinclair and Zelda."

"Were any of the staff waiting on you?" I asked.

"Two of the girls. I don't remember their names."

"Kimi and Banks?" Alana asked.

"I think so."

"So you were here in the lounge. Was everyone drinking?" I asked.

Raymond nodded.

"Things were tense, especially after Tiffany's blowup with Reese and Sinclair," he said.

"Why was Tiffany mad at Sinclair?" Alana asked.

"I don't know. She never told me anything about it."

"When you left the lounge, did everyone come down to the cabins with you or were there still people here?"

"I was the first to leave. I was exhausted, especially after being sick the night before. I wanted to go to bed earlier, but I was worried about Tiffany and Reese fighting."

"Did you hear anyone else come down later to the cabin area or were you already asleep by then?" Alana asked.

"I went to sleep as soon as my head hit the pillow. I did wake up at some point, though. I thought I heard fighting. Then I heard someone walking down the hallway in front of my cabin door."

"When you say fighting, do you mean a physical fight or a verbal fight?" I asked.

"They were yelling...well, maybe not yelling, but speaking louder than normal. I got up and looked out into the hallway. I saw the door to Tiffany's cabin was open. I looked inside but didn't see anyone there, so I walked back up here and saw her."

"And no one was in the lounge then? Just Tiffany?" I asked.

Raymond nodded.

"That's right."

"Forgive me for asking this. I know it's a really sensitive question, but was Tiffany still alive when you found her?" Alana asked.

"No. I don't think so. I shook her, but she wouldn't wake up."

"A minute ago, you said you heard yelling down below in the guests' cabin area. Could you make out what they were saying?" I asked.

"Not really. I was mostly asleep. By the time my mind cleared enough for me to know what was going on, I heard the footsteps walking past my cabin."

"Running? Not walking?" Alana asked.

"I'm not sure. They were just loud."

"After you looked into your daughter's bedroom, you came straight up here or did you go anywhere else first?" I asked.

"Straight here."

"Mr. Calloway, other than the verbal altercation with Reese earlier this evening, can you think of anyone who was upset with Tiffany or who may have wanted to hurt her?" Alana asked.

"No. There was no one."

"I know this is hard, but we need to speak with the other guests. Can you go down to your cabin now? We'll come see you as soon as we can and let you know what we've learned," Alana said.

Raymond didn't answer her. He looked past us toward his daughter's body. I watched as his eyes filled with tears.

"She was my only child. I loved her more than anyone," he said.

"I'm sorry, Mr. Calloway. I'm truly sorry," I said.

Chapter 13
Sinclair Dewey

"I think we should speak with Reese next. He seems like the most obvious suspect," Alana said.

I knew exactly what Alana was getting at. It wasn't just the fact that we'd heard Reese speaking ugly to his fiancée just a few hours before her death, but boyfriends and spouses were the ones most likely to have committed violent crimes against women. In fact, I believe the violent crime statistic is more than fifty percent, and of those murders, about a third of them occurred directly after a heated argument.

"Might I make another suggestion?" I asked.

"Sure. What is it?"

"We assume Reese's argument with Tiffany had something to do with Tiffany's comment to Sinclair."

"Yes. The one where she said 'I know what you did.'"

"Exactly. Maybe we should talk to Sinclair next. Find out what Tiffany was talking about. We know Reese is going to deny he had anything to do with killing Tiffany. Let's hit him with the knowledge that we already know exactly what he and Tiffany were fighting about."

"That's a good idea. There's something else I want to do, and we're going to need Foxx's help."

"What is it?"

"You don't stab someone in the neck without getting blood all over yourself. Did you notice anyone with blood on them while we were all standing around the dining table?"

"No, and I made a point to look at their clothes and their hands. I didn't see anyone with cuts," I said.

"I didn't either. The killer obviously changed clothes, which means the bloody clothes have to be somewhere."

"Unless they tossed those overboard, too."

"It's certainly possible, but maybe not. Perhaps they were too afraid to venture out of their cabin. They'd have known it was only a matter of time before someone found Tiffany's body. They probably didn't want to risk being seen wondering the yacht with bloody clothes in their hands."

"What did you say to Captain Piadelia when you two went off to the side?" I asked.

"I asked him about video cameras on the yacht. I'd assumed they'd be on the main parts of the yacht, but I didn't notice any."

"I haven't seen any either, which surprises me. What did he say?"

"They don't have them. In fact, he said it's one of their major selling points to their guests. The rich want to make sure no one is secretly recording them while they're on vacation."

"You mean while they're drunk and committing all sorts of sins they don't want the tabloids to see."

"Of course. He said the marinas have cameras, which is the main time they actually need security."

It made sense, sort of, but I thought I'd still have found a way to discreetly hide cameras if this had been my yacht. The thing was worth tens of millions of dollars. I found it irresponsible to not have some form of video surveillance.

On the other hand, maybe the owner wasn't as concerned for his guests as much as he was worried about himself. Who knew what kind of boss he was. Maybe he was a world-class tyrant, and he worried his staff would be the ones actually leaking incriminating video of him. It didn't take much to ruin people these days. I think we've all seen one inappropriate video on YouTube destroy a career in a matter of hours.

I walked down to the cabins to find Sinclair, but I made a stop first to speak with Foxx and fill him in on the plan. Hani was sitting on top of the bed. Her hands had finally stopped shaking.

"I can't believe this has happened. Who do you think did this?" she asked.

"I don't know, but I feel pretty confident Alana will figure this out."

"Maybe not. I mean it could have been anyone. Nobody on this ship liked Tiffany, especially the crew. You should have heard some of the things they were saying about her while they were making dinner."

"What did they say?" Foxx asked.

"That they thought she was going out of her way to belittle them, Angela especially. Apparently, she has a history with Tiffany."

"Did you ask Angela about that?" I asked.

"I did. She said she's known Tiffany for years."

"Did she say how they knew each other?" Foxx asked.

"No, and I didn't ask. Angela thinks that Tiffany only booked this yacht because she knew Angela was chief stew on it and Tiffany wanted to humiliate her by making her wait on her."

That was interesting, and it suddenly opened the lists of suspects up to members of the crew, or at the very least one crew member in particular.

"Did you tell Tiffany about this yacht or did she specifically request it?" I asked.

"She asked for it by name. Actually, she didn't ask for it. She demanded it. She said if the yacht wasn't available the week she wanted, then she was more than willing to move the date for the wedding ceremony on Kauai."

"How hard would that have been to do?" Foxx asked.

"Extremely hard. That resort on Kauai is the most popular one on the entire island. It's the most glamorous, and it has the best views. It books up several months in advance. If she'd wanted to move the wedding date to accommodate the yacht's availability, it probably would have resulted in delaying the wedding for a long time, maybe even a year."

"Did you let her know that?" I asked.

"Of course, but she said it didn't matter. She had to have this yacht. She was even willing to move the wedding to another island if she had to."

"Did you ask her why it was so important?"

"I did, but she didn't give me a specific reason. She just repeated that it had to be this one."

"Just curious, when you booked this cruise, how did you do it?"

"There's a booking service you go through. They put me in touch with the woman who manages the schedule for the yacht, as well as the pricing. We discussed the specific dates and a proposed itinerary. I also had to negotiate bringing us on the cruise since Tiffany wanted the entire trip documented. They quoted me an overall package, and I forwarded that estimate to Tiffany for her final approval."

"How about payment for something like this? Is it all in advance?" I asked.

"They paid a deposit of fifty percent several months in advance. The second half was due about thirty days out."

"So the party had to pay the entire bill before they even set foot on the yacht?" I asked.

"That's right, but it's pretty standard for this type of thing. The gratuity for the crew comes at the end of the voyage."

"Who paid the invoice? Did the two families split it?" Foxx asked.

"No. Raymond Calloway paid the entire thing himself."

"I know you've done several big weddings now. Is that normal for the bride's family to pay for the entire thing? I know that used to be the tradition, but I assumed that wasn't the case anymore," I said.

"It just depends. Usually the families divide the costs, but sometimes one family will pay for everything, especially if that family is decidedly better off."

"Did you notice any tension between the two families regarding the money?" I asked, remembering the argument I'd overheard between Raymond and Artemis on the first night.

"No. I didn't hear anything like that."

"Back to Angela. Did you hear her make any kind of threat to Tiffany?"

"No."

Hani paused a moment.

Then she said, "Actually, Kimi said something. When Angela was making dinner last night, Kimi mentioned that they should put something in Tiffany's food that would make her sick again, but I just assumed she was joking."

I'd worked in restaurants myself, and I'd heard fellow waiters talk about slipping things like eye drops into annoying customers' drinks to make them sick. I never saw anyone do that, though. Of course, that didn't mean it didn't happen.

I turned to Foxx.

"I'm going to get Sinclair and Zelda now, but I know Alana wants to interview them one at a time. You ready to do your thing?"

"Absolutely."

I left the cabin and walked to the area where the guests were staying. The door to Sinclair's and Zelda's cabin was shut, so I knocked on it. Zelda opened the door a few seconds later. I saw Sinclair sitting on one of the beds in the background. Both of the women looked shaken, but I already expected that to be the case. I asked them to go with me to the upstairs lounge. Alana had decided to conduct the interviews as far away as possible from the main lounge where Tiffany's body still was.

I walked Zelda just outside by the tanning deck and told her we'd interview her shortly. She sat on one of the deck chairs that wasn't too far from where Alana and I had been sleeping just an hour or so before.

I walked back into the lounge, shut the sliding glass door behind me, and saw Sinclair had already taken a seat on the sofa beside Alana. I sat on a matching chair off to the side.

"First, I'd like to say how sorry I am for your loss. I know you were very close to her. How long did you know Tiffany?" Alana asked.

"Most of my life. Zelda, Tiffany, and I met in first grade. We went all the way through high school together. We even went to the same university."

"That's impressive that you've stayed friends this long. I know how easy it can be for people to drift apart, especially as they get older and careers and families take them in different directions," Alana said.

"We made a pact not to let that happen to us."

"Do all three of you live in the same city?" I asked.

"Zelda lives about thirty minutes from Tiffany and Reese's condo in New York. I live in another state now. I got a marketing job in Chicago."

"How often did you and Tiffany see each other before you moved?" Alana asked.

"At least once a week. We'd try to meet for drinks every Friday night after work. Zelda and Tiffany are both lawyers, and the agency where I used to work wasn't that far from their firms," Sinclair said, and then she teared up. "I don't know how I'm ever going to get used to talking about her in the past tense."

"I know it's hard, and I'm sorry to have to press you for information, but we have to ask these questions," Alana said.

Sinclair wiped her tears away with the back of her hand.

"You said that you ladies would meet after work," Alana continued.

"Yes. Sometimes Reese and Tiffany would invite us over for dinner on the weekend."

"So it wasn't a surprise to you when Tiffany asked you to be a bridesmaid," I said.

"Not at all. We were good friends."

"I'm afraid we have to ask you a difficult question. Tonight, after dinner, we heard Tiffany mention that she knew what you did. She seemed very upset. What was she talking about?" Alana asked.

Sinclair hesitated.

Then she said, "I'm not sure."

"You're not sure or you don't know?" Alana asked.

"I don't know. I hadn't done anything to her."

"That's a bit strange since that was such a specific statement for her to have made," Alana said.

"I'm not sure how close you were paying attention. I don't even remember seeing you in the room at that point, but Tiffany had several glasses of wine at dinner. She wasn't exactly herself when she said that."

Sinclair turned to me.

"You saw how drunk she was. Tell her."

"She was intoxicated. I'll agree to that, but she didn't seem sloppy drunk. She had no problem walking, and her words were very clear," I said.

"You didn't know her like I did. She could be very cruel sometimes, especially when she had too much to drink."

"Why stay friends with someone like that?" I asked.

"Because I'm not going to throw away a friendship of over twenty years because of the occasional drunk comment. Most of the time she would never even remember the next morning what she'd said. I guarantee you everything would have been fine this morning if…."

Her words trailed off as she began to cry. This time even harder. She was sobbing within seconds. Zelda must have heard her because the sliding glass door to the lounge opened, and she walked quickly over to the sofa. Zelda sat beside Sinclair and wrapped her arms around her.

The interview was basically over now as I assumed it would take Sinclair a while to recompose herself. We hadn't learned much beyond the fact that the three women were old friends and two of them lived in New York, presumably New York City, while the third friend had moved to Chicago.

The big reveal, if Sinclair could be trusted, was that Tiffany's accusation of "I know what you did" was nothing more than a drunk, nonsensical outburst. Did I believe Sinclair? Well, there are two prevailing theories when it comes to things said while drunk. Some believe that one's true feelings emerge when one has had too much to drink. Others declare that you should never listen to what an intoxicated person has to say.

What are my feelings on the matter? I believe you have to take it on a case by case basis. Sinclair was right when she'd said that I'd seen how Tiffany was. She did have a lot of wine that night, but she'd come across as someone who could handle her drinks. I tended to believe there was much more behind her words.

"I know what you did."

It had to mean something.

Chapter 14
Zelda Cameron

It took several minutes for Sinclair to calm down and stop crying. She said she wanted to go back to her cabin to rest. I couldn't come up with anything to say to try to delay her. I wasn't sure how much time had passed since we'd all been in the upper lounge. Maybe Foxx had already done his search of their cabin, as I'd requested him to do.

I doubted Sinclair or Zelda would have been the one to kill Tiffany, but if there was one thing I'd learned from previous investigations, it's that you just never know what someone is capable of doing when they're under pressure. Husbands kill wives. Wives kill husbands. Friends turn on friends. You simply cannot predict human behavior, especially when heightened emotions come into play.

Sinclair left the lounge, while Zelda stayed seated on the sofa at Alana's urging. I hadn't been looking in Zelda's direction during our interview with Sinclair, so I didn't know how much eavesdropping she might have done. The glass door looked fairly thick, though, so maybe she wouldn't have been able to hear anything even if she'd tried.

"Sinclair told us about how long the three of you have been friends," Alana said.

Zelda didn't respond. She just stared off into the distance.

"Do you know how long Tiffany and Reese have known each other?" Alana continued.

"I guess it's been about ten years. I remember they met our freshman year in college."

"Were you with her when they met?" I asked.

"I was. We were at a fraternity party."

"What university did you attend?" I asked.

"Harvard."

She said it without the slightest hint of pride or arrogance. I wasn't sure what I was expecting her to say, but I was caught a little off-guard by the answer. I don't know why, but I was. Her answer meant one thing. We were dealing with very smart people, which just made this task of uncovering Tiffany's killer that much harder, if it was someone in the wedding party, that is.

"Had they been dating all this time?" Alana asked.

"They were off and on the first few years. Then steady after that. They got engaged last year on Tiffany's birthday. Reese took her to Paris. He proposed to her under the Eiffel Tower."

An engagement in Paris? I'd done the same thing, and I wondered if I'd inadvertently contributed to a cliché.

"Sinclair mentioned that she recently moved to Chicago for a new job," Alana said.

"Yes. She works in advertising. New York is the capital of that field, of course, but she got an incredible opportunity in Chicago that she couldn't turn down."

"It must be hard to be away from her friends in New York," I said.

"It is. That's one of the reasons we were all so excited about this trip."

"When we spoke with Mr. Calloway, he said that he heard people arguing in the cabin area, which is what caused him to get up and look for the source of the disagreement. He said he assumed it was Reese and Tiffany. Did you hear anyone arguing?" Alana asked.

"I wouldn't have if it was in the cabin area. I came up here to sleep, right here on this sofa."

"Why would you do that?" I asked.

Zelda hesitated.

"You're rooming with Sinclair, aren't you?" I asked.

She nodded.

"Sinclair wanted the cabin to herself? Why?" Alana asked.

"She and Reese wanted to talk in private."

"They wanted to talk?" I asked.

"It was about the argument Tiffany had with Sinclair just after dinner."

I decided to try a tactic that had worked fairly well for me in the past. It's not a revolutionary idea, but it tends to be effective if you use it with conviction. It goes something like this: When you're interviewing someone, assume you already know the truth and you're just coming to them for confirmation. Truly convince yourself that you have it right so that you can convince others of the same.

"Sinclair admitted to the affair. What I don't understand is how Tiffany found out about it," I said.

I saw Alana look at me out of the corner of my one good eye. She'd been subtle, but I'd noticed it.

Zelda didn't respond, and I knew she was running through the odds in her mind and asking herself all sorts of questions. Would Sinclair have admitted that to us? Was that why she was crying? Was I lying about knowing? If I was, then how had I figured it out so quickly? Had someone else told me? If so, who?

"What exactly did she say?" Zelda asked.

Nice countermove, Zelda. Nice.

"She admitted her feelings for Reese. I'm sure it was hard for her to suppress them, especially with the wedding approaching," I said.

How was that for a vague answer? Hopefully, it hadn't appeared too vague.

"It happened before she moved away. Tiffany had gone out of town for business, but Sinclair and I decided to meet for drinks anyway. Reese met us there as well. We all had too much to drink. Sinclair called me the next morning. She was really upset. She said that she and Reese had hooked up. They'd both regretted it, but she didn't know what to do. She asked me if I thought she should tell Tiffany what she'd done. I convinced her not to."

"Why would Tiffany suspect something now?" Alana asked.

"It was Trenholme's fault. He made a comment at dinner."

"What did he say?" I asked.

"He's always had a big mouth, and he was drunk. He brought up the fact that he didn't think he could ever forgive someone cheating on him. His mother said that she agreed with him, and then Trenholme asked Tiffany how she could be so forgiving. I couldn't believe it."

"Did Tiffany ask him what he was talking about?" I asked.

"No, and I didn't know if that's because she already knew or if she just assumed Trenholme was being stupid because he'd had too much to drink."

"Why would Trenholme try to sabotage his brother like that?" Alana asked.

"He's always been jealous of Reese. That's the only explanation I can come up with. I don't know how he would have found out about Sinclair and Reese because I can't imagine Reese being careless enough to have told him about it."

"Maybe he was talking about someone else," I suggested.

"I don't know. Maybe."

"Did Tiffany ever express to you that she had suspicions about Reese and Sinclair or any other woman for that matter?" I asked.

"No. Never."

"Did she ask you about them after dinner tonight?" I asked.

"I expected her to, but she didn't."

"We left the lounge after Reese insulted her. Did things escalate from there?" Alana asked.

"Not really. They both kind of ignored each other after that. Tiffany was on one side of the lounge with me and her father, and Reese was with his family on the other. It was pretty awkward."

"Where was Sinclair?" I asked.

"She was with Reese's family, but I think she made it a point to sit near his parents. She stayed away from Reese."

"Did Tiffany and Reese argue a lot?" I asked.

"I'm not sure. They had fights like everyone does."

"Has Reese ever had a history of violence with Tiffany?" Alana asked.

"No. No way."

Zelda hesitated.

Then she asked, "Is that what you think? You think Reese killed Tiffany?"

"We all witnessed them arguing and apparently it was about Tiffany's possible knowledge of an affair between Reese and Sinclair. He was the man she was about to marry, and Sinclair was a bridesmaid. That's quite a betrayal," Alana said.

"He would never hurt her. There's no chance of that."

"Then who on this yacht would want to hurt her?" I asked.

"I can tell you exactly who. It was Kurt."

"Why do you think that?" Alana asked.

"Because I heard him threaten her. He did it to me, too. That's why Tiffany reported him to the captain."

"When did this happen?" I asked.

"Yesterday morning. I told Tiffany and Sinclair about Kurt and me. They thought it was funny."

"Funny?" Alana asked.

"Well, not exactly funny. We all remarked shortly after we boarded how we thought Kurt was cute. I got to talking to him that night. He was up here in this lounge by himself. I was walking around the boat, and I ran into him. He made me a drink at the bar over there. He had one, too. After a while, he invited me to come see his cabin. I knew what he really wanted, but I thought 'why not? I'm on vacation.'"

"When you told Tiffany, she didn't have a problem with it?" I asked.

"No. Why would she? She actually joked with him about it when she ran into him the next morning. Kurt found me and threatened me. He demanded to know why I would tell her about him and me."

"What did you say?" Alana asked.

"I told him not to worry about it. I told him that no one would say anything to the captain. We weren't trying to get anyone fired."

"Had he asked you not to say anything when you were with him?" I asked.

"Yes. I was leaving his cabin, right before I ran into you in the hallway. He said not to tell anyone about what we'd done. He said he could get in a lot of trouble."

"You said he threatened you. What exactly did he say?" Alana asked.

"He found me after Tiffany had let on that she knew about us. He called me a dumb bitch and said that we better not say anything more. He said we'd regret it if we did."

"So you told Tiffany this?" Alana asked.

"Of course. She went right to Reese, and they both went to see the captain. He was horrified to hear what Kurt had said. He told them he would take care of it."

"Kurt's actually still on this yacht," I said.

"I know. We saw him when we got back from the beach. He was coming out of the galley. Tiffany asked him why he wasn't gone. He said that she'd cost him his job. She said she was going to the captain to find out why he wasn't off the boat."

"Did you witness the conversation between Captain Piadelia and Tiffany?" I asked.

"No. I have no idea what his excuse was, but the whole thing is crazy. Why would he allow someone like that to stay? Now Tiffany is dead."

"So you're pretty convinced Kurt did this?" I asked.

"Who else could it be? We all loved Tiffany. Why would any of us want to hurt her?"

Zelda turned to Alana.

"I don't know why you haven't arrested him yet. I'm terrified he's going to come after me next," Zelda said.

Alana looked over to me.

"Poe, would you please escort Zelda back to her cabin. I'm going to find Captain Piadelia and talk to him about Kurt. Why don't we meet back here in the lounge in twenty minutes?"

"Sure," I said, and Zelda and I stood.

I walked her below. We didn't run into anyone on the way. It was like we were on a ghost ship. Zelda opened the door to her cabin, and I saw Sinclair inside, lying on the bed. She looked over to us but didn't say anything.

"Do you think she's going to arrest Kurt?" Zelda asked.

"I don't know, but I feel confident she'll make sure he doesn't bother you."

"She didn't look after Tiffany."

I didn't respond. I knew it was an unfair thing to say, but I also knew Zelda had just lost one of her best friends. She was allowed to be unfair in these circumstances.

I left Zelda and Sinclair and walked back to my cabin. Foxx and Hani were inside.

"Did you find anything?" I asked.

Foxx shook his head.

"Nothing, and I was able to go through the entire cabin."

"Do you think anyone saw you?"

"No."

"Did you learn anything from talking to them?" Hani asked.

I told them both about the one night stand between Reese and Sinclair, as well as Zelda's theory that Kurt was the only one with motivation to harm Tiffany.

"Why would he threaten them like that?" Hani asked.

"He kind of came after me too when he thought I might have been the one to talk. Some guys are just hotheads. There's no other explanation," I said.

"You want me to keep an eye on him?" Foxx asked.

"Maybe leave the door to this cabin open so you can see if he tries to leave his, but be careful. If he did kill Tiffany, he might not think twice about killing again."

"You think he did it?" Foxx asked.

"Maybe he went upstairs to get something to eat or drink after he thought everyone had gone to bed. He ran into Tiffany in the main lounge, and she was alone. She'd have been an easy target."

"And she was drunk. Maybe she insulted him, and he just lost it," Foxx added.

It was a plausible theory, and it certainly wouldn't be the first time someone took the life of a relative stranger. Some people simply couldn't control their anger. It was a sad commentary on human nature.

Chapter 15
Reese Lockwood

"What did the captain have to say?" I asked, as Alana walked back into the upper lounge.

"He confirmed what Zelda said. Tiffany came to him yesterday morning and told him that Kurt had threatened her and Zelda. She also went to him after they saw that Kurt was still on the yacht after their day at the beach."

"I assume you asked him if Kurt had ever done anything like that before."

"I did. He said he didn't know about Kurt threatening anyone before, but this wasn't the first time he'd had sexual relations with a guest. It's strictly forbidden."

"Apparently it's not that strict if Kurt got away with it multiple times."

"Agreed."

"Did you ask him why he didn't immediately kick Kurt off the boat?"

Alana nodded.

"He said it was a mistake on his part. He says the owner wouldn't have agreed to the cost of the flight."

"That seems completely ridiculous, especially with the kind of money they're pulling down on these charters."

"You're right, but maybe the captain was just too lazy to get it all done. He hasn't impressed me as being on the ball."

"What's your gut feeling on all of this? Was it Kurt or Reese or someone else?" I asked.

"I'm still leaning toward Reese, but that's mainly based on past experience.

Good job on getting Zelda to reveal Reese's affair with Sinclair."

"It was luck, nothing more."

"Luck or not, it still worked. Do you think it was just the one time as Zelda claimed?"

"No chance, but she might not have been lying about that. Sinclair might not have admitted any other possible encounters to her."

"That was my thought, exactly. Which begs the question: Was Tiffany really in the dark about it until last night?"

"I would say so. I can't imagine her asking Sinclair to be a bridesmaid if she knew in advance that she'd had sex with her fiancée," I said.

"Okay. Who's next on your interview list, the fiancée or the bosun?"

"Let's go with Reese, especially if that's what your gut is telling you."

I walked downstairs to get Reese. I found him outside his cabin and talking to his parents and brother, Trenholme, in the hallway. They all immediately clammed up as soon as they spotted me. Unfortunately, I hadn't been able to catch anything they were talking about.

I told Reese that Alana wanted to talk to him. He hesitated at first, and I wondered if he or anyone else in his family was going to pull the I-want-to-speak-to-a-lawyer-first card. It would have halted our investigation in a split second. Fortunately, he didn't do that.

He followed me back to the lounge. Alana stood when he entered and asked him to have a seat on the sofa. He did as she asked. She sat beside him, and I took the chair off to the side again. Alana repeated her opening line of condolences. Reese didn't respond, at least not verbally, but he gave a slight nod.

"Zelda told us that you and Tiffany met in college," Alana said.

"That's right. At a party."

"She also told us about your engagement in Paris," Alana said.

"It was Tiffany's favorite city. She'd been several times. I knew that's where the proposal had to take place."

"Why did you and Tiffany decide to get married in Hawaii?" I asked.

"We both loved the islands. It was our first vacation together. We went to Oahu. I'd been a few times with my family before."

"First trip with a girlfriend. That's always a big step," I said.

"Yeah. You learn a lot about a person when you travel with them."

"I guess you learned some good things about her since you got engaged later," Alana said, and she smiled.

"Actually, we broke up after the trip."

Reese chuckled as he probably relived the trip in his mind.

"Can you believe that?" he continued.

"Why did you break up?" I asked.

"Things didn't exactly go well on the vacation."

"What happened?" Alana asked.

"Tiffany could be...demanding. I wasn't sure she was for me. We broke up, but then we ran into each other six months later and got back together. Everyone has flaws, don't they? I guess you just have to decide whether the positives outweigh the negatives."

I found his statement to be a wise one, and it was an observation I'd made myself some years ago when I was contemplating whether or not to break up with an ex-girlfriend. She beat me to the punch and broke up with me first. How unfair and inconsiderate of her, don't you think?

Fortunately, this wasn't something I had to debate with Alana. The list of her positive traits was quite long, and her negatives were all fairly trivial things. I'm sure you're wondering what some of them are, and I don't mean to get distracted from the main tale. Here's one, though. She will not change the toilet paper roll even if her life depended on it. She intentionally leaves just a few squares so she can claim, falsely I might add, that it's not completely empty. I know a lot of people do that, but it really works my nerves, as I'm sure you can tell by me needlessly ranting about it here. Okay, back to our story.

"Let's talk about the weeks running up to your wedding. I know the planning of a wedding can get very stressful. Were you and Tiffany dealing with it okay?" Alana asked.

"Yes, because I just agreed to whatever she wanted, and she'd hired a wedding planner. But you already know that."

"Ms. Hu said that Tiffany insisted on this charter and that she was even willing to move the wedding to another island if need be. Do you know anything about that?" I asked.

Reese looked away.

"I'm assuming you do, based on your reaction," Alana said.

"I didn't know why Tiffany was so insistent on this yacht. There were others that seemed just as nice. It wasn't until I was onboard that I realized what was going on."

"You had no idea Angela was a member of the crew?" I asked.

"No. None. Tiffany never said anything. I was pretty upset when I saw her because I knew exactly what was happening."

"And what was that?" Alana asked.

"Tiffany, Sinclair, and Zelda wanted to torment the poor girl."

"Why?"

"Angela and I used to date for a while when we first started college. I was actually with her at the party where Tiffany and I met."

"You broke up with Angela to be with Tiffany?" I asked.

"Not exactly. Angela and I cared for each other, but we were more friends than anything else. There wasn't that chemistry, not like I had with Tiffany. I would have broken up with her whether I'd met Tiffany or not."

I assumed the presence of the beautiful Tiffany just made it a lot easier for Reese to let Angela go.

"I felt somewhat guilty for breaking up with her after that party, but that was a long time ago, and I'm sure she's over it by now. I haven't seen or spoken with her in years. Angela's a nice person," Reese continued. "She doesn't deserve the ridicule she got the last two days. That's really what made me get angry with Tiffany last night. I was tired of how she was treating Angela and the rest of the crew. It was petty and beneath her. I just wanted this to be a nice trip. I didn't understand why she had to turn it into a drama."

"Let's talk about last night, specifically after your dinner. Tiffany seemed upset with Sinclair. We've spoken with her and Zelda already. It seems your brother made a comment at dinner about cheating and forgiveness that hit a nerve with Tiffany," Alana said.

She paused and waited for Reese to respond. He didn't.

"We know about your affair with Sinclair," Alana continued.

"I'd hardly call it an affair," Reese countered.

"What would you call it then?" I asked.

"It happened one time. That's it. It doesn't make it right, but we both knew it was wrong and it never happened again. Tiffany was out of town. She and I would usually meet Sinclair and Zelda for drinks. Zelda left early that night because she had something to do in the morning. I don't remember what it was. Sinclair and I drank for a couple more hours. We made a mistake."

"Was this incident what your brother was referring to at dinner?" I asked.

"I'm sure. The asshole can't keep his mouth shut."

"Do you and your brother have a bad relationship?" Alana asked.

"I thought it had gotten better. I guess it hasn't."

"Had you told him about you and Sinclair?" I asked.

"No, because I knew he would try to sabotage my relationship with her. He's always been jealous of me. Whether it be girls or jobs or whatever, he has always wanted what I had."

"If he was trying to hurt you at dinner, what do you think set him off?" I asked.

"He was flirting with Sinclair the entire time we were on the beach. She wasn't interested. I suspect his pride was damaged."

"If you didn't tell him about the one night stand, who do you think did?" I asked.

"I don't know. It doesn't make sense that Sinclair would tell him."

Reese paused, and then he said, "It was probably Zelda. The girl loves to gossip. She can't help herself. Maybe Sinclair said something to her, and she told Trenholme."

"Had Tiffany suspected something between you and Sinclair before? If Trenholme just alluded to your cheating, why did Tiffany assume it was with Sinclair?" I asked.

"Sinclair has always been flirtatious with me. It's not just me, though. She is with a lot of guys. I told Tiffany she just likes the attention. I guess Tiffany just assumed it would have been with her."

"So Tiffany had confronted you about Sinclair before?" I asked.

"Not exactly. She made a comment once or twice that she thought we'd been talking to each other too much, but she never accused us of an affair."

"Talking too much?" Alana asked.

"Sometimes Sinclair would call me. It was a little weird since she was more Tiffany's friend than mine."

"What would she call you about?" I asked.

"Work stuff. She valued my opinion, I guess."

"What happened after you went to bed last night? Did Tiffany come with you?" Alana asked.

"No. I went back to my cabin on my own. I was there maybe an hour or so when I heard knocking on my cabin door. I thought it might be Tiffany, but then I realized that she wouldn't bother knocking. I answered the door, and it was Sinclair. She said she was worried that Tiffany knew about us and wanted to know what we should do. I told her we should go to her cabin to talk."

"Why her cabin? Why not just have the conversation where you already were?" Alana asked.

"Because I didn't want Tiffany coming back and finding Sinclair in our cabin."

"Someone mentioned that they heard arguing in the cabin area. Was that you and Sinclair?" I asked.

"No. It wasn't us. I didn't hear any arguing. I did hear Mr. Calloway yell. Maybe that's what the other person heard."

"So you heard him yell and then you went upstairs to the main lounge?" Alana asked.

"That's right. He was kneeling on the floor beside Tiffany. I didn't know what to do. I just sort of froze."

"Who do you think killed your fiancée?" I asked.

"The only guy I can think of is the crew member who Tiffany complained about. I know he was angry with her. I didn't think for a second he was mad enough to kill her, though."

"You're talking about Kurt," I said.

"I think that's his name. I can't think of anyone else."

We asked Reese a few more questions, but nothing helpful emerged from his answers. Alana thanked Reese for his time and promised to do her best to bring Tiffany's killer to justice. He made a comment just before leaving about having a hard time processing that she was really gone. He also said he didn't know how he'd be able to move forward without her.

They were things you'd expect the fiancée to say, but it had come across like his comments in the main lounge when we were all around Tiffany's body. There was simply no passion behind the words. They seemed like empty or clichéd phrases delivered by an actor who wasn't very good.

Another odd thing about the interview was that I didn't really have a gut instinct when it came to Reese Lockwood. He didn't seem like a good guy or a bad guy to me. He was just there, almost like a shadow without detail. I don't know if that makes any kind of sense. I just didn't have a feeling for his guilt or innocence. Could he have killed her? Of course. Did he? I had no idea. I'd gotten pretty good at these interviews, which was one of the reasons I was so frustrated by my lack of instinct in regards to Reese.

The important thing when conducting these interviews was to listen. That may seem like common sense, and I'm sure you're saying to yourself, "Poe, of course you should listen. Everyone knows that."

What I'm referring to, though, is the process of taking your listening skills to another level. Most of the time, we only halfway listen to what someone is saying. It's very easy to get distracted by all sorts of things, including how the person looks, such as facial tics or a hair out of place, as well as background interferences like noise or the movement of other people.

Furthermore, we start formulating what we're going to say next in anticipation to them concluding what they're talking about. The basic point is that we think we're doing a good job of listening, but we're really not.

So, what did I notice about these past few interviews now that I've touted my listening skills? A few key things, actually.

The first thing that jumped out was Reese's comment that he told Sinclair they should have their conversation in her cabin since he didn't want Tiffany coming back and seeing Sinclair in his cabin. That made sense, but it also contradicted what Zelda had said.

She'd claimed that Sinclair had asked Zelda to leave their cabin so that she could talk to Reese alone, meaning Sinclair had anticipated going to see Reese and then inviting him back to her cabin. If that was the case, then why wouldn't Sinclair have been the one to suggest that they have their private conversation in her cabin versus Reese saying it?

I believe it wasn't a conversation at all. Instead, I think they went there for another round of wrestling on the mattress. Sure, that would have been really risky, but I still thought it likely. Reese knew Tiffany was in the upstairs lounge. Maybe he assumed she was passed out from too much drink and wouldn't be coming downstairs anytime soon. He could easily slip into Sinclair's cabin for some fun and games and no one, except maybe Zelda, would have any idea what had happened.

There's another reason I thought this. Reese had made a comment that Sinclair had come to his cabin and had claimed "She knows about us." I'd paid very close attention to the wording of that statement. Sinclair hadn't said, "Tiffany knows what we did that night." Instead, her phrasing made it sound, at least to me, that there was still something going on between them, and Sinclair was afraid that Tiffany had finally figured it out, thanks to Trenholme's big mouth.

Sinclair certainly displayed her nervousness when Alana and I were talking to her. Our questions about Tiffany's remark of "I know what you did" had jarred her. The more I thought about it, the more I started to suspect that Sinclair had faked the waterworks to cut our interview short.

Yeah, she was sad about her friend. Any friend would be, but that didn't mean that was the main reason she started sobbing. The tears hadn't seemed entirely real to me. We've all heard people sobbing before. We know what it sounds like. There's full-on wailing, the chest and abdomen rising and falling as the person gasps for breath between sobs, and, forgive me for saying this, but the snot starts flowing. That hadn't happened with Sinclair.

Again, I'll use the bad actor comparison. I felt somewhat guilty for thinking that when she was crying, and I also felt a bit awkward when the tears started flowing. All guys feel that way when women start crying. My awkwardness had dulled my instincts and kept me from further pursuing the thought that Sinclair was faking it. But now that she was gone, I was pretty convinced that it had been a show, at least mostly a show.

Need further proof of the relationship between Reese and Sinclair? What about those phone calls to Reese that prompted Tiffany to wonder if something was going on. That seemed really weird to me. Alana doesn't have a huge number of friends, but the ones she does have never call me. I know them all, and I'm on good terms with them. Maybe you'd even say that I'm friends with them, too. Nevertheless, if they needed something from me, whether it be information or a strong back to move furniture, they would contact me through Alana. It would be different if they were my friends first and then became friends with Alana. They would never call me directly otherwise. It was just an unwritten code. Maybe you think I'm being old-fashioned when it comes to that, and maybe I am, but I still think the rule applies.

That wasn't the case with Reese and Sinclair. Sinclair had been friends with Tiffany for over a dozen years before she'd even met Reese. Regardless of that, she seemed to have no issue with violating the rule I just talked about.

The more I thought about it, the more I was convinced Sinclair and Reese were going to have one last go of it before the wedding. That was the main reason they'd gone to her cabin for a "private" meeting. Yeah, it was private all right.

I'm sure you're accusing my imagination of running wild, but it was just a feeling I had and now I couldn't let it go.

There was also Trenholme's humiliation at Sinclair rejecting him. He hadn't lashed out at her, as some insecure men are prone to do. Instead, he'd taken a shot at his brother. Why? I propose that it's because he suspected that Sinclair wasn't interested in him because she was already interested in his brother.

Alana and I heard from both Reese and Zelda that Trenholme was jealous of his brother. It seems likely to me that the jealousy extended to Reese's relationship with Sinclair. There was also Reese's claim that Trenholme always wanted what Reese had. I'm sure that extended to women and not just material things.

Both Reese and Zelda claimed not to have known how Trenholme was aware of the one night stand between Reese and Sinclair, yet Trenholme had somehow known. Maybe he didn't know. Maybe he'd guessed at the affair after observing their behavior for a long time. Perhaps his comment was nothing more than him tossing out the theory that Reese was cheating on Tiffany.

Trenholme had accomplished two things at once. He'd gotten back at his brother for possessing something that he wanted, and he'd taken a shot at the woman who'd rejected him as recently as earlier that day on the beach.

My photo session with the lovely Sinclair would have only made him angrier as he watched her pose in her skimpy bikini for some other guy. Granted, we weren't involved in any kind of romantic way, but she was posing for me when Trenholme desperately wanted her to be with him.

Let's talk more about Trenholme. Reese made the remark that he thought his relationship with Trenholme had gotten better, but after dinner last night, he'd realized it hadn't. Why would Reese ask Trenholme to be his best man if he had a bad relationship with him? Wasn't there anyone else he could have asked? Maybe he'd felt obligated to ask his brother, but I doubted it.

Either way I analyzed it, it didn't make sense. If Reese didn't like his brother, then why ask him to be his best man? If he did like his brother, then why would he say tonight that they didn't get along? It was baffling.

Chapter 16
Kurt Parrot

I told Alana about my suspicions that Reese and Sinclair still had a romantic thing going. She agreed with me and said that she'd had the same thoughts during our interview with Reese.

"Unfortunately - well, maybe that's not the right word to use - but if Reese was in the cabin with Sinclair as they both claim, then that provides a pretty solid alibi for him. It doesn't sound like he could have killed Tiffany," I suggested.

"Unless Sinclair is lying to help protect him."

"Why would she do that?"

"With Tiffany out of the way, she and Reese are free to be together."

"By that logic, then Sinclair could be our killer. If she was, though, then why would Reese cover for her?"

"Maybe we're overthinking this. Maybe the simplest explanation is the correct one."

"You mean Kurt did it," I said.

"I think it's time we met with Mr. Parrot."

I walked below deck to grab both Kurt and Baakir. As I waited for them to exit their cabin, I looked down the hallway. I could see directly into my cabin. Foxx was sitting on the edge of the bed and looking at me. I didn't need to say anything to Foxx or even give him a signal. He knew exactly what I wanted him to do. He nodded. I didn't bother nodding back.

I escorted the two crew members to the upstairs lounge. I asked Baakir to wait outside by the tanning deck while Alana and I spoke with Kurt first.

"Thank you for meeting with us, Kurt," Alana said.

Kurt looked nervous as he sat down on the sofa beside Alana. Was that a sign of guilt? Not necessarily. Alana's death stare can make anyone nervous, including me.

"I assume you know why we want to talk to you," Alana continued.

"I didn't kill that lady," he said.

Well, he didn't bother wasting time getting right to the point.

"We have two people who say you threatened Tiffany Calloway," I said.

"That's not true."

"You're going to deny it?" Alana asked.

"Why would I have threatened her?"

"Because you didn't want her or Zelda Cameron to reveal your one night stand to Captain Piadelia," Alana said.

"It's true that I asked Zelda not to say anything. I knew I'd get in trouble, but I certainly didn't threaten her or the other lady."

"Okay, if that's the truth, then why would Tiffany have reported you to the captain? I doubt she would have cared one way or the other if you'd had sex with her friend. It didn't affect her in any way. I spoke with Captain Piadelia. He specifically said that Tiffany came to him and said that you'd threatened her and Zelda. He also said how angry Tiffany was when she saw you after their day on the beach," Alana said.

"I did run into them outside the galley, but I sure as hell didn't threaten them. Why would I?"

"Because you'd been fired at that point. I seems like a good motivation to me," I said.

"I wasn't fired. That's the thing."

"I'm sorry? You're going to claim you weren't fired?" Alana asked.

"Ask the captain. He told Tiffany that he'd fired me and Bucky, but he hadn't. Not really. Why do you think he didn't put us on the first flight back to Maui? We were going to get off when we got to port, but we'd get right back on for the next charter."

"You're suggesting that Captain Piadelia pretended to fire you for show?" I asked.

"I'm not suggesting anything. It's a fact. It's the whole "The customer is always right' bullshit, only they aren't. Sometimes you need to pretend to cave in to keep them happy. I get it."

"You're forgetting something. I ran into you outside your cabin the morning that you'd been fired. You came at me pretty hard," I said.

"That's because Zelda denied telling the captain, so I assumed you must have been the one. I didn't threaten you, though, did I?"

"No. You didn't."

"And I didn't threaten either of those ladies. I knew I still had my job. This is a great gig. You can't make these kinds of tips in some restaurant job. I'm not going to risk screwing this up."

"Only you did. Whether you threatened anyone or not, you still had sex with Zelda, despite knowing it was against your supervisor's policy," Alana said.

"So? It's not the same thing as murdering anyone, is it? Besides, she threw herself at me that night. What was I going to do? Say no?"

"She threw herself at you?" I repeated since I wasn't sure I'd heard him right.

"Yeah. I was up here in this very lounge. She walked in, saw me, and went directly to the bar. She made us two drinks. I wasn't even halfway through mine when she suggested we go to my cabin."

"I didn't realize you were so charming," Alana muttered, and it took everything in me not to laugh.

"You can make fun of me if you want, but everything I'm telling you is the truth. Ask Bucky. He supposedly got fired, too, only he didn't, not really. He was going to get his job back, just like I was."

"Where were you when Tiffany Calloway was killed?" Alana asked.

"In my cabin with Bucky. He can vouch for that. The captain yelled at me when I was on the main deck when the guests came back. I got it. I was ruining his plan, so I wasn't about to move my butt out of that cabin again until we got back to Maui."

Alana concluded the interview with Kurt and asked him to wait outside while we talked to Baakir or Bucky. He backed up Kurt's story. I wasn't sure if that was because the two of them had hatched this scheme to keep Kurt out of handcuffs. Granted, I had no way of knowing if Baakir would have covered for a co-worker like that. Still, they'd had plenty of time to come up with some kind of story.

Our interview with Baakir didn't last very long. Neither of us thought he'd done the deed. Yes, he'd also been fired, or maybe I should say allegedly been fired, for preparing a rotten meal that got the guests sick. Nevertheless, he seemed to take the firing in stride. He was either a really laid back guy or Kurt was telling the truth when he stated that the captain was pulling one over on all of us.

Alana and I walked up to the bridge after we finished our brief conversation with Baakir. The captain was the only one there. He turned to us as we entered.

"Captain Piadelia, may we have a word?" Alana asked.

"Of course," he said, and his voice sounded as tired as he looked.

"We just spoke with two of your crew members, Mr. Parrot and Mr. Rajan. They both claim that you didn't really terminate their employment. They said you pretended to fire them in order to pacify Ms. Calloway. Is this correct?" Alana asked.

Piadelia didn't respond.

"I'll take that as a yes," Alana continued.

"You must understand the position I was in," he said.

"And what position is that?" I asked.

"It's difficult to find good crew members. They've both been with me for a few years now. I didn't want to lose them."

I could certainly understand his take on not wanting to lose two good employees, but neither one of them seemed to fit that description, even in the vaguest terms. The chef had made everyone sick with his lamb dish, and the bosun had a habit of bedding the guests. I guess one could be crude and say that Kurt was willing to go the extra mile in the customer service department, but it was probably only a matter of time before one of these ladies he had sex with decided the next morning that he'd taken advantage of them after they'd had too much to drink.

"Why would you lie to me?" Alana asked.

"Because at the time I thought you were just wedding planners. I didn't want to upset you if you knew I hadn't really fired them. Besides, I had fired them from this charter. Isn't that what the guest really wanted?"

"You're trying to excuse your dishonesty with a technicality. That doesn't fly with me," Alana said.

"I apologize, detective. Still, I don't see how this matters. No one on my crew harmed Ms. Calloway."

"How do you know that? Where were you when she was murdered?" I asked.

"I was asleep in my cabin. The first mate was here on the bridge."

"So you have no idea who killed Tiffany Calloway," I said.

"No. I don't but the manner in which she was killed was a crime of passion. No one on my crew disliked her that much. We're used to difficult charters. Her demands were nothing out of the ordinary. In fact, they were rather minor compared to some of our clientele."

"And her verbal attacks on Angela? That seemed rather personal," Alana said.

"I agree that I was unaware that the charter guest and Angela had a prior history, but she's a professional. Angela can take the criticism. That's what she's paid to do, and she makes very good money for it."

"At what point did Angela know the guests were the Calloways and Lockwoods?" Alana asked.

"Not until I presented them with the client sheet."

"What is that, exactly?" I asked.

"It's a brief description of each client, including their activity and food preferences."

"Who prepares that?" Alana asked.

"Our booking agent. She takes down all of the information from the client."

"What was Angela's reaction when she saw the names of the guests?" Alana asked.

"She didn't have one."

"Really? She said nothing?" Alana asked.

"No. She informed me that she knew them."

"You're saying that she displayed no emotion to having to spend a week with them in a relatively small space?" I asked.

"No. She had none at all. In fact, I asked her how she thought the charter would go, and she indicated that she thought everything would be fine."

"Yet you had to fire or pretend to fire two employees after the very first day. That doesn't sound fine to me," I said.

Captain Piadelia shrugged his shoulders.

"Angela had nothing to do with that. If you recall, she bailed this charter out when she stepped up and assumed the chef's position last night."

He paused. Then he said, "What are you trying to get at? Do you think Angela had something to do with this?"

"We're not saying that at all," Alana said.

"Then why all the questions about Angela?"

"Because we don't leave anyone out, not in a murder investigation," Alana said.

"Forgive me for saying this, but it sounds like you have no idea who killed Ms. Calloway. I am still the captain of this vessel. Please remember that."

"What is that supposed to mean?" Alana asked.

"I must insist that you not speak to any more members of my crew without my permission."

"Don't try a power play with me, captain. You'll regret it."

I waited for his response, wondering if this was about to turn into a test of wills between Alana and the captain. The captain said nothing back to her. Did that mean that he'd acquiesced to her position? I wasn't sure.

He turned from Alana and me and looked out the window. I guessed that was his sign that he was done talking to us.

I followed his gaze and looked out the window myself. All I saw was the black ocean.

Chapter 17
Kimi Lange

The interview with the captain had confirmed everything that Kurt had said, at least in terms of the firing. I must admit that I'd never heard of anything like that before. What kind of employer fires someone on a temporary basis? Did I think this got Kurt off the hook as far as him being a murder suspect? Not at all. I still considered him one of our top two candidates.

Alana and I left the bridge and made our way back down to the lounge. We found Foxx waiting for us.

"I have something to show you," he said.

He walked over to us and held out his phone.

"Check this out," he continued.

Alana took his phone. Foxx had pulled up a photo of three glass bottles that looked like they were inside a black bag.

"Magnesium citrate?" I said, reading the label on the bottles.

"I had to look it up. It's a laxative," Foxx said.

"You found this in Baakir's and Kurt's cabin?" Alana asked.

"Yeah. It was inside a gym bag under the lower bed. I don't know whose bag it is."

"Who needs three bottles of a laxative?" I asked.

A possible answer dawned on me a second later.

"Is this what got everyone sick the other night?"

"Take enough of that and you'll be running to the toilet all night long," Alana said.

ROBERT W. STEPHENS

"So who put it in the food or drink? Kurt or Baakir?" Foxx asked.

"They'll both deny it, and does this relate to the murder in any way? There's a huge difference between making someone use the bathroom and sticking a knife in their throat," I said.

"Absolutely, but if you don't have a problem poisoning several people, maybe you don't have a problem killing someone," Foxx said.

I understood his logic, but I still thought it was too far of a leap to make. I didn't think Kurt had tampered with the food since the dinner was apparently tainted before he'd hooked up with Zelda and had subsequently gotten fired. As far as Baakir went, why would he have done it since a rotten dinner could only make him look bad and lead to his termination?

"You're right, Poe. They'll do nothing but deny it, but we still need to talk to them about it at some point," Alana said.

She turned to Foxx.

"Would you mind going below deck again and finding Kimi? Something tells me we should interview her next," Alana said.

"What do you think she knows?" Foxx asked.

"Poe has told me numerous restaurant stories from when he worked as a waiter. It seems to me that the staff hears everything. They're both in and out of the kitchen, and people have a tendency to stop paying attention to their presence. They seem to have no problem with saying things around them when they should keep their mouths shut until the staff walks away."

That was a true statement if I've ever heard one. I was once pouring wine for a couple when the wife suddenly asked her husband for a divorce. I don't know if she timed it that way, hoping the husband wouldn't have an outburst in front of me. Maybe she'd been so filled with anxiety and apprehension that she hadn't even noticed me standing there. Either way, I'd felt uncomfortable as hell. I remember putting the bottle down before I'd finished pouring the wine. I just sort of backed away from the table and didn't come back for half an hour. I was tempted to pay their bill for them so I wouldn't have to interact with them again. On another note, it had been the wife who'd made the selection of that particular bottle, and it had cost fifty dollars. I wasn't sure why she hadn't picked a cheaper bottle since she had to have known they wouldn't have been able to enjoy anything after that sudden declaration. Can you see how I overthink things? I told you I did that.

Foxx left the lounge in search of Kimi while I turned back to Alana.

"What do you think of Captain Piadelia's admission that he hadn't really fired Kurt and Baakir?"

"I wish I could say I'm surprised but not really. The man seems like an incompetent captain."

"Does this knock Kurt off your list?" I asked.

"I'm not sure. Maybe. Seems like it might have been hard for him to be truly mad at Tiffany when he knew he'd secretly pulled the wool over her eyes."

"Well, he would have lost his share of the cash tip."

"Who kills people over a lost tip?" she asked.

I'd heard stories in the news of people getting killed over five dollars in their pocket, but I understood her point.

"So, it's back to Reese?" I asked.

"I think so since I don't know who else it could be."

"I think I'm going to grab a bottle of water. Do you want one?"

"Yeah. That would be great."

I walked over to the bar and grabbed two bottles from the tiny refrigerator under the counter. I walked back to Alana and handed her one of the bottles. I twisted the top off of mine and swallowed the water in just a few long gulps.

"Some wedding party this has turned out to be. We should go check on Mr. Calloway after this. I can't even begin to imagine what he's going through," Alana said.

I was about to make a comment when Kimi walked into the lounge.

"Foxx said you wanted to speak with me."

"Yes. Please have a seat over here," Alana said.

Kimi walked across the lounge and sat on the sofa.

"Would you like something to drink?" I asked.

"No. I'm fine."

I put my empty bottle on the bar counter and then walked over to join Alana and Kimi.

"How are you holding up?" Alana asked.

"Fine, all things considered."

"How long have you worked with Captain Piadelia?" Alana asked.

"A couple of years now. This is a good job. I really enjoy it."

"It must be hard, though, especially with all of the demanding guests," I said.

"It can be, but how many people get to work a job like this? I'm surrounded by beautiful locations every day, and I get to live on an island. I think I can put up with a few snotty people from time to time."

"So you live on Maui?" Alana asked.

"Yes. I rent a room from Angela."

"Really? You two have an apartment?"

"No. Angela owns a small two bedroom house in Kihei. She stays there, and I'm in a studio apartment in the back of the house. It's tiny, but I don't need much. A lot of my time is here on the yacht."

Alana hesitated a moment. Then she said, "We want to ask you some questions about the last couple of nights, if that's okay."

"Of course."

"The night the guests got sick from dinner, has that ever happened before?" Alana asked.

"No. Not that I can remember. Sometimes people get hungover, especially after their first night here. They tend to overdo it when they get on the ship. They just go crazy."

"I'm sure they hit the bar pretty hard," Alana said with a smile.

"Definitely. It can sometimes get a little awkward. It's not like we're going to cut them off like a public restaurant would. We had this one group that went through three cases of Grey Goose in just under a week."

Three cases of Grey Goose? That's a hell of a bar tab, I thought.

"Regarding the first night's dinner, did you sense any tension between Baakir and the guests?" I asked.

Kimi didn't respond, but she did touch her left forearm with her right hand. It was clearly a subconscious maneuver, sort of like closing herself off from the interviewer.

"It's okay, Kimi. We're not trying to get anyone in trouble," Alana said.

"He was upset with them, but he had good reason."

"Why was he upset?" I asked.

"Mrs. Lockwood said something about him."

"What did she say?" Alana asked.

"She called him a BLANK."

Okay, for those new readers, I sometimes leave the offending words as BLANK so I don't cause sensitive readers to clutch their pearls. I wouldn't want to give anyone a heart attack when they're supposedly reading this book for enjoyment. I will say this. It was a pretty offensive remark, and I think you know me well enough by now to realize I don't offend easily.

"Why in the world would she say that? What happened?" Alana asked.

"I don't know. I was in the galley with Bucky. Angela came in. We could tell she was upset. I asked her why, and she said Mrs. Lockwood said something that made her mad. I asked her what it was, but she wouldn't tell us, not at first."

"But she eventually told you," I guessed.

"Yes, after I pressed her about it. Mrs. Lockwood said that Bucky better make them American food and not that Indian garbage, except she didn't say his name. She said that slur."

"What was his reaction?" I asked.

"He was mad. I could tell by the look on his face."

"Did he say anything?" Alana asked.

"Not really. He just kept working on the dinner. Believe me, it's not the first time he's heard something like that. More than one guest has been racist toward him. To the captain's credit, he hasn't been tempted to replace Bucky, at least I don't think he has."

I don't mean to sound politically correct here, especially after touting just a few paragraphs ago that I wasn't an overly sensitive type. However, is it racist to keep calling the guy Bucky when you know that's not his real name? I mean everyone knows it's Baakir. It's not like it's a difficult name to say. It's two syllables for God's sake. And why would the captain replace him because of his ethnicity? Just to appease the guests? Who does that? Granted, you're catering to guests who want things exactly the way they want them, but that sure as hell doesn't mean they get to pick who does and doesn't work on the yacht.

"We found three bottles of liquid laxative in Baakir's cabin," Alana said, breaking me out of the rant that was just taking place in my mind. "Do you think that he might have added that to their dinner?"

"You mean to get back at them?"

"Possibly. That was a pretty horrible thing for her to say. I could understand his desire to do something," Alana said.

"I don't know. I can't see him doing that, even after Mrs. Lockwood said those things. Besides, why would he even have those bottles to begin with?" Kimi asked.

It was an argument I'd already thought of myself. However, if Baakir was the type of guy willing to drench his guests' food or drink with a laxative, maybe he was also the type of person who would keep a steady supply of it in his bag.

"Do you think someone else might have spiked the food?" I asked.

"Who?"

"I don't know. Maybe Angela? She was the one to actually hear the racial slur. Maybe she was just defending a friend and co-worker," I suggested.

"I don't see how she could have done it. I was in the kitchen, too. Bucky gave us the plated food, and Angela, Banks, and I took it out to the guests. I would have seen her do it."

"What about the drinks? Perhaps the laxative wasn't in the food at all," Alana said.

"Banks and I made the drinks. That's one of our responsibilities. They had pitchers of margaritas."

Margaritas with lamb? These people have no class, I thought.

"Just a couple more questions. We've heard there was arguing in the guests' cabin area. This was right before Ms. Calloway was murdered. Did you heard anything?" Alana asked.

"No. The guests' area is too far away. They would have to be pretty loud in order for me to hear them."

"But you heard Mr. Calloway yell when he found his daughter?" I asked.

"I did. We're much closer to the main lounge, and I had my door open when he screamed."

"Why did you have your door open?" Alana asked.

Kimi hesitated.

"I feel a little awkward saying this."

"We're not here to judge you," Alana said, but wasn't that exactly what we always did during these little interviews?

"I was saying goodbye to someone."

"Who?" Alana asked.

Kimi hesitated. Then she said, "Foxx."

"Foxx?" Alana asked.

She turned to me, and I did my best to keep a neutral look on my face.

"We were in my cabin for a while," Kimi said.

"Oh," Alana said, finally getting it.

It seemed Ms. Kimi Lange was fairly well preoccupied when Tiffany Calloway was knifed to death. At least we could scratch Foxx and Kimi off the suspect list, not that they were ever there to begin with.

On that somewhat embarrassing note, Alana concluded the interview with the young stewardess. She thanked Kimi for her time, and we watched as Kimi stood and exited the lounge.

"Did you know about Foxx and Kimi?" Alana asked.

"Yes. About the first time, not the second."

"They've hooked up twice?"

"Apparently."

"Why didn't you tell me?"

"Well, there was that discussion about a possible romance between Foxx and Sinclair. I decided to keep my mouth shut after everything went south with that."

Alana pointed to my watch.

"Is it too early to have a drink?"

"That depends."

"On what?" she asked.

"Well, it's almost four A.M. It's one of those weird times. Are we counting this as night or morning? If it's night, I think we could safely have an adult beverage."

"Never mind. A beer might put me to sleep. I'm barely hanging on as it is. So, did we learn anything?"

"Not much. Sounds like neither Kimi nor Angela nor Banks could have doused the guests' food with laxative."

"Maybe that wasn't it. Maybe it was just bad meat," Alana said.

"And Baakir has the world's worst constipation?"

Alana laughed.

"That would be some blockage."

"You definitely don't want to be anywhere near him when that thing blows."

"God, we're both so tired we think this is funny."

"Poop jokes are always funny, no matter what time it is," I said.

"To guys."

"Yeah. I can't argue with that."

"I think it's most likely Baakir who added it to the lamb. That was a pretty horrible thing Catherine said about him. He knew, or at least figured, that Captain Piadelia wouldn't fire him for good. Maybe he was okay with losing a tip just to get back at her," she said.

I thought there was another thing we learned, but I saw no reason to mention it out loud. Mrs. Lockwood was a world-class bitch, but we already knew that, didn't we?

I was about to go back to the bar for another bottle of water when Kimi ran back into the lounge.

"Something's happened. Reese has disappeared," she said.

"Disappeared?" I asked.

"They've searched everywhere below. He's nowhere to be found."

Angela and Banks walked in a second later.

"Have either of you seen Reese?" Angela asked.

"No," Alana answered.

"And you both have been in this lounge?" Angela asked.

"Yes, for a while. We spoke with Reese about an hour or so ago. We haven't seen him since," Alana said.

"His parents first noticed him missing. They went to talk to him and his cabin was empty, so they went to the main lounge, and he wasn't there either. They found me, and we started a search," Angela said. "I better go see the captain and let him know we have a potential man overboard."

She walked past me and headed straight for the stairs that would take her to the bridge.

I turned to Kimi and Banks.

"Has this ever happened before?"

Kimi shook her head.

"Never," Banks said.

"When was the last time you two saw him?" Alana asked.

"When we were all around Tiffany's body," Banks said.

Alana turned to Kimi.

"And you?"

"Probably around the same time. You told us all to stay in our cabins. I only left to talk to you up here," Kimi said.

I was about to ask a question of my own when we all almost fell over as the boat immediately slowed down.

I ran out of the lounge and over to the railing. I looked out at the water below. It was black as ink, and I couldn't see a thing. The yacht turned hard to the port side, and I assumed they were going to retrace the earlier course of the yacht. I had no idea how long or how far we'd traveled since Alana and I had spoken to Reese. The yacht moved at a pretty good pace, and I thought we might have covered several miles.

I looked over the side again. I still couldn't see anything, but I could hear the waves smashing against the hull. Even if the captain perfectly retraced our journey, there was no telling how far Reese could have been pulled away by the ocean currents. He could be anywhere, if he was still even above the water.

We heard clicking sounds as several lights on all sides of the yacht turned on and bathed the ocean around us in shafts of white light.

Banks ran out of the lounge and joined us at the railing.

"The captain is asking for everyone to stay outside and be on the lookout for Reese."

"So we've definitely decided he's overboard at this point?" Alana asked.

"Yes. We've gone over every inch of this yacht twice now. He's not here," Banks said.

"Will the captain put out a distress call?" I asked.

"I'm sure he's already done that. It's standard protocol to contact other vessels in the area, as well as the Coast Guard. There's flashlights below. I'll grab them and start passing them out."

"Where should we go?" Alana asked.

"I'd come down to the main deck. The first mate can show you to your positions."

Banks ran off.

I turned to Alana.

"Reese is overboard? Did you ever see that coming?"

"No. Not in a million years, and I already know what you're going to ask me next. Did he jump or was he pushed?"

"What's your guess?" I asked.

"I don't know, Poe."

She turned from me and looked out at the ocean.

"My God," Alana continued. "I can't believe he might actually be out there."

I looked out at the water myself. The lights of the yacht were almost blinding, but they did relatively little to that massive field of darkness that was the Pacific Ocean. The dark waters seemed to suck up that light and render it useless.

If Reese was still alive, he wouldn't stay that way for long.

Chapter 18
He Would Have Told You

"Do you know the one person who isn't up here looking for Reese?" Alana asked.

I looked around, which wasn't a real helpful thing to do since I knew there were people positioned on both sides of the yacht. There was simply no way for me to currently see everyone. Then I realized who she was probably talking about.

"Raymond?"

"I didn't see him. Did you?"

"I don't believe so, but it's been pretty chaotic."

"Maybe he's still down in his cabin. Maybe he went there after pushing Reese overboard," she said.

"Do you think he's strong enough to have done that? Reese is a big guy. I would really struggle to do it myself."

"So you're thinking Reese jumped?"

I looked overboard at the waves rolling into the hull of the ship. I couldn't imagine the depth of despair or guilt it would take to make that leap.

"I don't know, Alana. That was the first thought that crossed my mind, but I could easily be wrong. Jumping overboard? That's a hell of a decision to make."

"People jump all the time. Not that different than putting a gun in your mouth."

"I'm going to have to disagree with you on that one. Things end pretty quickly with a bullet to the brain. How long would it have taken him to die in those waters?"

"Probably not as long as you think."

Fear came rushing through my body, and it wasn't hard for me to figure out where it had come from. During my first investigation, a man had taken me miles out into the ocean and forced me into the water. I won't go into the details of why he did that, but I vividly remembered those long hours desperately trying to keep my head above water. I'd been tempted to give up many times, but I couldn't imagine voluntarily opening my mouth and letting that cold water wash down my throat and into my lungs. Could Reese have? Maybe, but that would have been a hell of a thing to do.

"Do you want to go look for Raymond? I can stay up here and keep looking for Reese," I said.

"You should come with me. I could use the backup."

Alana looked out to the water.

"I don't mean to sound cruel, but Reese is gone. There's no way they'll find him," she continued.

I didn't know what to say, so I didn't respond. I knew she was right. It just seemed so final to voice those thoughts out loud. I looked at the dark water one last time before going below. Was he still out there clinging to life? I just couldn't let my mind go there.

We walked down to the guests' cabin area and found Raymond's cabin. The door was shut.

Alana knocked softly on the door.

"Mr. Calloway. This is Detective Hu. I'd like to talk to you."

Raymond opened the door a few seconds later.

"May we come in?" Alana asked.

Raymond nodded. He turned from us and walked back into the cabin. We followed him inside. He sat on the edge of his bed. Alana and I stayed standing. I shut the door behind me while Alana took a few steps closer to the bed.

"Is that it? Is it basically over now?" Raymond asked.

"No. They're still conducting the search for him," Alana said.

"That's not what I mean. I was referring to my daughter's murderer."

"You think Reese committed suicide over his guilt?" Alana asked.

"He knew what he'd done. He knew it was only a matter of time before you had proof. You want to know something? He never came to me tonight. Our cabins are just a few feet apart, yet he never said anything to me about Tiffany's death. I remember standing in the doorway to my cabin. I looked right at him. He looked back at me but then immediately looked away. He walked into his cabin and shut the door. The boy was a coward."

"Did his parents say anything to you? Did Trenholme?" Alana asked.

"No. None of them. They knew their meal ticket was gone. They weren't going to get anything else from me."

"Their meal ticket? You think that's how they viewed Tiffany?" I asked.

"Of course. I didn't want her marrying Reese, but what could I do? My daughter was not about to listen to what anyone else thought."

"Why do you think Reese was just after her money?" Alana asked.

"It wasn't just Reese. It was the whole Lockwood family."

"We didn't mention this before, but Poe and I overheard an argument between you and Dr. Lockwood on the first night of the cruise. It sounded like you were arguing over money," Alana said.

"Then you heard me say that I was paying for this whole trip."

Alana nodded.

"Among other things."

"Artemis Lockwood is broke. Tiffany told me how he'd made one bad investment after another. The golf course was the last straw."

"The golf course?" I asked.

"Reese convinced him to go in on this golf course. Tiffany told me about it. I know a thing or two about golf courses. I've closed many a deal on one. The region he was talking about was already saturated with courses. It didn't need another one. That's a basic rule of investing. Be the first guy in, not the last. Neither Artemis nor Reese could get that through their thick skulls. They lost their shirts. Next thing you know, Reese is proposing to my little girl. I wonder why that was."

"Tiffany knew what had happened?" Alana asked.

"She knew, but she'd been after him to propose for a long time."

"Only you clearly thought he'd turned to her because he'd lost everything else. Did you tell her that?" I asked.

"No. I just sat back and waited for her to come to her senses. I'd hoped it would happen before the wedding. If not…well, then my daughter would be a divorcee. It's not the worst thing in the world. This is my fault. I never thought he'd do what he did. I should have put a stop to her relationship a long time ago."

"Did Dr. Lockwood ask you for money? What specifically was the argument about?" I asked.

"He wanted me to introduce him to some investor friends of mine. He knew I'd done well, and he wanted in on it. There was a part of me that considered it. I didn't want my daughter having to support her husband, but I couldn't go through with it. I've worked too hard and for too long to have my name associated with Artemis and Reese Lockwood, at least not in terms of my business."

I thought he'd overestimated people's ability or willingness to draw the line between family and business. Reese Lockwood was going to be a part of the Calloway family, whether Raymond wanted that or not. I was fairly certain that Reese would have tried to start cashing in on that Calloway connection the second after he said "I do" at the ceremony.

A new theory, or maybe I should say a more defined theory, popped into my head after hearing Raymond's story about the Lockwoods being broke. Money is one reason for murder. Perhaps Tiffany had threatened to call off the wedding after learning of Reese's secret sexual relationship with one of her best friends. Reese would have been panicked to lose the financial security she represented.

You may suspect that would cause him to fall on his knees and beg for forgiveness. That would have been the smart move, but people don't always act in a logical way, do they? He could have easily lashed out at her as he saw those dollar bills slipping out of his grasp. It wouldn't take much to snatch up a nearby dinner knife and strike out at her before he'd truly realized what he'd just done.

It went a long way to explaining his bizarre behavior at the scene of her death. It also explained why he'd gone out of his way to avoid Raymond in the cabin area. Perhaps Reese's parents and brother knew or at least suspected what he'd done. That had been their reason for not giving Raymond comfort either. Maybe Reese even admitted to one of them what he'd done so they could help cover it up.

"Why didn't you say any of this to us before?" Alana asked.

"How can you ask me that? I'd just been holding my dead girl's body, and I'm supposed to remember everything?"

Alana didn't respond to his outburst.

"I'm sorry. I don't mean to yell. I know you're trying to help. It's not just Tiffany, though. I've been thinking about my wife all week. She should have been here for Tiffany's wedding. She died a decade ago in a car accident. A drunk driver came across the median when my wife was driving back from an event. She'd asked me to take her, but I said no because I was too tired. Maybe I would have been able to swerve out of the way, and she'd still be alive today. She didn't like driving at night. I should have been there. Tiffany and I spoke a lot about her recently as she was planning the wedding. She missed her mother so much."

"I'm sorry for your loss," Alana said.

"They're both gone, and I've got nothing left. I'd give the Lockwoods all my money if it meant getting those two women back."

"Mr. Calloway, you said Reese avoided you after Tiffany's death. Did you ever say anything to him? Did you go near him?"

Raymond laughed.

"You mean did I push that asshole overboard? No. I've been in my cabin the last two hours. If you want to know if I would have done it, then the answer is yes. I hope he's sitting at the bottom of the ocean right now. I hope the sharks are feasting on his corpse."

It was a stunning thing for Raymond Calloway to admit out loud. Nevertheless, I would have felt the same way if I were in his position.

"Is there anything else you want to know?" he asked.

"No. Not at this moment," Alana said.

"Am I free to go once we get to the marina?"

"I'd ask that you stay on the island for a few days, at least until we can officially wrap this up."

"How will you do that? It's not like there was a confession letter, at least I didn't hear of one. The man killed my little girl. Now he's robbed me of justice, and I'll never really know why he did it."

"I'm sorry again for your loss, Mr. Calloway. I better get back to the main deck and check on the status of the search," Alana said.

I expected Raymond to make another comment, but he didn't.

Alana turned from him and walked toward me. I opened the door, and we exited the cabin.

We were halfway down the hallway when she spoke to me in a low voice.

"Do you think he pushed Reese overboard?"

"He certainly hated him enough, but I don't think he did it."

"Why?"

"Because he would have told you if he did, as crazy as that might sound. You heard the man. He's lost everything. He's probably ready to die himself."

"You really think that?" she asked.

"I do. I saw it in his eyes. He's done."

Chapter 19
Angela Toppliff

Alana said that she wanted to go to the bridge to find out how much longer Captain Piadelia was going to conduct the search. She invited me to go with her. I got as far as the upstairs lounge before I begged off. I just didn't have the stomach to be around that captain anymore. I was beyond exhausted, and I needed to sit down for a few minutes. Alana had somehow caught a second wind. She was like that on these investigations, relentless and driven. I didn't know how she did it.

I told her I'd wait for her in the lounge. I walked over to the sofa and sat down. I was on my back two seconds after that. I stared at the ceiling and felt sleep overtaking my body. I tried fighting it, but the fatigue was winning. I heard Alana walk back into the lounge. I turned on my side to see what she needed.

It wasn't Alana, though. It was Angela.

"Oh, hey there," I said.

"You okay?"

I sat up.

"Yeah. Just tired."

"I'm sure. We all are."

"Did you just come from the bridge?"

"Yes. I was asking about the search."

"That's what Alana just went to do."

"I know. We crossed paths when I was coming down here."

"How are you doing?" I asked.

Angela sat down on the chair beside the sofa.

"I'm okay."

Neither of us said anything for a few seconds.

Then she asked me, "What will she do next?"

"You mean Alana?"

Angela nodded.

"I'm not sure. There's a theory going around that Reese jumped overboard because he felt guilty for murdering Tiffany."

I studied Angela for a reaction, but I didn't get one.

"How well did you know Reese?" I asked.

"We dated a short while in college. He was in one of my classes, and he asked me out."

"Reese told me that you guys broke up when he met Tiffany."

"If you knew Reese and I had dated, why did you ask me how well I knew him?"

"I was trying to get a sense of whether it was an intense relationship or just a few dates."

"What does that matter?"

"I guess it doesn't."

"So you were just curious?"

She didn't ask her question in an accusatory tone. Rather, she was more matter-of-fact about it, which I found kind of odd. Unfortunately, I was smack in the middle of an awkward place in the conversation. These interviews, and that's what I intended this to be, always went one of two ways. Most people want to be helpful, so they tend to answer your questions freely, even if they aren't sure where a specific question is coming from. The second way for these interviews to go is for them to question every question you ask. Why do you want to know that? What are you getting at? Are you accusing me of something? Do I need my lawyer present?

Angela sort of fit into the second category. She wasn't going to blurt out answers unless she knew what my motivations were, but she wasn't exactly going to be hostile toward me, either.

What was my response going to be? I decided to go philosophical on her.

"The more people I meet, the more I find human nature so interesting. Take Tiffany for example. When I first met her, I found her to be a difficult person, but then we had a long talk the same night she died. I realized there was a different side of her, like there might have been a good reason she was the way she was."

"Is that right?"

I didn't reply.

"Let me tell you something about Tiffany. What you saw was exactly what she was. She could be mean. No. I take that back. She could be vicious, and I don't use that word lightly."

"How long did you know her?" I asked.

"I met Tiffany, Zelda, and Sinclair in high school. I thought they were my friends. Turns out they weren't. I'm not trying to imply that Reese was the love of my life, not by a long shot, but that doesn't excuse Tiffany for doing what she did."

"I'm guessing Zelda and Sinclair sided with her on the matter."

"There was never any question about that."

"Why be friends with someone you thought was vicious?"

"Because that's what teenagers do. They search for acceptance with the cool kids even if those cool kids are bastards. Only when we get older do we realize how foolish that is."

"And Tiffany's friends were the cool kids?"

"The coolest of the cool."

"Is the breakup with Reese the thing that ended your friendship with them?" I asked.

"For the most part, but I left school after my freshman year. I haven't seen or spoken to them since."

"Why did you leave college?"

"I worked so hard to get into Harvard. Then I got there, and it wasn't what I expected it to be. There were other things I wanted to do with my life, and I decided not to wait three years before I did them."

"What were they?"

"I wanted to travel, to see the world, and I didn't want to be saddled with a mountain of debt from school loans. I didn't come from money, and I didn't want to spend all my time working to pay off those loans. So I left."

"I guess that's how you ended up with this job. You get to travel and be paid for it."

"Exactly. It's hard to beat."

"Was this your first job on a yacht?"

"No. I moved around a lot after I left college. Did a bunch of bar and restaurant jobs. I ended up moving to Oahu since I figured I might as well have nice weather if I was going to be broke. I met this guy who worked as a first mate on a yacht. He got me a job when one of their stews quit just before a charter. I couldn't believe how much money I made, so I asked if I could stay on for more charters. They liked my work ethic."

"That was this yacht?"

"No. I bounced around to a few different yachts. I've been on this one for a while because I really like Captain Piadelia."

"Why move to Maui from Oahu?"

"Because the yacht's docked out of there, and the island's a bit cheaper than Oahu. The traffic's a lot less, too."

It was an observation I'd made myself on a couple of trips to Oahu. Honolulu routinely ranked as one of the worst cities in the country for traffic. That traffic made people want to live in the city, which only served to make the real estate prices even higher than the astronomical rates they already were. Hawaii was paradise, all right, but that paradise came at a steep price.

"How do you think Tiffany found out you worked on this yacht?" I asked.

"I don't know. I intentionally try to keep my life private, which is why I stay off social media. You have to be a bit closed off with this job. It's best that the guests not know too much about you."

"Why is that?"

"It's hard to describe. There's a level of wealth here that you can't understand. They pay a small fortune to spend a week on these yachts. They expect to be treated like royalty. They act like they own you. I don't like them knowing details about me. I don't want them to have anything they can use against me."

"Use against you? I'm not sure I understand."

"People can be cruel. It's that simple."

I found her words ironic. The job gave her freedom, at least the freedom to travel and fulfill her dreams, but it did so at a high price. In a way, she was a slave to these people and their crazy whims.

"It's more than the clients," she continued. "The owners also do extensive background checks on us. They can't have anyone who might project a feeling of…instability."

"I understand."

"I don't think you do," she said.

"It must have been a shock to you when you found out who was coming on board."

"That's an understatement."

"Hani said Tiffany was insistent that she charter this particular yacht."

"I know. Hani told me that, too."

"Does that surprise you?"

"Actually, yes. I always thought Tiffany wanted what others had. That's why she went after Reese. She saw him, and she wanted him. She got him. Fine. But that was a long time ago. I don't know why she'd still have it out for me."

"So you think she chartered this yacht just to torment you?" I asked.

"No. I suspect that was just an added bonus."

"I saw you and Reese talking at the bar the first night of the cruise. Do you mind me asking what you were talking about?"

"He was apologizing for Tiffany's behavior. I don't think he knew that I worked this charter."

"That's what he told me. So you believed him?"

"Sure, why not? It didn't really make a difference. They were here. What was I going to do? I just had to grin and bear it. I'm actually pretty proud of myself. I think I did a pretty good job, considering the circumstances."

"You know, we found something interesting in Baakir's cabin."

I paused and waited for her to ask me what it was. Why did I do this? Because I thought she might already know, and I wanted to study her reaction. Again, she didn't really have much of one, nor did she seem all that interested in knowing what we'd uncovered.

"We found three empty bottles of magnesium citrate," I continued.

"I don't even know what that is."

"It's a laxative."

"Why would he have three bottles of that?"

"That's what we were trying to figure out. Then we thought he might have put it on their food or in their drinks to get back at them after Catherine Lockwood's racial slur."

"I guess Kimi told you about that."

"She did."

"I never met Reese's parents until this trip. They're a real piece of work, at least the mother is."

"Why do you think she would say such a thing?"

"Someone asked what was for dinner. I think it might have been Zelda. I don't remember exactly. Before I could answer her, Mrs. Lockwood made that comment."

"What did you say?"

"I didn't say anything, and I regret that. But it's what we're told to do. Sit back and take the abuse. You know what my first captain said? He said when someone pays me two hundred grand for a week, they can treat my people however they want. It's a pretty shitty thing, but it's the way it is."

"Do you think Baakir might have made them sick on purpose?" I asked.

"I don't know, but a part of me hopes he did. It would be kind of funny, wouldn't it?"

"Any chance Kimi or Banks would have done it?"

"No. No chance. I would have seen them if they tried."

"I know you were in the galley cooking dinner the night Tiffany died, but did you serve the guests drinks after dinner?"

"For a little while. They were all drinking, and the girls were having trouble keeping up. I spent most of my evening in the galley."

"I heard Reese and Tiffany apparently had a disagreement about his possible cheating," I said.

"Is that what was going on?"

"You didn't know?"

"How would I? I had my hands full after the captain let Bucky go."

"Apparently, Tiffany thought there might be something going on between Reese and Sinclair."

"Is that right? You don't know how happy that makes me to hear. Tiffany being betrayed by a friend? How ironic," Angela said.

"You didn't hear anything specific when you were around them?"

"No. You learn how to tune things out. I listen for my name, or I wait for them to make eye contact with me."

"So, what's your best guess? Did Reese jump overboard?" I asked.

"I'm sorry, but I just don't know. It makes sense, though, since I don't know who else would have killed Tiffany. Zelda and Sinclair worshiped her, and I don't see how a member of his family would have done it."

"What about your crew? She wasn't the nicest lady to them."

"No. She wasn't, but she was nothing compared to some of the nasty little pieces of work we get here. If the crew went after everyone who demeaned us, there would be a lot more dead bodies."

I saw Alana enter the lounge behind Angela. Angela must have seen my eye movement because she turned around.

"Sounds like we have several more hours before we'll be heading back to the island," Alana said.

Angela stood.

"The captain told me the same thing. They're not going to abandon the search anytime soon, especially now that the sun is about to rise," Angela said.

Angela turned back to me.

"Is there anything else you wanted to know?"

I shook my head.

"Then I'm going to check on Kimi and Banks and see how they're doing."

Angela left the lounge, and Alana sat beside me on the sofa.

"You had a talk with her?"

"Yeah."

"Learn anything interesting?"

"Just that Angela is a deeply private person, and she apparently had no idea that Tiffany and company had chartered this yacht until right before they showed up."

"That's what we already heard," Alana said.

"Yeah. I know."

We walked down to the main deck and helped look for Reese. I watched as the sun rose over the horizon. It was a beautiful sight, beyond beautiful, actually. The sky was a deep red, and it reminded me of an old sailor saying I'd heard years ago: Red sky morning, sailor's warning.

Did that mean we were in for another tough day? Yes, if you believed the saying. Did I? Not especially, but something told me we were going to have a bad one. Reese might have killed Tiffany, and he might have killed himself afterward. All signs seemed to point in that direction, but I thought this was far from over. I had no good explanation for that. It was just a feeling, however remote and fleeting.

Chapter 20
I Loved Him

I'm not sure how long we stood at that railing and scanned the waters for Reese. I do know it was at least an hour for the sun was much higher in the sky, and the black water had turned to a magnificent shade of blue. The wind had started to die down, and it was finally beginning to warm up. There was still no sign of Reese, nor had we heard anything from any of the other vessels searching for him. A few had passed us while Alana and I were on the deck. They ranged from yachts like ours to smaller sailing vessels. I knew the Coast Guard was out there somewhere, but I hadn't seen them yet.

Alana eventually left since she wanted to contact her department and give them an update on the search and our projected time to return to Maui. I kept looking for several more minutes after Alana left but then decided to go below deck and see how Foxx and Hani were doing.

I turned from the railing and almost bumped into Sinclair.

"Oh, I'm sorry," I said.

"It's my fault. I should have announced my presence."

She paused a second. Then she said, "There's something I was hoping to talk to you about."

"Sure. What is it?"

"It's about Reese."

She paused again, and I waited for her to continue. She didn't.

"Do you know something about Reese's death?" I asked.

"No. Not his death, but I wasn't completely honest with you and the detective when we spoke earlier."

Was that a surprise? Of course not since her friend had already contradicted her about her relationship with Reese. Did I think that made Sinclair the worst liar to ever walk the earth? No. I got why she didn't say anything. She was ashamed. Clear and simple.

"What do you want to tell me now?" I asked.

"I knew what Tiffany was referring to when she said 'I know what you did.' She found out about Reese and me. I still don't know how she did."

"So you and Reese did have some kind of romantic attachment?" I asked, even though I already knew the answer.

"Yes. It started when Tiffany was out of town for work. It was just a one-night thing. Neither of us thought it would go beyond that."

"Are you just telling me this now because Zelda admitted to you that she already told us about you and Reese?"

"No. She did tell that she told you about that night, but she doesn't know the whole story."

"What does she not know?"

"That night happened a couple of months before I moved. Reese and I pretty much avoided each other after we slept together. We were both terrified Tiffany would find out. I got that job in Chicago, and I thought that was the end of it. I mean I stayed in touch with Tiffany, and we planned to see each other as often as we could."

"So what happened?"

"Reese called me one night. He said he was coming to Chicago for a week for work. He said he wanted to get together and talk."

"He wanted to talk," I repeated.

"Yes. He said he felt really bad about how things had gone down. He said he felt like he'd gotten in the way of my friendship with Tiffany. He wanted to apologize to me and see if we could find a way to move forward."

"I'm not sure I understand. It seems pretty clear you guys had two options, either tell Tiffany or keep it a secret. You both obviously had a lot to lose if she found out, so why not just pretend it didn't happen?"

"I told him basically the same thing. He said he understood, but he insisted on seeing me. I agreed to meet with him. I met him at the restaurant in his hotel."

I think we all know where this was headed, and I'm sure Sinclair did as well. So why was she putting on this act and dragging it out? Maybe she was worried about her reputation, even though it didn't matter what I thought. Who was I going to tell? Maybe she just enjoyed the drama of making me wait. Who knew?

"I assume something happened that night," I said.

"He told me he hadn't been able to stop thinking about us. I admitted that I'd thought of him a lot, too. We went back to his room and had sex. I'm ashamed to admit this, but I spent every night with him that week. I was even in the room when Tiffany would call him before she went to bed. I felt so guilty."

Why do people say that when you know they don't mean it? How guilty could she have really felt if she'd had sex with her best friend's fiancée every night he was in Chicago? Good Lord, this was worse than a reality TV show.

"Did Zelda know about this?"

"No. She only knew about the one night in New York. I didn't tell her about Chicago. I didn't tell anyone."

"So why are you telling me this now?"

"To try to explain why I didn't come forward before."

"Come forward about the affair?" I asked.

"No. There's more."

Really? Is this where she told me that she and Reese got secretly married in Chicago?

"Reese came to me last night. He was really upset. He was banging on the door. I opened it, and he was drenched with sweat."

"Did you ask him why he looked like that?"

"Of course. He said he'd gotten into an argument with Tiffany. He said it was about me and him. He swore she didn't know anything for certain, but she'd threatened to call off the wedding."

And the pieces began to fall into place, I thought.

"Did you get a good look at his clothing? Was there blood on it?"

"No."

"No there wasn't blood or no you didn't get a good look?"

"He was wearing a black shirt, and my cabin was kind of dark, but I didn't see any blood on him."

"So what did you say?" I asked.

"I told him to calm down. I told him not to worry about the wedding. I knew Tiffany wouldn't cancel it."

"Why wouldn't she, especially if she believed he was having an affair?"

"Do you have any idea how many people were coming to that wedding? There was no way she'd cancel it and be humiliated. I told him all of that. I thought he believed me because he slowly started to calm down. I told him to go back to his cabin and try to get some rest. That's when we heard Mr. Calloway yelling."

"When you saw that Tiffany was dead, did you think it was Reese who'd killed her?"

"I wasn't sure. I thought it might have been, but I couldn't let my mind go there."

"Why not? You knew they'd been fighting just minutes before Reese came to your cabin. You'd seen what he looked like."

"Don't you see? I loved him. I couldn't believe he would do such a thing, especially to my friend," she said.

"And now?"

"He must have done it. It's the only thing that makes sense."

"When we were on the beach yesterday, you told me there was some man who assured you that your relationship was over. You were talking about Reese, weren't you?"

Sinclair nodded.

"I was a fool. It's not easy to admit that. Here I was, on his wedding trip, and I was still holding out hope that he'd leave Tiffany for me."

"If he'd told you that he wanted to leave her, would you have gone with him?"

"Yes. Yes, I would have."

Our conversation ended shortly after that. There really wasn't much more that she could say. There wasn't much farther she could drop in my eyes.

I gave her the advice that she'd given Reese. I told her to go back to her cabin and lie down.

I stayed on the deck, stared out at the ocean, and tried to collect the thoughts that were spinning through my head at a million miles per hour.

Tiffany was gone. Reese was gone. Could it really have all been over a love affair? I didn't see why it couldn't. Emotion. Uncontrollable emotion. That's what murder often boiled down to. It was seldom logical, not that that would excuse one person taking the life of another.

Tiffany had stolen a man from her friend. Why? Because she wanted to. Reese had betrayed his love with another woman. Why? Because he wanted to. Sinclair had made love repeatedly with the fiancée of her friend. Again, because she wanted to. A brother and best man had brought those secrets into the light because he was jealous of another man. Those revelations had led to a man plunging a knife into the neck of his wife-to-be. It then led him to climb over the railing and drop into the cold waters below.

It would only be a matter of time before Captain Piadelia abandoned this hopeless search and took us back to Maui. I would gather my things and climb off this boat. I would go back home and try to forget I ever met the Calloways, the Lockwoods, the Sinclairs, and the Zeldas. They were a disgusting bunch, and I had no desire to let them stain my soul any more than they already had.

Chapter 21
Trenholme Lockwood

I went back to my cabin. Foxx and Hani were still there. I brought them up to speed on everything I knew, including the recent revelation by Sinclair that she'd encountered an agitated and sweating Reese moments before Tiffany's lifeless body was discovered just off the main lounge.

"Do you believe that she'd cover for him like that?" Foxx asked.

"I'm not sure."

"I do," Hani said. "You'd be surprised what people will do for love, especially if they're desperate for that other person to love them back. Maybe she thought Reese would see how much she cared for him if she helped him."

"But that would imply that she already knew Tiffany was dead. She couldn't have known then," Foxx said.

"I understand but she obviously knew something had happened. She might not have thought it was a physical attack, but she still wanted Reese to know she was there for him. She knew Tiffany had found out, and Sinclair wanted Reese to see that she was a better choice for him. I wouldn't be surprised if Sinclair asked Zelda to let it slip that Sinclair had been sleeping with Reese."

"They were both part of Tiffany's wedding party. You really think they'd be that petty?" I asked.

Hani laughed.

"You really haven't been around women that much, have you?"

"Wow, am I that naïve?" I asked.

Foxx patted me on the shoulder.

"Yeah, buddy, you are."

The cabin door opened, and Alana walked in.

"Judging by the look on your faces, I can tell I just missed something funny," Alana said.

"We were just trying to explain human nature to Poe," Foxx said.

"Oh, yeah, what's the reasoning behind that?" Alana asked.

"He wanted to know if Sinclair would be conniving enough to break up Tiffany's marriage to Reese," Hani said.

"Really? And why would you be talking about that?"

"I had a brief conversation with Sinclair on the deck. She came to see me a little after you left to see the captain," I said.

I filled Alana in on everything Sinclair had told me about her passionate week with Reese in a Chicago hotel.

"So Reese was even more panicked than we thought," Alana said.

"Sounds like it. Every time Tiffany would look at them, I'm sure he imagined her walking in on the two of them in that hotel room," Foxx said.

"Do you think she even knew they'd seen each other in Chicago?" Alana asked.

"She probably suggested it," Hani said. "I can almost hear her now, 'Reese, darling, you should look up Sinclair and have her show you the sights.'"

"She showed him the sights, all right," Foxx said.

I decided to change the subject before this conversation went any lower.

"What did you learn from the captain?" I asked.

"They're going to continue the search for Reese until the sun goes down. Then we'll head back to Maui."

"Does he have any hope of finding Reese?" Hani asked.

"I don't think so, but he has to try," Alana said.

"So is the case essentially closed? Reese killed Tiffany because she threatened to call off the wedding and then killed himself over his guilt?" I asked.

"That's the theory I'm going with. Still, we have a long time before we're back at the marina. I think it's worth talking to a few more people and try to tie up a few loose ends."

"Who are you going to talk to?" Hani asked.

"I still need to speak with Trenholme and his parents."

"Do you mind if I tag along?" I asked.

"I assumed you would. Why don't you grab Trenholme and bring him to the upstairs lounge? I'll be there waiting."

I knew what Alana was getting at. It seemed a touch more intimidating for me to bring him to Alana versus the other way around, kind of like being summoned to the principal's office in high school.

It took me several minutes to locate Trenholme. I found him on the deck behind the main lounge. He was standing at the railing and looking out at the ocean. Tiffany's covered body was just ten feet away. I found it an odd location for him to have picked to search for his brother.

I informed him that Alana wanted to speak with him. I thought he might decline, saying that he didn't want to temporarily stop searching the waters. He didn't say that, though. He just turned from the railing and told me to lead the way.

We walked to the lounge, and he took a seat beside Alana on the sofa. I sat back down on my chair.

"I just spoke with the captain. We're going to keep searching as long as we have light," Alana said.

Trenholme nodded.

"Thank you for talking with us. There are a few things we'd like to go over with you," she continued.

"What do you want to know?" Trenholme asked.

"There's been some discussion about a comment you made at last night's dinner. Apparently, you made a reference to Tiffany's willingness to forgive Reese for cheating. Is that correct?" Alana asked.

"Yes, and I'm going to regret saying that for the rest of my life."

"Can I ask why you would say that?" Alana asked.

"I was angry with Reese and Sinclair."

"Why were you angry with them?" Alana asked.

"I found out about them. I always had my suspicions, but they were nothing more than that until this cruise."

"How did you find out?" I asked.

"They were flirting with each other pretty hard at the beach. Then it got even worse at the restaurant. I couldn't believe it. They were being so disrespectful to Tiffany. When we got back to the ship, I cornered Zelda and asked her if she knew anything. She denied it at first, but then she admitted that Sinclair and Reese had slept together."

"Do you have feelings for Sinclair? Is that one of the reasons you reacted so strongly?" Alana asked.

"There's nothing between Sinclair and I."

That certainly wasn't the answer to Alana's question, at least it wasn't a direct answer. There's nothing quite as embarrassing as expressing your feelings for someone and having them reject those feelings. Trenholme may not have voiced his affections for Sinclair out loud, but it seemed pretty clear that everyone knew what they were. She'd made her choice clear, too, only it had been for a different Lockwood man.

"Did Reese say anything to you after the dinner?" I asked.

"No. There really wasn't anything he could say that wouldn't cause a scene."

"Did Sinclair say anything?" Alana asked.

"No, but Zelda did. I walked out onto the deck to get some air and try to get away from everyone for a minute. Zelda came out and let me know exactly what she thought of my comments. She thought they would come back on her. I told her I was sorry."

"After you saw that Tiffany had been killed, what did you think?" Alana asked.

"I thought Reese had done it."

"Why did you think that? Was it because you thought Tiffany might have confronted him?" I asked.

"I'm sure she did. Reese has a terrible temper."

That was interesting, and it was the first time we'd heard that.

"Had he ever hit Tiffany before?"

"Not that I know about, but he's been in several fights. He's kicked the hell out of me more than once. He hasn't done it in a long time. I started hitting back."

"All brothers fight. Are you talking about childhood fights or something more recent?" I asked.

"Nothing in the last few years," he said.

"The last few years? So you've had fights in your twenties?" Alana asked.

Trenholme nodded.

"What about?" I asked.

"Different things. Stupid things. The reason didn't ever matter. It had more to do with if he'd been drinking or not."

"You said you suspected Reese might have killed Tiffany. Did you say anything to your parents about it?" Alana asked.

"No, but they came to me. They told me that Reese couldn't have done it."

"They said that? Why did they think that?" I asked.

"They didn't give a specific reason. They just said that Reese loved Tiffany, and he could have never done such a thing."

"What did you say to that?" I asked.

"Nothing. I knew what they were getting at. They were telling me to keep my suspicions to myself."

"Did you confront Reese?" Alana asked.

"I did try to talk to him. You guys were interviewing people. Reese wasn't in his cabin, so I went looking for him. I found him near Tiffany's body."

Trenholme turned to me.

"He was right where you found me a few minutes ago. He was standing at the railing like I was. He had an empty bottle of Jack in his hand. I went to say something to him, and he told me to get lost. His words were so slurred I could barely understand him."

"So did you walk away?" I asked.

"I did. I knew there was no use talking to him in that condition."

"In your opinion, do you think Reese took his own life?" Alana asked.

"It wasn't something I ever thought him capable of, but I think he probably did. The guy was so wasted. He wasn't thinking clearly."

"Is that what your parents think?" I asked.

"No. They refuse to believe it. It's no secret Reese was their favorite. He could do no wrong in their eyes."

Trenholme hesitated.

Then he said, "I should have forced him away from that railing. I should have physically dragged him back to his cabin. Instead, I just left him there, and now he's gone. He's never coming back."

"It's not your fault. Reese made his own decisions," I said.

"Maybe, but I was his family. I'm supposed to look out for him."

We all sat in silence for a few more moments. None of us seemed to know what to say next. Alana eventually thanked Trenholme for his time. She expressed her condolences again.

Trenholme stood and left the lounge, perhaps to go back to searching the ocean for his brother.

"Well, that looks like the confirmation we were looking for that Reese probably jumped. His brother puts him at the railing with an empty bottle of liquor in his hand," Alana said.

"And this was just a handful of feet from his fiancée's dead body."

"He came back to the scene of the crime. Killers do that all the time."

"It's also pretty clear that Reese was a violent guy. Who the hell has a fistfight with their brother when they're in their twenties? That's crazy."

"And Trenholme said it happens when Reese had too much to drink. It's only a matter of time before the guy everyone says would never hit a woman suddenly loses control and does it."

"Are you still going to talk to his parents?" I asked.

"Eventually, but not right now. You heard what Trenholme said. Reese could do nothing wrong in their eyes."

Alana stood.

"I think I'm going back to the cabin and rest for a bit. I'm finally starting to crash. Are you coming?"

"I'll meet you down in a little while. I want to help with the search."

"Okay. I'll see you soon."

Alana left, and I walked outside to the tanning lounge. I walked past the white cushions where we'd tried to sleep the first night and went to the bow. I stared out at the ocean. The waves had picked up a bit, and the boat rocked harder back and forth. My stomach started feeling queasy, which was probably a combination of the boat's movement and the lack of food and sleep.

I closed my eyes and hoped that my insides would settle if I stopped looking at the horizon bouncing up and down. It didn't work.

Chapter 22
Dream Job

As far as I knew, the case was essentially closed. I thought about going back to the cabin and resting with Alana. Something held me back, though, and I was pretty sure I knew what it was. There was still a mystery to solve.

Actually, there were two mysteries, but I didn't care about one of them. The first mystery involved the empty bottles of laxative. Who dosed the guests' food or drink with it? I thought the answer to "why" was pretty obvious, but the "who" was still missing. This was the question I was more than willing to put on hold since it didn't seem to directly connect to the murder-suicide. Of course, I could be wrong, but I saw it more as a cruel prank than anything else.

The second mystery was one that had been quickly cast aside by Alana and me, but in hindsight I felt that it might just prove to be significant. I'm sure you'll accuse me of exaggeration when you hear my thoughts on the matter. That would probably be a fair assessment. My brain is often prone to flights of fancy, and I've been guilty more than once of concentrating on something that never amounted to the proverbial hill of beans.

The mystery I'm referring to was how did Tiffany Calloway know that Angela worked on this yacht? That question was driving me crazy. There were only two possibilities. Option one was that someone told her. Both Sinclair and Zelda claimed they hadn't heard from Angela since college. Had they lied to me and Alana? That was certainly a distinct possibility, and I could see why they would have done so. They would have looked really small if they'd fessed up to the fact that they were the ones to suggest to Tiffany that she turn her wedding cruise into a chance to emotionally torture Angela.

The second option was that Tiffany discovered Angela's job on her own. If she had done that, then how? Perhaps she'd simply stumbled upon Angela's name while searching for Hawaiian yachts. Angela was a chief stew, which as far as I knew was a senior member of the yacht crew. Maybe that meant she was likely to be mentioned on the website for The Epiphany.

I walked back to the upstairs lounge and sat at a small table by the two bookcases. There was a laptop for guests. I logged onto the internet. The Wi-Fi connection was predictably slow since we were out at sea, but it still worked.

The first search I did was for this yacht. I typed the words Epiphany, yacht, and Maui into the search box. I found several listings for the yacht, as well as several photographs various guests of the yacht had posted on social media websites.

I clicked on the link that took me to a listing for several potential yachts one could charter for a tour around the islands. I clicked on the link for The Epiphany and found a general description of the yacht and several professionally taken photographs. There was also a short video that wasn't much more than the same photographs I'd already seen edited to Hawaiian music. It should have been charming, but I found it a bit cheesy instead, especially considering the price potential guests would have to pay to get on this thing.

The listing for the yacht didn't show any of the crew members as I thought it might, not even the captain. I went back to Google and typed in the name Angela Toppliff as well as Epiphany and Hawaiian cruises. I found the same links to various cruise lines, as well as the link for the website I'd just searched. There was nothing, though, that had Angela's name or photograph, at least not on the first page of the Google results.

I scanned through several additional pages since I thought that a previous guest might have mentioned Angela in a review of the cruise or perhaps even a personal social media post. I went through a total of eight pages of Google results, but I didn't find a single mention of Angela. Did I think that odd?

Sure, but the results were the results and beyond anyone's manipulation, unless they worked at Google.

I decided to switch gears and did a search for Tiffany Calloway. Do you have any idea just how many Tiffany Calloways there are on the World Wide Web? It took me several minutes of scanning through the dozens of results to find a website that listed the Tiffany I was interested in. I discovered she was a lawyer for a law firm in New York called Blackburn, Peal, and O'Brien. They specialized in a variety of things, but Ms. Calloway's area of expertise was listed as family law. I saw that she was a graduate of Harvard Law, which I already knew. I found it a bit odd that she'd want to concentrate on officiating people's prenuptial agreements and divorces, especially after getting a degree from Harvard. Yeah, it's a dirty job, and someone has to do it, as people like to say. Nevertheless, I would have predicted that Tiffany would have gone on to be a corporate lawyer or intellectual property lawyer or even criminal lawyer. I could easily see her love of verbal sparring to translate to success in the courtroom.

She'd shunned that in favor of family law. This, of course, brought up the inevitable question of why someone who dealt with divorces day in and day out would want to get married. I wasn't sure if I admired Tiffany's optimism to walk down the aisle or if she'd just been incredibly naïve. Another question popped into my head. Did Tiffany have an ironclad prenuptial agreement? She probably did, especially if she had all the money, and Reese was broke from his bad investments. That didn't mean she wouldn't help get him out of debt, but their marriage seemed more and more unlikely to me the more I thought about it. It just wasn't a good deal for her, both emotionally and financially, but love is blind, isn't it?

I logged onto my Facebook account and did a search for Tiffany. I got similar results to the Google search. There were a ton of Tiffany Calloways. Some women, such as those from a different race or age, were easy to dismiss. Other Tiffanys had non-human photographs for their profile picture, including dogs and cats or some attractive scenic location. I checked all of them but didn't find the correct Tiffany. I ended up looking at all the Tiffany Calloway pages and came to the conclusion that she didn't have one. Was that odd? Maybe, but perhaps she didn't want potential clients or angry ex-spouses of those she represented to learn personal details about her and come looking for revenge.

I moved on to another subject and typed Zelda Cameron's name into Google. It was a more unique name, and I was able to find her law firm quickly. She was listed as a tax attorney in case you're wondering. I found it a surprising choice, especially considering her personality. In full disclosure, I couldn't come up with many jobs that I thought would be more torturous than tax attorney, maybe the poor soul who is responsible for emptying human waste out of porta-johns.

I went back to the Google results for Zelda and scanned through the various social media links. Our Zelda was a very active lady. She was apparently obsessed with politics, and she posted to Facebook and Twitter several times a day to express her opinions. I had no idea how she managed to keep her job as an attorney with all the posting she was doing. She also liked to link to several articles on CNN, the New York Times, Politico, the Washington Post, even the comical website The Onion. Zelda was a news junkie. In case you're wondering, she leaned far to the left.

I scanned through Zelda's Facebook posts and saw no mention of her trip to Hawaii. There were some older posts showing her, Tiffany, and Sinclair, but nothing that mentioned Tiffany's engagement to Reese. Odd? Hell, yes, especially since Zelda was the maid of honor. You would have thought that she would have wanted to wish her friend happiness.

A thought then popped into my head. Perhaps Tiffany had specifically asked her not to mention the engagement on social media. If Tiffany was a deeply private or careful person, then it made sense she wouldn't want her friends giving anything away, either.

I clicked the back tab a few times until I got to the website for Zelda's law firm. I looked up the physical address for the firm on the contact page. I clicked on it, and it took me to a Google map of Manhattan. I opened a second web page and typed in the name of Tiffany's firm. I found their address and pulled up their location on another Google map. I compared the two maps. The law firms were just a few blocks away, which confirmed what

Zelda, Sinclair, and Reese had told me. It would have been very easy for them to meet for drinks on a Friday night.

I went back to Google and searched for Sinclair Dewey. It was a bit more common of a name than Zelda's but still nowhere as common as Tiffany's. I decided to look through Sinclair's work-related search listings first.

I found some old posts that mentioned Sinclair's work on different types of advertising jobs. She'd apparently worked for an agency in New York called Kirkland & Company. They had some monster accounts with the country's largest discount store and a national insurance company that's known for its humorous commercials. I won't mention the store's name because I break out in hives every time I go in there, which isn't very often.

As far as the insurance company goes, I hate them, too. I actually used them for several years until they refused to reimburse me for a fifty-dollar light after a moving truck plowed into my SUV in Virginia. It ripped the front bumper off and almost knocked my entire vehicle onto its side because it had hit it so hard. Somehow, the insurance adjuster didn't think that the moving truck could have possibly cracked my turn signal light in the process.

I knew all too well what they were doing. Fifty bucks doesn't seem like that big of a deal, especially for a huge insurance company. If you rip off thousands of customers for fifty bucks each per day, then your cost savings suddenly become significant. Sure, they all do it, but that didn't mean I couldn't enjoy giving this company the middle finger of righteous indignation and switch insurance brokers.

Back to Sinclair, though, and I apologize for getting distracted. I guess you can tell I'm still upset after all of these years about that damned turn signal light. Anyway, Sinclair was listed as a copywriter for Kirkland & Company in New York. I had a general idea of what she did, but I searched the definition anyway. It turns out a copywriter reports to the creative director and writes for a variety of mediums, including print and online ads, brochures, and commercial scripts.

I went back to the Google search for Sinclair and found the new job she had in Chicago. She was mentioned in a press release by an agency called Peanut Butter Jar. No, you're not reading that wrong, and I swear that I'm not drunk as I write this. It was the God's honest name of the company. I was so sure that the press release had gotten it wrong that I did a separate search for Peanut Butter Jar and Chicago ad agency, and I found their website.

Sinclair Dewey was listed under the "Our Team" page on the website. I was absolutely convinced that she would be listed as the creative director for this company since I didn't see how she would be willing to work for such a ridiculously named agency. She wasn't a creative director, however. She was still a copywriter.

I looked under the "Our Clients" page and found a few hospitality companies and a brand of tequila I'd never heard of before. I hadn't heard of the resort companies, either. They weren't named Marriott or Westin or even the Holiday Inn.

Peanut Butter Jar had a page on its website that showcased some of the print ads it had done. The website also had several commercials with embedded YouTube links, and I watched most of them. They weren't bad, but they certainly didn't come close to matching the quality of those commercials for the insurance company that I eluded to earlier in this chapter.

Sinclair had told Alana and me that she'd left New York and her best friends for a job in Chicago that was too good to pass up. She'd either lied to us or she was suffering from a head injury. I could only conclude that she might have been fired from Kirkland & Company and had gone to Peanut Butter Jar out of desperation.

The question was: Did this mean anything in regards to the murder of Tiffany Calloway and the apparent suicide of Reese Lockwood? I didn't see how it could, and I thought I'd just wasted the last hour sitting in front of this laptop.

Chapter 23
Blood

I'm not sure what caused me to drive on with this investigation. I've been accused of listening to that strange little voice in the back of my mind way too often. The voice wasn't really talking to me now per se. It was more a lack of the voice that left me feeling a touch uneasy.

I'll explain it more like this. It's sort of like when you open that box that has the sticker that says "some assembly required," only the box has no less than ten thousand pieces in it. You look at the instructions and see that you're supposed to slide piece A into piece B. It doesn't go in as easily as you think it should, but it looks like it fits. There aren't any cracks or gaps or any other signs that would seem to indicate something is wrong.

That's how I felt with this case. Tiffany was dead. There was no denying that. The murder weapon had vanished, but we still knew it was a sharp object, almost certainly a knife. Reese seemed to be the only one with a motive strong enough to kill her in such a passionate way. We also knew that Reese was no longer on the yacht. Granted, we didn't know if he'd jumped out of remorse for his actions against Tiffany.

The thing that bothered me was that although part A seemed to fit nicely into part B, and I couldn't see any of the aforementioned gaps or cracks, I still hadn't heard that nice clicking sound you hear when something truly fits perfectly.

I left the upstairs lounge and made my way down to the main lounge. There was no one in there. I'm not big into physical evidence, which I realize makes me sound like I'm ignoring a big part of the investigative process. I don't mean to imply that physical evidence isn't important, but I don't have access to the high-tech labs and equipment that law enforcement does. Yes, I'm often the recipient of that information when Alana decides she wants to share it with me.

The thing that has always allowed me to crack cases where the police have failed is my stubborn desire to stick to analyzing the emotional evidence. People kill for emotion. Someone has rejected their love. Someone has stolen their money or prized positions. Someone is trying to keep them from getting the power they feel they deserve. Figure out the motive, and you'll figure out the killer.

Now, let me contradict all of that in a maddening way and state that my only reason for coming to the lounge was to look for the physical evidence that I just so callously dismissed. I'm guessing you can see just how desperate I was at this point in the journey.

Trenholme had told us that he'd seen Reese standing at the yacht's railing several feet from Tiffany's body. He also mentioned that Reese had been drinking heavily. I walked over to the railing. It came up to about the level of my waist. I leaned against the railing. I didn't see how I could possibly fall over, even I'd been drunk. I'm six-foot-two. Reese was probably two to three inches taller than me. Regardless, he'd have to intentionally jump over if he were to end up in the water.

There was another possibility. He was pushed. Check that. He was tossed overboard. A person would have had to lean Reese's intoxicated body halfway over the railing and then lift his legs, presumably one at a time, up into the air so that the weight of his body and gravity would carry him over.

That led to an interesting question. Who would have the strength to do that? Drunk people are essentially dead weight. Reese had easily been over two hundred pounds. Granted, a person wouldn't be lifting the entire weight of his body if they could have somehow gotten him slumped over that railing, but it still would have been a difficult thing to toss the rest of him up and over. I probably could have done it. Foxx certainly could have. Trenholme had the capability. Raymond and Artemis probably could have done it, too, but their ages would have made it a bit trickier, especially if they had bad backs.

I decided to go through that list one by one. I knew that neither Foxx nor I killed Reese. I didn't see any conceivable reason why Artemis would have pushed his son overboard. That left Trenholme and Raymond.

Trenholme had been angry with Reese for his presumed affair with Sinclair who Trenholme apparently had a thing for. All things considered, that didn't seem like a strong enough reason to me. That left Raymond Calloway. He had good reason, especially if he believed Reese had just murdered his daughter.

I'd dismissed Raymond earlier because I didn't see any attempts that he'd made to conceal his disdain for Reese when we'd interviewed him in his cabin. He openly stated that he'd wished he'd killed him. A killer certainly isn't going to admit to wanting someone dead, or was I being foolish to believe that? Was Raymond just being a good actor? I'd done several cases in my brief career as an investigator. I'd met very few people who I considered brilliant in disguising their true selves. Most of the time it was simply a matter of finding motivations, which had remained hidden from me.

I looked at the decking around me and quickly found the drops of blood which I'd spotted immediately after Tiffany's murder. It had been several hours since then, but the droplets still looked wet and sticky. Can something look sticky? I'm not sure, but that's how they seemed to me. I didn't see any fresh blood that might have been from a potential struggle between Reese and whoever might have thrown him to the sharks.

I got down on my knees and looked for scuff marks on the deck boards. I saw nothing. I also searched the railing and the railing posts for scuff marks or paint chips but had the same result: zilch. The railing looked freshly painted and everything was as clean.

I crawled on my knees and checked the main deck railing on the entire backside of the yacht. Granted, just because Trenholme had seen Reese at that part of the deck, it didn't mean that's where a potential struggle had ensued. Either way, I didn't find anything that would indicate a fight took place. If someone had fought Reese, they'd left no evidence or they'd done a good job of cleaning it up.

I looked back to Tiffany's covered body. Even in the dark of the night, it would have been impossible to miss those dark red stains on the bed sheet that covered her. Reese had picked a hell of a place to stand and get drunk. I didn't know why he would have done such a thing unless it was for the specific reason of torturing himself.

I decided to do another pass on the deck and railing before accepting the fact that Reese had most likely been the murderer of Tiffany Calloway. I'd searched about five feet of railing again when I saw something I'd missed before. I knew why I'd missed it, too. It was incredibly hard to see given its position. There were three partial bloody fingerprints on the underside of the railing. The fingertips were pointed toward me, which made perfect sense since the person, presumably Reese, had been standing on the inside of the railing. They would have wrapped their hand around the railing, and the fingers would have inevitably ended up pointing back at the person.

The killer would have seen the bloody palm print on the top of the railing and would have wiped it clean. They might have even looked over the railing to see if the print extended to the other side, but they might not have seen the underside in the dark. Hell, I'd missed the prints on my first pass, and I'd been looking in the bright sunlight.

A thought then occurred to me. Maybe this print had been left by Reese after he'd stabbed Tiffany. He'd walked over to the railing with the explicit purpose of tossing the knife into the ocean. He might have inadvertently grabbed the railing to steady his shaking body.

I looked at the deck again and saw that the blood drops from the murder weapon were several feet away from the bloody fingerprints. I didn't see why Reese would toss the knife over at one point along the railing and then walk down the deck and stop at another point. It was improbable but not impossible. Stranger things have happened, and it wasn't as if Reese would have been calm and reasonable.

Nevertheless, it was a distinct possibility that someone, possibly Raymond, could have stabbed Reese and then pushed him over. Reese might have grabbed the railing as he struggled to stay on the yacht. Raymond would have cleaned the deck and the railing but might have easily overlooked the fingerprints under the railing. Was my imagination running wild? Maybe.

I bent over and took several photographs of the prints with my cell phone. I was about to go find Alana and tell her about my discovery when I heard a disturbance behind me. I turned around and saw Artemis and Catherine entering the main lounge on the far side of where I was. Raymond Calloway was on the other side. I wondered how long they'd been standing there and whether or not they'd watched as I'd photographed the bloody prints.

That question quickly vanished as a more pressing issue popped up. That would be Artemis's vicious attack on Raymond.

"You told her we're desperate? You think we want anything you have to offer?" Artemis growled, and he ran across the lounge.

Raymond instinctively walked back a few paces until his body was pinned against the wall, and he had nowhere to escape. He was completely unprepared for Artemis's aggression. He didn't even put up his hands to defend himself. Artemis' fist connected with Raymond's jaw. The force of the blow snapped Raymond's head back hard against the wall, and I saw his eyes glaze over.

I moved across the lounge to pull the two men apart, but Alana beat me to it. She'd entered the lounge from the side door just as Artemis struck Raymond. Alana grabbed Artemis from behind. He was a big man, and he easily tossed Alana to the floor. She hit her head on the granite countertop of the bar as she fell. I saw her eyes close, and she was completely motionless on the carpet.

This is a question for the husbands reading this book. If someone tossed your wife on the floor, what would you do? I reacted the same way you would have. I smashed my fist into Artemis's stomach. I heard the air escape his lungs, and I hit him a second time on the bridge of his nose as he bent over. I felt the cartilage break, and the blood flowed freely. Catherine, at least I think it was Catherine, screamed behind me.

I was about to tend to Alana when I got hit myself. I couldn't tell who it was because the blow had come from the side of my face where my eye was covered with the patch. In full disclosure, it hurt like hell, and I dropped to one knee. I rolled away to avoid the second blow that I was sure was coming.

I looked up just in time to see Foxx grab Trenholme from behind. He did something that I didn't think I'd ever see in my entire life. He lifted Trenholme over his head and slammed his body against the ceiling of the lounge. He then dropped Trenholme to the floor. It had to have been an eight-foot drop. Trenholme was a strong guy, and the blow didn't knock him unconscious. Instead, he groaned in pain and rolled back and forth, clutching the small of his back. I didn't see him being a problem anymore.

I crawled over to Alana, and Foxx joined me.

"Alana, are you all right?" I asked.

She didn't move.

"That son of a bitch," Foxx said, and he moved toward Trenholme again.

"Foxx, no. It was Artemis."

We both looked over to him. He was on his knees on the floor, and Catherine was trying to help him stop the flow of blood. I'd broken the nose badly, and blood drenched the front of his shirt and pants and had spilled onto the carpet.

"Looks like he already got payback," Foxx said.

I looked back at Alana. A large goose egg was quickly forming on her forehead.

"Wake up, Alana. Wake up."

Chapter 24
Lawsuits, Felonies, and Concussions

Alana was still unconscious after a few minutes. I wasn't panicked, but I was close. She'd been beaten to within an inch of her life the last time I'd seen her in a state of unconsciousness. I knew this was nothing like that, but she'd hit her head, and that made it serious. I checked her pulse. It was steady, and her breathing seemed normal.

"You better hope she's okay," Foxx said to Artemis.

"Look what you did to my son," Catherine screamed.

Trenholme was still on the floor, clutching his back and moaning.

"I don't give a rat's ass about your son," Foxx yelled back. "He got what was coming to him when he attacked my friend."

That was the thing that I admired most about Foxx. He was loyal, and he'd walk through hell for those he cared about.

"I'm going to sue you for this," Raymond said to Artemis.

"And I'll sue you for character assassination," Artemis shot back.

His voice sounded nasally through the broken nose and blood.

"Character assassination? For telling the truth about your finances?" Raymond asked.

"You had no right to talk about my personal business," Artemis said. "None of it's true, not one damn word."

Artemis turned to me.

"And your ass is going to be sued. Look what you did to my nose."

"I don't see how you're going to sue me from jail," I said.

"Jail?" Catherine asked.

"He assaulted a police officer. That's a felony," Foxx said.

That shut them up.

"Foxx, can you take them downstairs? Make them stay in their cabins," I said.

"My pleasure."

"We're not going anywhere. My son can't walk in this condition," Catherine said.

"He's a big boy. I'm sure he'll be okay."

Foxx grabbed the back of Trenholme's belt and lifted him to his feet. Trenholme stumbled, which made it even easier for Foxx to shove him hard against the wall. He fell to the floor again.

"What are you doing?" Catherine yelled.

"You're right, Mrs. Lockwood. He does seem unsteady," Foxx said as he kicked Trenholme's legs. "Come on now, buddy. You need to go back to your cabin," he continued.

Trenholme struggled to his feet. A spasm of pain hit him and he grabbed his lower back.

"You'll be fine. Now move it."

"I'd ask Kurt and one of the other deckhands to stand guard. I'm sure he would welcome the assignment," I said.

Foxx led the Lockwoods and Raymond Calloway out of the lounge and back to the cabin area.

I heard Alana moan. I looked down at her just as she opened her eyes.

"Lie still. Don't try to stand yet."

"What happened?" she asked.

"Artemis shoved you, and you hit your head on the corner of the bar as you fell."

"How long was I out?"

"Maybe five minutes. Not long."

Alana touched her head and winced.

"Look at the two of us, you with your head injury and me with my eye patch."

"Hani's going to owe us big for this," Alana said.

She turned her head and looked around the lounge.

"Where is everyone?" she asked.

"Back in their cabins. Foxx and Kurt are making sure they don't go anywhere. You should have seen what Foxx did to Trenholme."

"He didn't throw him overboard, did he?"

I laughed.

"No, but I wouldn't have put it past him. It was like something out of a professional wrestling match. I'm going to need to ask him about it when we get back to Maui."

I helped Alana to her feet.

"Oh, I'm dizzy."

"Here, let's get you to the sofa."

We walked several feet to the sofa, and Alana sat down.

"I hope Artemis Lockwood realizes it's a felony to assault a police officer."

"Oh, he knows," I said.

"How? Did he say something?"

"No. We informed him he was going to be arrested the moment we docked at the marina."

"You did?"

"Yeah. It was right after he threatened to sue me for breaking his nose."

"You broke his nose?"

"Right after you hit the bar. Then Trenholme sucker-punched me from my blind side, and Foxx did his thing with Trenholme and the ceiling."

"The ceiling? What are you talking about?"

"We'll have to get Foxx and Trenholme to reenact it later. I'm sure they'd both be up for it. What in the world happened between you and the Lockwoods? I saw them rush into the lounge, and then Artemis attacked Raymond."

"I interviewed them, and we spoke about their finances. They admitted they were having some issues but said it was nothing like Raymond described."

"Did you ask them about money being a potential reason Reese was marrying Tiffany?"

"Not in those exact words, but they're not dumb people. They knew what

I was getting at. Catherine got really offended and said money had nothing to do with Reese's love for Tiffany," Alana said.

"She seems to elevate getting offended to a new level."

"Yeah. She's a pro at it. I also asked them if they thought Reese was capable of taking his own life."

"How did they answer that?" I asked.

"Artemis didn't say anything, but Catherine swore he would never do it, even if he had been heartbroken over Tiffany's death."

"Did she think him falling overboard was an accident or intentional?"

"She's convinced Raymond did it. Trenholme told them that he'd seen Reese drinking heavily, just like he told us. Catherine thinks Raymond snuck up on a drunk Reese and shoved him over the railing."

"It's a plausible theory, but maybe not exactly the way she described."

"What do you mean?" Alana asked.

"I think Reese was stabbed first to incapacitate him. Then he was lifted over the railing."

"Stabbed?"

I told Alana about my discovery of the bloody fingerprints under the railing and how I thought they were the result of Reese grabbing it as his body was shoved toward the ocean.

"Show me," she said.

"I don't know, Alana. You still seem pretty weak."

"Nonsense. I'm tougher than you think."

Alana stood and immediately grabbed my arm as a wave of dizziness washed over her.

"Okay, tough guy. Let's take it slow," I said.

I led her past Tiffany's body and over to the railing where the fingerprints were.

"I'm going to take your word that they're there and not try to bend over to see them myself."

"Here. Let me show you on the phone," I said.

I pulled up the photo and handed Alana my phone.

"Tough to tell the size of the person based on these partial prints," she said.

"I agree, but I think they have to belong to a man. The tips of the prints are way too wide for a woman."

"Easy explanation. Reese stabbed Tiffany and then he grabbed the railing when he walked over to toss the murder weapon into the ocean."

"I thought about that, but I think he would have been too careful to have touched the railing. The killer obviously knew they had to get rid of the murder weapon. I don't think they would be so careless to leave prints on the railing," I said.

"Killers make mistakes like that all the time. They've just taken a life. The adrenaline is rushing. They think they have it covered, but they miss some obvious thing."

It was definitely something that I'd considered already, but I still found it unlikely.

"Here's another thing," I said. "Look how far apart the blood splatters are on the deck boards and compare their position to where we are at the railing. The killer tossed the knife back there. Why would they walk six or seven feet to this position and grab the railing? I don't buy it. This was left during a separate incident."

"Maybe. I don't want to shoot down one of your theories. We both know how right you often are, but it's still pretty thin. We'll test the prints when we get to Maui and forensics comes on board."

"Unfortunately, if they are Reese's prints, as I suspect they are, it doesn't prove whether he left them after killing Tiffany or when he, himself, was getting murdered," I said.

We both turned when we heard the sound of footsteps. It was Foxx.

"Glad to see you're up and about," he said.

"Thanks."

Foxx looked at Alana's head.

"That's some bump you got there."

He touched the side of her face.

"Look at me. I want to see your eyes," he continued.

"What's going on?" she asked.

"He's checking you for a concussion," I said.

"You know how many of those I've seen on the field. I lost count of how many I've had myself," he said.

It was something Foxx and I had spoken a lot about in the last year with all the news of NFL players suffering debilitating brain disease from repeated blows to the head. Foxx was terrified it would happen to him.

"Your eyes look a little glassy. I think you should sit down and rest."

"I'm fine," she said.

"Let me tell you a quick story. We were in the locker room at halftime, down twenty-one to three. Our quarterback got smashed between two linebackers. Everyone knew he had a concussion, but the coaches wanted him to go back out there in the second half. Our backup stunk, and there was no chance that guy could lead us back. The quarterback was so out of it, but he thought he was perfectly fine. I watched that guy walk into a wall and then into his locker door. He had no idea where he was. I'm not sure he even knew who he was. You think you're fine, but you're not. Trust me. Listen to me. Sit down and take it easy. Neither Poe nor I want you stumbling around on a rocking boat with the real chance you fall off this thing. Got it?"

"Got it," she said.

"I'm impressed, Foxx. She never listens to me like that," I said.

"Let's get you back to the cabin so Hani can keep an eye on you," Foxx said.

"Do you mind taking her down? I'll be there in a few minutes," I said.

"Sure."

I watched as Foxx helped Alana through the main lounge and down to the cabin area. She wasn't completely out of it, not by a long shot, but I thought she'd just been regulated to the sideline for the rest of this game, to use Foxx's football analogy.

I kneeled on the deck and looked under the railing again. I studied the fingerprints for a few minutes. I compared their size to my own fingers. They were about the same, which reinforced my earlier belief that they belonged to a man. Was this proof that Reese killed Tiffany? Maybe, but I didn't think so. Why? Because I hadn't heard that clicking sound when part A perfectly fits into part B.

There was one problem. Actually, there were lots of problems, but I was only willing to concentrate on one at the moment. I didn't know if Reese's death was a revenge killing for his presumed murder of Tiffany. I thought that's what it was, but here was the problem. If Raymond didn't kill Reese, and I don't think that happened, then who killed him?

Another thought popped into my mind, and it was one I found very intriguing. Perhaps the person who murdered Reese also killed Tiffany. If so, had that been their plan all along? If someone had killed them both, then what was their motivation? Why kill a future bride and groom on their wedding cruise?

Unfortunately, I had tons of questions and no answers at the moment. I didn't see how that was going to change, not unless some incredible piece of evidence popped to the surface. That seemed extremely unlikely as I stood on this yacht in the middle of the Pacific Ocean.

Chapter 25
Peapods and Other Things

I'm sure you're like me in that much of your childhood schooling has vanished to the deepest recesses of your mind. I tend to only remember the things I use every day. For example, I made it up to calculus in high school, but now I'd be lucky if I could figure out the most basic algebra equation. I'm still pretty decent at adding and subtracting but forget about multiplication and division.

There was one lesson, though, that I tended to remember. It was from junior high biology class. Our teacher told us about a monk named Gregor Mendel who paved the way for modern genetics. Perhaps you remember that lesson as well. He had a garden at his monastery where he mixed various types of peas and came up with the basic theories of dominant and recessive genes. I remember our teacher used the example of brown eyes versus blue eyes. Say the mother has blue eyes but the father has brown eyes. In all likelihood, their offspring will be born with brown eyes since it's the dominant gene.

So what? You might ask. What does this have to do with two dead people on a yacht? Well, I'm about to get to that.

I decided not to immediately check on Alana since I knew she was in good hands with Hani and Foxx. Instead, I made my way up to the bridge to ask Captain Piadelia for an update on our return to Maui. I wanted to get Alana proper medical care. I also wanted to ask him to contact the police department and inform them of Alana's injury and the assault perpetrated on her by Artemis Lockwood.

When I got to the bridge, I found the captain, his first mate, and Banks, our friendly third stewardess.

"Is the detective going to be all right?" Piadelia asked.

"Word travels fast on this yacht."

"Kurt informed us of what happened."

I confirmed the fight between the Lockwoods and Raymond Calloway, as well as Alana's injury at the hands of Artemis. I left out the part about me breaking his nose in return, as well as Foxx military pressing Trenholme into the ceiling. I forgot to mention this before, but there was a large dent in the ceiling from Trenholme's butt. I wasn't going to say anything, but if the crew noticed it, I would tell them to add it to the invoice for the cruise.

"What time do you think we'll resume our course to Maui?" I asked.

"We're going to continue our search for another few hours and then we'll head back," Piadelia said.

"I assume you've heard nothing from the other vessels."

Piadelia shook his head.

"I'm afraid not. It would be a miracle if we found him now."

The captain turned to Banks.

"Could you get me a cup of coffee? I need the caffeine."

"Of course, captain."

"Thank you, Pele."

Banks left the bridge.

"If the detective needs immediate medical attention, I can divert us directly back to the island. There's no reason to jeopardize her health when we have little to no hope of finding Mr. Lockwood."

"She might have a concussion, but I doubt she'd want you abandoning the search now. I appreciate your concern, though."

"Of course."

We spoke for a few more minutes. Nothing worth repeating here since it was mostly small talk.

I left the bridge and ran into Banks in the upstairs lounge. She was on her way back to the bridge with the coffee for Piadelia.

"Excuse me a second, but did the captain call you Pele?" I asked.

"That's right."

"That's the name of the soccer player. Why would he call you that?"

"Yeah, it's a famous soccer player, but it's also the name of the Hawaiian god of fire."

"He refers to you as the god of fire?"

"Not exactly. He says I'm like a spitfire. All the stews have Hawaiian names," she said.

"Why is that?"

"We decide at the beginning of the charter whether we're going to tell the guests our real first names or if we're going to go by our Hawaiian names."

"I think Angela said she didn't like the guests knowing too much about her."

"It can be a real problem, especially on the all-male charters."

"You have all-male charters?" I asked.

"Rich guys who want to turn this place into a brothel. They think their money and this yacht is going to guarantee they land gorgeous girls on the islands. It usually doesn't, so they turn their attention to us. It's disgusting."

"Do you mind me asking what Kimi's alter ego is?"

"Summer."

"Summer? That's Hawaiian?" I asked.

"Not exactly, but there is no Hawaiian word for it."

"So why didn't she pick something else?"

"She said she just liked the name. Angela was mad because she said that was going to be her stripper name."

"Stripper name? Now you've lost me."

"You know? Strippers give themselves ridiculous names like Bambi or Sugar or Cinnamon."

Cinnamon? Now that was an interesting name.

"What did Angela end up going with?

"Makani. It means wind."

"It's also the name of that restaurant we went to on the Big Island," I said.

"I'm pretty sure that's why she picked the name. She loves that place. We try to eat there every time we go to the Big Island."

I thanked Banks for her time, and she left to give Captain Piadelia his coffee.

I was almost out of the lounge when a thought occurred to me. Maybe I hadn't found anything for Angela during my online searches because I was simply using the wrong name. She'd told me that she kept information about her off the web so guests and potential employers wouldn't know anything about her. Maybe that was only a partial truth. Perhaps she had an online presence but as a different person.

I walked back to the small desk with the laptop and logged onto the internet. I did a Google search for the word makani. I found results for a power company called Makani, as well as a kite named Makani that supposedly created wind power. I clicked on the second page of search results and saw that there was also a catamaran company by that name. The most interesting result I found was that a killer whale at Seaworld was also named Makani. There was definitely nothing that tied back to Angela, though.

I logged onto Facebook and did another search for the word makani. Dozens of results appeared. The first few were a couple of restaurants by that name, one of which we'd visited on the island, and an artist who looked like she specialized in the art of tattoos.

I scanned down the list and found a ton of people who either had Makani as a first or last name. It wasn't until I got near the bottom of the list that I saw a name that jumped out at me: Summer Makani. Summer Wind.

I clicked on the name and saw a profile shot of a woman with her back to the camera. She had long hair that was metallic gray. So far, so good. I clicked on the photo tab and saw several shots of Angela at various places across the island of Maui. I recognized the black sand beach travelers can see along the road to Hana. There was also a shot of her standing at the crater's edge of Mount Haleakala at sunrise. Another photo clearly showed the Iao Needle in the background.

Then I found something that really got my interest. Angela was standing behind a boy. He, in turn, was standing behind a birthday cake and was clearly about to blow out the candles. It was that classic shot we've all taken dozens of times.

I continued to scan through her shots and saw many more of her and the boy. Some of them included Kimi in the images. I remembered she'd told me that she rented a studio apartment behind Angela's house. I found a shot that looked like it had been taken in their backyard. There was a tiny swing set and a lanai in the background.

Here's where Gregor Mendel fits into this equation. The boy had blonde hair and blue eyes. I was pretty sure Angela had brown eyes. I didn't know her true hair color, so it could have been brown or blonde or even black. I doubted it was red since her skin tone didn't seem to match what I'd seen on most of the redheads I'd known.

According to Mendel and my eighth grade biology teacher, the darker genes were the dominant ones, but that certainly didn't mean a recessive gene couldn't squeak through. Granted, Angela could have been carrying a gene for blue eyes in her DNA, but I thought it far more likely that the boy's blue eyes had come from his father. Anyone remember the color of Reese's eyes? I sure did.

I've never been that good at guessing the age of kids, but I didn't have to in this situation. I double-clicked on the photograph of the birthday boy and saw that it had been uploaded about a month ago. I then counted the number of candles on his Star Wars birthday cake. He'd just turned nine.

It wasn't hard to do the math. Angela had left school ten years ago either during or after her freshman year. Give nine months for the pregnancy. That meant she'd gotten pregnant during college.

She'd told me that she'd left Harvard because it hadn't been what she'd thought it would be. She'd also wanted to travel the world. I didn't see how she'd have been able to do that with a baby to care for. Yes, she could have left the child with her parents, but something told me she probably hadn't done that.

She'd lied to Alana and me, and I could only come up with one reason for her to have done that. She hadn't wanted us to know that she had a child right after college. Why? I didn't know the answer to that. I thought he most likely was Reese's child, or his father was another blue-eyed college student. That had to mean something.

Of course, she might not have told us because she didn't want it getting back to Reese. Maybe he didn't know, and the last thing she wanted was for him to try to get parental rights to the child. If Reese hadn't known, then that almost certainly meant Tiffany hadn't known either. There she'd been, tormenting and taunting Angela, all the while having no idea that Angela was the mother of Reese's child.

I took the next ten minutes to scan through Angela's - aka Sumer Makani's - social media posts. She was clearly a foodie as many of her posts were photographs of what she was about to eat. So, what were her favorite meals? I'll give her credit. She likes a nice variety of food, including sushi, Thai, seafood, and salads. She also had a good eye for photography. Usually the amateur posts you see about food are often underlit and look completely unappetizing.

There were several mentions of movies she'd taken her son to see. There was the aforementioned Star Wars film and one from Pixar called Coco. It was all typical stuff that young boys like. There was also an outing they'd enjoyed at the Maui Ocean Center. I'd been there several times myself. It's a great place.

Everything I'd seen so far was pretty typical for social media, but there was an interesting thing that was absent from her posts. There were no shots of the yacht, no mention of any of her crewmates outside of the few images of her roommate Kimi, and not one hint at what she did for a living. The yachting career didn't even exist, at least in terms of her life as depicted on social media. I understood her desire not to show her co-workers since I believed Facebook could tag people from their facial images. She wouldn't want to risk anyone tying her to the yacht and inadvertently making her personal information accessible to weirdo clients.

I continued to scan through her timeline until I found a long list of birthday wishes for Angela herself. I say a long list. There were maybe fifty names, not as many as some, but probably pretty decent for someone who lived on an island and liked to keep her work life excluded from her private one.

That was where I found the second bombshell in Summer Makani's world.

There was one particular wish that was from someone I knew. The post was just two words: Happy Birthday. There was no exclamation point after it. No smiley face emoji. No mention of Summer or Makani or Angela. Just a simple and concise "Happy Birthday."

That wasn't the bombshell, though. That would be who wrote those two words.

Sinclair Dewey.

Chapter 26
Father

I headed immediately back to my cabin to tell Alana what I'd learned. When I opened the door, I heard the sound of vomiting coming from the bathroom. I looked around the cabin and saw Foxx and Hani.

"That's the second time she's thrown up," Foxx said.

"That's another sign of a concussion, isn't it?" I asked.

Foxx nodded.

I turned when I heard the bathroom door open. Alana wiped her face with a wet washcloth as she exited.

"Are you okay?" I asked.

It was a dumb question since it was obvious she wasn't.

"Here, let me help you," Hani said, and she held Alana's arms and walked her back to the bed.

"What can we do?" I asked Foxx.

"She needs rest. That's the best thing for her right now."

Foxx walked over to the door and turned the lights out.

"We need to keep the room dark. The bright lights will stimulate the brain. She doesn't need that right now. She needs to remain calm and undisturbed, nothing that will cause her stress."

Foxx turned to me.

"We should probably get out of here so she can have quiet."

"I'll watch over her," Hani said.

"What's going on out there?" Alana asked me.

"Nothing. Everyone is in their cabins, waiting to get back to Maui."

"And the case?"

"Don't worry about that," Hani said.

"The case, Poe. What's happening with that?" Alana asked again.

"It's solved. You were right. Reese killed Tiffany and then committed suicide," I said.

Alana didn't respond. She just laid her aching head back on a pillow.

"Let me know if you need anything," I said to Hani.

"I will. I won't let anything happen to her. I promise," Hani said.

"Thank you."

Foxx and I left the cabin. My anger grew as I thought about what Artemis Lockwood had done to her.

"What you said back there about the case being solved, is that true?" Foxx asked.

"I don't think so."

"About which part? Reese killing Tiffany or him committing suicide?"

"Maybe both."

"Really?"

"I'm not sure," I said.

"Is there anything I can do to help?"

I thought about that for a moment.

Then I said, "Yes. I think there is something."

I'd reached the point in the investigation when it was time for follow-up interviews to try to catch people in lies and prove the various theories that were forming in my mind. I had a vague idea of what had happened, but it was still like a cloud that was slowly shifting and forming different pictures. I knew I couldn't think too hard or else the answer might not ever appear. I needed to find a way to relax my thoughts and let my subconscious do the work. Maybe that makes sense to you. Maybe it doesn't.

I decided to see Kimi first. Actually, I wasn't going to be the one seeing her. I realized I'd thoroughly blown the first interview with her. We'd been distracted by the tainted food or drinks, and we'd gone down a line of questioning that was completely wrong. Now I knew what I really needed to ask her. Would she lie to me? I was about to find out.

One of the things about lying is that it's an art form. Most people simply aren't good at it. They think they are, but they always have some tell that gives them away. Maybe they don't make eye contact with you, which is the most obvious giveaway but still something people do all the time. Perhaps they have some physical tell like an arm touch or a hand through the hair or an eye twitch.

I worked with this one guy at my architecture firm who would rub his thighs whenever he was lying. Yes, you saw an S on the end of the word thighs. He rubbed both legs. In fact, he rubbed them so vigorously that I was often convinced his pants were going to burst into flames. It wasn't sexual at all. I say that because I realize it sounds like I'm describing a cheesy scene in a porn film. Instead, it was nervousness, pure and simple. I always felt the need to look around for the nearest fire extinguisher whenever I saw him walking toward me. The guy was a world-class idiot, too, but that's a story for another day.

The easiest way to spot a lie is to ask rapid follow-up questions, the more detailed the better. Most people come up with a basic lie and a couple of supporting fake facts, and they usually structure their lies on a main event. For example, a guy might tell his girlfriend that he's going to the movies with his friends when he's really going to see his side chick. The supporting fact would, of course, be the name of the film he saw and the people he saw it with. He would have given his friends the heads-up so they could cover for him in case the girlfriend called to check up on him, but he wouldn't tell his friends much more than those few things.

It would be a waste of time for the girlfriend to ask him questions that pertained to the big lie. He would have already practiced his deceptive responses dozens of times in his head. The best thing to do, therefore, is to ask him questions he hadn't prepared for: What trailers were shown before the movie? Did his friend buy popcorn or just candy or did he buy nothing at all? You get the point.

Foxx and I didn't have decent signals on our cell phones, but that didn't mean the little devices were useless. It's kind of scary when you realize practically everyone is carrying around a recording device. The guy who used to rub his pants at work also had the habit of secretly recording people during meetings and hallway conversations. We all knew he was paranoid, but no one could figure out why. A few people started recording their meetings with him as well in case he tried to manipulate the recordings. It was pretty weird. I'm sure you're accusing me of exaggerating, but now you can see why I was actually relieved when I got laid off.

I asked Foxx to put his phone on record mode for his conversation with Kimi. I knew there was little chance she'd be honest with me, but maybe she'd be honest with the guy she'd had a one night stand with.

This is the recording on his conversation with Kimi:

"She's on the deck. It's a little windy out there. Hopefully, you'll be able to make this out," Foxx said into the phone. "Okay. Here goes nothing," he continued.

I heard the wind cutting across his phone and thought I'd never be able to eavesdrop on his conversation with Kimi. Then the wind suddenly died down.

"Hey there. How's it going out here?" Foxx asked.

"Nothing so far. I don't think there's any way we're going to find him."

"How long have you been standing here?"

"For a couple of hours. Banks is about to relieve me."

"I know the cruise is going to be cut short a few days now. When are you guys going back out?"

"We had a day to turn the yacht around before the next charter. I guess we have longer now. Is this your way of asking if I want to get together?"

I thought I heard a nervous laugh from her after asking the question.

"You caught me. I wanted to invite you to my bar. I'll buy you a drink."

"I'd like that."

"You should bring Angela, too."

"I'll mention it to her. I'm sure she'd like to come."

"We're in Lahaina, so it's not that far from you."

"I know. I remember you telling me."

"Oh, yeah. I forgot. Hey, if you guys have any other friends or relatives you want to bring, let me know. We're always trying to spread the word about Harry's."

"Okay. Sounds good."

There was a pause in the conversation.

Then Foxx asked, "Do you?"

"Do I what?"

"Do you or Angela have any relatives on the island?"

"No. It's just us."

"Really? I thought someone told me Angela had a son."

There was another pause. It hadn't been the smoothest way for Foxx to introduce the subject of Angela's son, but I was more than willing to cut him some slack since I knew I wouldn't have been able to come up with anything better.

"Why are you asking me that?" Kimi said.

"No reason. Just making small talk. I like you and want to get to know you better. That's all."

"What does Angela's son have to do with me?"

"You live with them. I thought that would be kind of cool to be around a kid. I have a child myself. I know how much they bring to your life."

"Who told you about her son?"

"I don't remember."

"I find that hard to believe," she said.

"I think you're making a much bigger deal out of this than it is. I was just curious. It's nothing more."

"Who told you? I want to know."

"It might have been Banks," Foxx said.

"Might have been or was?"

"I don't remember."

"I don't believe you. Banks would know better than to talk about Angela's son. She knows how private Angela is."

"Who takes care of the boy when you guys go on these charters?" Foxx asked.

"Didn't you just hear what I said? Angela doesn't want people to know about her. I'm not going to talk about her son. What's going on here? Why are you so interested in this?"

I figured this would be the end of the conversation as Foxx would probably say he was going to drop the matter and walk away. He didn't do that. He went for it and tossed our script away.

"Look, Kimi. I like you, and I don't want you to get caught up in all of this."

"Caught up in what?"

"How can you ask me that? What have you been doing the last several hours? A guy has gone overboard. There's a dead woman in your main lounge. Do you have any idea what's going to happen when word gets out about these deaths? It will. All it takes is for one member of your crew to leak it to the media. I guarantee you someone has already taken dozens of photographs of Tiffany's dead body and the blood stains on the deck. This is a worldwide story. Hawaii and dead bodies and super yachts. Kimi, your name and the name of everyone on this boat is going to be plastered on every news website. Your privacy and Angela's privacy are gone. Your life as you know is over. Trust me on this. I have a little bit of experience in this matter. The Epiphany is done. No one wants to pay big bucks to charter the Death Boat. You're out of a job."

There was a long pause in the conversation, and I didn't need to be on that deck to know Kimi was shaking in her little shorts and Epiphany polo shirt.

"What's going to happen to me?" she finally asked.

"Everyone on board is a suspect. The police are going to make your life a living hell."

"Why am I a suspect? I was already interviewed by that detective."

"That was just the warm-up act. You think that's all she's going to do?"

"I haven't done anything wrong," she said.

"I believe you, but sometimes that doesn't matter."

"How can it not matter?"

"Because people lie, Kimi. They can implicate you, even if you had nothing to do with it. That whole concept of innocent until proven guilty is a joke. Innocent people end up in jail all the time."

"What is it you want to know?"

"Just one thing. That's it. What do you know about the father of Angela's child?" Foxx asked.

"Nothing. She refuses to talk about him. Her mother let it slip once that the guy was someone Angela knew in college. You should have seen how Angela reacted. She didn't talk to her mother for weeks."

"Does her mother live on Maui?"

"Yeah. She lives in Angela's house. She's the one who watches her son when we're on these charters. That's all you wanted to know?"

"Yeah, for now. Thank you."

"You'll talk to that detective for me? Tell her I had nothing to do with either of those deaths?"

"I'll vouch for you."

There was a pause in the conversation.

Then I barely heard Kimi ask, "Do you really think I'm out of a job?"

Yes. That's what she asked. Two people were dead, and Kimi was more worried about her employment status. People can be heartless, but I'm sure you already knew that.

Chapter 27
Uneasy Alliance

Foxx and I had agreed to meet in the upstairs lounge after his conversation with Kimi. That's where I'd listened to the recording.

Foxx closed the audio recording app on his phone and slipped it back into his pocket.

"How do you think it went?" he asked.

"I don't think it could have gone any better. You did a masterful job of getting her to talk. I was surprised I was able to hear as much as I did. It's pretty windy out there."

"I shielded the phone with my hands. I thought I was being pretty obvious. I practically had the phone just below her mouth like it was a news interview. I couldn't believe she didn't notice."

I wasn't surprised in hearing that. People clutch onto their phones like they're their children. Everyone just takes the behavior for granted these days.

"Was my monologue a bit too dramatic?" he continued.

"No. I think it had just the right amount of drama."

"What next?"

"I'm going to have a little talk with Raymond Calloway and Trenholme Lockwood."

"Trenholme," he repeated with disgust.

"Yeah. It might be best if you skipped this one."

"I'll go check on Alana. See how she's doing."

"Thanks. I'll let you know what I find out, if anything."

Foxx and I both headed below deck. He turned one way toward the crew cabins, and I went toward the higher-end guests' cabins. The hallway was completely empty, and all of the cabin doors were shut. I didn't know who was stowed away in their cabins and who was still on the deck looking out for Reese.

I stopped in front of Raymond's cabin and knocked on the door. He opened the door, and I involuntarily winced when I saw his face.

"That bad, huh?" he asked.

"It's a shiner, all right."

"He got me right on the cheek bone. Those always make for the worst black eyes. You don't look so good yourself."

"I guess between the two of us we have a matching pair of shiners. May I come in? I'd like to ask you a couple more questions."

Raymond walked back to his bed and sat down. I stayed standing.

"I heard you say that Artemis was going to get arrested for felony assault on a police officer. Is that true or were you just trying to scare him?"

"It's really up to Detective Hu. Actually, I take that back. It's probably up to the officers who board this vessel when we get back to Maui. Once they see the condition she's in, I suspect they'll arrest him."

"Is she going to be okay?" Raymond asked.

"I think so, but she's got a concussion. She's pretty out of it."

"I'm sorry to hear that. She seems like a nice person."

"She's the best."

"She's your wife, isn't she?"

"How could you tell?" I asked.

"I saw the look of rage in your eyes when Artemis threw her into the bar. You only see that look in a husband's or father's eye when some man hurts someone they love. You're too young to be her father, so that leaves husband as the only choice."

"We just got back from our second wedding anniversary. Hani asked us to help with this cruise just a couple of hours after we landed back on Maui."

"Second wedding anniversary. You two are still in the honeymoon phase. My wife and I never left that phase. People never believe me when I said that, but it's the truth. I loved her more every day."

"I believe you. I can hear it in your voice."

"What did you want to know from me? I'm sure you didn't come here just to see how I was feeling after getting punched by Lockwood."

"Actually, that was the main reason, but there was something else. Do you remember Tiffany ever mentioning anything bad about Reese while they were at Harvard?" I asked.

"Bad? Like what?"

"Anything serious he might have gotten into? Possibly something that got him arrested?"

"No. There was nothing like that. Not even close."

"They dated all though college, didn't they?"

"I think so. They might have had one or two breaks. I don't know. Her mother and I tried not to smother her. She wanted to be independent, so we gave her space."

"He didn't do anything to her that would have gotten your attention?" I asked.

"You mean something violent?"

"Yeah."

"You asked me that before. If there had been something like that, I never would have allowed her to stay with him. I would have driven to that school and put a stop to it myself."

"Okay. I appreciate your time again. I hope that black eye heals quickly."

"It's the least of my concerns."

I thanked him again and turned toward the door.

"What's going on? I thought you two already determined that Reese murdered my daughter. Are you just trying to build a stronger case against him, or is there something else you're not telling me about?

"Alana has to write a report when we get back. I'm just trying to make sure I know all the facts so I can help her, especially now that she has a head injury. I don't know if that concussion is going to play games with her memory."

Raymond hesitated a moment and then he nodded. I wasn't sure if he'd bought my excuse. The truth was I wasn't really sure of anything.

I exited Raymond's cabin and walked a few feet down the hallway to Trenholme's. His door was also shut, so I knocked on it.

"Who is it?" I heard him yell from inside.

"It's Poe. The guy whose brains you tried to bash in a little while ago."

How's that for an answer?

The door flung open, and I saw a furious Trenholme standing in front of me.

"Don't have your big ugly friend with you this time?"

"I wouldn't say that too loud if I was you. He has an anger management problem," I said.

Trenholme winced and grabbed his back as if the act of talking about Foxx caused him to relive the moment he was slammed into the ceiling. I still couldn't believe Foxx had done that.

"Are you all right?" I asked.

"No, I'm not all right. I fell eight feet to the ground. How would you feel?"

"I think you're forgetting you weren't the only one hurt up there. You gave me a hell of a punch."

"You deserved it. You broke an old man's nose."

"Well, that old man gave my wife a concussion."

He didn't reply. Maybe he just couldn't come up with something witty or cutting to say.

"Are we going to argue here in the hallway, or are you going to invite me inside?" I asked.

"Tell me what you want first."

"I'd love to, but not here."

Trenholme reluctantly stepped back a few paces, and I went inside the cabin. I reached behind my back and shut the door since I didn't want to take my eyes off the angry young man. I wouldn't put another attack on yours truly past him.

"Are you going to tell me now?" he asked.

"When you spoke to Detective Hu and me before, you said that you thought Reese killed Tiffany."

"No. You're putting words in my mouth. I said he might have done it. I don't have proof either way."

"You did say he had a vicious temper."

"So? A lot of people do. That doesn't mean they're murderers."

"True, but there doesn't seem to be another legitimate suspect, even after talking with everyone on this yacht."

"Is that why you came down here? To tell me my brother killed his fiancée?"

"No. I came here to ask a few more questions. When did Sinclair tell you she was moving to Chicago?"

"She never told me that. I heard it from Tiffany."

"Do you remember what she said exactly?"

"No. She said it had something to do about some job. She seemed more confused than anything else."

"Confused? Why was that?" I asked.

"She didn't know why Sinclair would want to leave New York, especially since all her friends were there. She also knew Sinclair loved the agency she worked for already."

"I was told the Chicago job was a promotion of sorts."

"I don't know. Maybe. You'd have to ask Sinclair."

"You didn't talk to her about it?"

"No. It all happened so fast. One minute she was in New York. The next she was packing her bags and hitting the road for Chicago."

"Did you ever tell her how you felt about her?" I asked.

"I told you I didn't. How many times are we going to talk about that? There was nothing between us. I wanted there to be. I'll admit it, but there wasn't. She made her intentions perfectly clear. She wanted Reese, not me."

"Did you ask Zelda about the Chicago job?"

"No. What would be the point?"

I walked a few steps toward Trenholme and stopped right in front of him. I thought I could almost feel his body grow even tenser before me.

"Did you kill your brother?"

"Go to hell," he said.

"You didn't answer my question. Did you kill your brother?"

He shoved me hard. It was something I'd been expecting, but I still almost lost my balance.

"We can have round two if you want, only this time I'll see you coming. You think that lower back can take another shot?" I asked.

"I didn't kill him. The guy was an asshole, but he was still my brother."

"If you didn't kill him, then who did?"

"No one. There's no one. He took his own life. Isn't that what everyone thinks?"

"Let me see your hands."

"Why?" he asked.

"Let me see them."

I grabbed him by the wrists. He tried to pull back, but I held on tight. I looked at his palms. They were clean and smooth. You could tell this guy didn't do manual work. I turned them over. The top of his left hand was also clean. The top of the right was bruised, which was probably caused by his fist hitting the bone under my eye.

I let go of him.

"I found a bloody hand print under the railing, right where you said you last saw Reese with the bottle of Jack Daniels. Was he bleeding when you saw him?" I asked.

Trenholme paused.

Then he said, "No. I would have noticed that. There was no blood on him. In fact, I specifically remember being surprised by that."

"Why?" I asked.

"Because he was wearing the same clothes as when we found Tiffany murdered. Her body was covered in blood. If it had been my fiancée, I would have gone to her. He didn't even touch her. He just stood there and watched, like he was detached from the whole thing. I was disgusted."

Trenholme paused again.

Then he asked, "Why would there be a bloody handprint under the railing? Do you think it was Reese's?"

"Maybe. I know it wasn't the killer's."

He didn't ask me how I knew that, and I didn't offer further explanation. The truth was I couldn't be one hundred percent sure it hadn't been left there by the person who killed Tiffany, but I was still playing another one of my hunches.

"I know we don't like each other. Hell, I hate your whole family, but I could use your help."

"And why would I ever agree to that?" he asked.

"What if your brother didn't kill Tiffany, and what if he didn't jump overboard?"

"Why do you even think that?"

"Will you help or not?"

"What do you need from me?" he asked.

Chapter 28
Zelda Cameron – Round 2

I found Zelda in her cabin. Sinclair was also there. I asked Zelda if I could talk to her, and Sinclair volunteered to leave. I told Sinclair that wouldn't be necessary since I wanted to speak with Zelda in the lounge where Alana and I had interviewed her before.

Zelda asked me what it was about, and I said I just wanted to do a final follow-up on a few things. I knew she could tell I was not being completely honest with her, but she agreed to go with me anyway. I don't know if she did that because she thought it might be suspicious for her not to or if she just assumed she could outsmart me. It was probably a little bit of both.

We left the cabin area and made our way up to the lounge. I looked outside the windows as we walked. The sun was much lower in the sky, and I knew it was only a matter of time before the captain abandoned the search for Reese and started the journey back to Maui.

We entered the empty lounge, and she sat on the sofa in the exact same spot as before. This time I sat beside her, which is where Alana had previously been.

"What did you want to know?" she asked.

"Why did Angela leave college?"

"I don't know. Maybe she was going to flunk out. It's a tough school. Only the best get in. Suddenly, you go from being one of the smartest in your class to being surrounded by people who are all smarter than you. It's a big adjustment. Some people can't handle it."

"You think that's what it was? She just couldn't deal with the pressure?"

"You should ask her. Maybe it had to do with finances. It's an expensive school, too. What does this have to do with anything?" she asked.

I looked over to the bookshelves on the opposite side of the lounge. Then I turned back to Zelda.

"There's a book over there that I was looking at earlier. It has a list of nautical terms and their backgrounds. It's all in alphabetical order, so one of the first terms I came across was Above Board. You've heard of that before, haven't you?"

"Of course."

"You know I always thought the term referred to the game of poker. People cheat by holding extra cards in their sleeves or maybe under the table. So I thought Above Board meant keeping all your cards or game pieces above the table or above the board game."

"Makes sense."

"But that nautical book said the term might have originated on the high seas. Pirates would often conceal their crew below deck to give other ships a false sense of security. The other ships wouldn't realize it was really a pirate ship until it was too late."

"I assume you didn't invite me up here to discuss the origins of Above Board. What is it you really want to know?"

"My apologies for delaying the real reason I wanted to talk. Sometimes I can get too dramatic. I want to know why you and Sinclair lied to me."

"We didn't lie to you," Zelda said.

"Oh, I think you did, and you lied about several things."

Zelda stood.

"I don't have time for this. My friends are grieving and need my support. I should be down there with them."

I waited for her to get most of the way across the lounge before I called out to her.

"Are you really going to head out that door?"

She stopped and turned back to me.

"Yes. I am."

"You don't want to hear what I have to say?"

"I don't care what you have to say."

"I think you do. Otherwise you would have ignored my question and kept walking, but I think you're dying to know what I know. I know you lied. You know you lied, only you're not sure exactly what I know. Maybe the lies aren't all that significant. Maybe they are. You can leave if you want. I'm not a police officer. I can't compel you to stay, but I can say this. There's no way the police are going to let you leave this yacht a free person, not after I have a talk to them."

Zelda hesitated. Then she walked back over to me and sat down.

"Let's start with the simple stuff," I said. "You and Sinclair both told me that Reese went to talk to Sinclair after dinner, but Reese said it was the other way around."

"What difference does that make? They talked. So what?"

"You're right. Not a big deal. That's why I said it was the small stuff, but it was still a lie. Tell a little one, maybe you'll tell a big one. Let's talk about Kurt next."

"What about him?" she asked.

"He claims you came up to this lounge and practically threw yourself at him."

Zelda laughed.

"Is that what he said?"

"I thought it was funny, too. He's a good looking guy, but look at you. You can have any guy you want, and no, that's not me hitting on you. It's just an observation. I found it hard to believe that you would be the one to pursue him when it was so much more likely that it would be the other way around."

"Is this what you do? You obsess about the romantic lives of others?"

"God, I hope not. That would make me creepy, wouldn't it? No, that's not my point at all. I think you and Sinclair are like those pirates who created a false illusion. Kurt was just the first part. You intentionally slept with him, so you could then tell everyone in an attempt to get him fired."

"Do you have any idea how ridiculous you sound right now? Why would I want to do that? The guy means nothing to me."

"I believe that, but it creates another suspect for the murder of Tiffany."

"That's right. He's a suspect, not me."

"He is. You're right about that part. There was also the big reveal to Trenholme that his brother had slept with Sinclair. You and Sinclair both knew how he felt about her. You knew it would crush him to find out what she and Reese had done. I couldn't figure out why you'd want to sabotage the wedding like that. You were friends with Tiffany, so why not keep your mouth shut, even when everyone told us you like to gossip?"

I expected her to react to that little dig, but to her credit, she didn't.

"You were trying to create your second suspect. You knew what Trenholme would do after hearing their secret. You knew he'd tell Tiffany to get back at his brother. She'd have a predictable reaction, too. She'd go after Reese and have a very public argument that everyone on this yacht would witness. That created suspect number two," I said.

"You've gone off the deep end, to use one of your nautical terms. This is all preposterous. You don't have proof of anything."

"Why did you and Sinclair tell everyone that she left New York for her dream job in Chicago?"

"Because she did."

"She was a copywriter in New York working on huge accounts that everyone has heard of. Now she's working for some ridiculous agency called Peanut Butter Jar. Who names a company that?"

I watched for a reaction in Zelda's eyes, and I got one. I'd figured out the name of the ad agency. What else did I know?

"Did she tell you some of the accounts she works on? I'm guessing not. It's embarrassing."

"She wanted a change of environment. What's wrong with that?"

"Nothing. Nothing at all. I moved from Virginia to Maui because I wanted the same thing, but I had a best friend and a new girlfriend waiting for me here. What did she have in Chicago?"

"It's a great city," she protested.

"It is. I've been there a few times myself. This isn't a Chicago-bashing discussion. I just want to know why Sinclair would leave her two best friends and a great job to go where she doesn't know anyone and work for a company with a stupid name."

I paused.

Then I asked, "How did Tiffany find out Angela was working on this yacht?"

"I don't know."

"You didn't tell her? You're the big mouth of the group."

"Go to hell!"

I reached into my pocket and pulled out my phone. I selected a photo I'd taken of Angela's Facebook page.

"Do you know who Summer Makani is?" I asked.

That got an even bigger reaction than my mention of Peanut Butter Jar. Zelda's face went pale as I handed her my phone.

"Happy Birthday from Sinclair Dewey to Summer Makani, and we both know exactly who that is. Sinclair found out Angela lived and worked on Maui. Maybe she told you. I'm guessing she did. Either you or Sinclair told Tiffany. I'm not sure why, but I'll find out. Would you like to tell me?"

"I didn't know Angela was here."

"Okay. I'm not sure that I believe that. Actually, I know I don't believe that. Why would Sinclair lie about it? A minute ago, you said I had no proof. That's proof in your hands. Sinclair was communicating with Angela even though she claimed she hadn't seen or spoken to Angela since college."

"Sinclair was ashamed of herself. She told Tiffany about Angela. She thought it was funny that Angela ended up working as a glorified waitress on a boat while we all went on to big jobs. Sinclair didn't expect Tiffany to charter this damn thing. She didn't think she'd take the joke that far," Zelda said.

"I suspect she knew that's exactly what Tiffany would do, but why did she want them back together? What was the real reason?"

"It was a bad joke, a chance to taunt and make fun of someone who'd done nothing to us. I'm deeply embarrassed by it, but that's all it was, a stupid prank. We didn't do anything beyond that. Yes, I told Trenholme about Reese and Sinclair. I was drunk, and sometimes I talk too much when I've been drinking. A lot of people do. And yes, Sinclair's embarrassed about her job. She was fired from the New York gig because she wouldn't sleep with her boss. He blackballed her at the other ad agencies in town. We talked about suing him. I told her I could help her find an attorney who specialized in lawsuits like that, but she just wanted to move on. What did you expect her to tell you when you asked about her job, that she'd been fired? No one wants to admit that."

"And Kurt?" I asked.

"He's lying. I had too much to drink. I hooked up with someone I shouldn't have. Maybe you've done the same thing. There was no grand scheme behind it. The guy chased me the next day, and I told him I didn't want anything more to do with him. I told him it had been a mistake. He threatened me. Told me not to tell the captain. Tiffany got involved and got him fired. That was the end of it."

She had an answer for everything, and a flood of insecurity washed over me. Had I gotten it all wrong? Was I trying to find a conspiracy where none existed? I've often touted the theory that the simple explanation is often the correct one. Well, we all knew what that simple explanation was in this murder, so why was I pushing for a more complex one?

"You've got an overactive imagination," Zelda said, as if she had the ability to read my mind. "I am getting off this yacht because I've done nothing illegal. Neither has Sinclair. We made some mistakes, some hurtful ones, but we haven't done anything beyond that."

Zelda stood, and this time she left the lounge.

There were two possibilities. I'd either gotten it all right or all wrong. There was no in-between. I figured I'd get the answer to that in the next hour.

Chapter 29
The Plan

As the minutes passed following my conversation with Zelda, I became more and more convinced that she'd lied to me again. She was a highly intelligent person, and that meant she was most likely a fast thinker. Her response, in particular, about Sinclair having been fired for not sleeping with her boss was a strong one. It was more than plausible, but I also thought it was untrue. Yes, those things happened to employees all the time, especially females. That doesn't make it right, but I didn't think it had happened to Sinclair. I didn't believe that she would have left New York over that.

I walked back to my cabin to check on Alana. She was asleep. Foxx was there watching over her since Hani had left the cabin earlier.

I sat down on the edge of the bed and waited for the next steps of my six-part plan.

Part one was my conversation with Zelda. We all know how that went. Part two involved Trenholme. We knew that Sinclair was still in her cabin after I took Zelda to the upstairs lounge. We had to get her out of there. I devised a story whereby Trenholme would go to her cabin and ask to see her in Reese's. It needed to be a story that she would believe.

Trenholme, reluctantly, told her about his feelings for her and how he understood and accepted the fact that she didn't feel the same way. He said he knew that she'd slept with his brother but that it was none of his business. He also told her that he knew how much she'd cared for Reese and that he agreed that Reese was a special person. The result had the desired effect, which was to make her feel uncomfortable and put her off-guard.

He showed her Reese's collection of watches. Trenholme told me that Reese liked to collect watches and always brought several with him when he traveled. He'd told me this after I asked him if he could think of any keepsakes in the cabin that Sinclair might want to remember Reese.

Trenholme showed her the collection of Rolex, Blancpain, Chopard, and Audemars Piguet watches and told her to pick one. She declined, as we both had expected her to do. That didn't matter. He'd accomplished our goal by getting her out of the cabin, which lead to part three.

Foxx entered Sinclair's cabin moments after Trenholme took her to Reese's. He opened the audio recorder app on his cell phone, hit the record button, and hid the phone. He then went back to our cabin. I joined him about twenty minutes after my conversation with Zelda.

"How did it go?" I asked.

"No problem. Trenholme did his job. Did you learn anything from Zelda?"

I told Foxx about the conversation, including her assertions that Sinclair had left New York because of her boss blackballing her with other agencies.

"Do you buy that?" I asked.

"I'm not sure. It could have happened."

"I buy it," Alana said.

Foxx and I both turned at the sound of her voice.

"Sorry to wake you," I said.

"I've been awake. I just wanted to see what you've been up to while I've been in here."

"That's sneaky."

"Look who's talking. What's going on?"

"You should rest. You need to keep calm."

"Don't tell me to keep calm. I'm the detective here, need I remind you."

"You don't need to remind me. I'm well aware. Need I remind you that you've suffered a concussion? This is serious. It's not to be taken lightly," I said.

"I am taking it seriously. I've been in here resting while you've been running around this boat. Now tell me what's going on."

"You might as well tell her. You know she's not going to let you out of this cabin before you do," Foxx said.

He was right, so I told her about my conversation with Trenholme, Zelda, and parts one through three of my plan.

"What's part four?" Alana asked.

The cabin door opened, and Hani walked inside.

"The captain wants to see everyone on the main deck," Hani said.

"That's part four," I said.

I'd asked Hani to go see the captain and get an update on when he would abandon the search for Reese. I already knew the answer to the question. He'd told me that he planned to quit once the sun went down. The captain didn't know that I'd already told Hani that, so it made sense that she would ask him, too.

Hani, as directed by me, asked the captain to speak with everyone on the main deck so they would understand why he was abandoning the search and what the next steps would be. I knew the families needed to be told, and I thought it would be better if they were all told at once. Plus, it had the added effect of getting Zelda and Sinclair out of their cabin so Foxx could retrieve his cell phone.

After Captain Piadelia made the announcement, Catherine Lockwood burst into tears. Trenholme went to her, not her husband. Artemis and Raymond were too busy glaring at each other, and I feared there might be a rematch about to commence. It was a somewhat chaotic scene, which made it unlikely that anyone, including Sinclair and Zelda, would notice Foxx's late arrival.

Captain Piadelia asked everyone to return to their cabins. He told us that he expected we would be back on Maui in a few hours.

Alana, Foxx, Hani, and I all went back to our cabin. We sat on the bed, and Foxx slipped his cell phone out of his pocket.

"Did it work?" I asked.

"I don't know. I haven't played the file yet."

"You have more restraint than I would," Alana said.

Foxx was about to hit play on the phone's app when there was a soft knock on the cabin door.

"Who do you think that is?" Hani said.

"I don't know," I said.

I stood and walked over to the door. It was Trenholme.

"May I come in?" he asked.

"Of course."

Trenholme entered. The room now had five adults, three of whom were well over six feet tall. Point is, it was exceptionally crowded.

Trenholme locked eyes with Foxx, and for the second time in five minutes, I got nervous about a potential fight.

"Don't even think about it, you two," Hani said.

Apparently, I wasn't the only one worried.

Trenholme looked over to Alana.

"I'm sorry that my father hurt you. I hope you're okay."

"Thank you."

Trenholme turned back to me.

"Did it work? Were you able to get the recording?"

"We're about to find out," I said.

Foxx started the recording again. He had to fast-forward through several minutes of nothing but room noise that was obviously recorded when I was talking to Zelda, and Sinclair was with Trenholme.

We heard the cabin door open after about eight or nine minutes. There were no voices, just the sounds of someone walking around the room. The footsteps were pretty loud, much louder than I would have expected.

"Where did you hide the phone?" I asked.

"Under the bed. I couldn't think of anyplace else," Foxx said.

We heard a loud squeak, and I assumed that was Sinclair lying down on the bed.

There was relative silence for a few more minutes, and then the cabin door opened again. It shut a second later, and we heard more footsteps.

"What did he want?" Sinclair asked.

There was no reply from the other person, which had to be Zelda, so Sinclair repeated her question.

"He knows," Zelda said.

"Knows what?"

"He's got it all figured out."

There was another squeak on the bed, which I interpreted as Sinclair sitting up.

"He told me that he knew we'd lied to him and that detective," Zelda continued.

"So what? He thinks we lied. Big deal. He knows nothing."

"He knows you were the one to get in contact with Angela. He showed me a Facebook post where you wished her Happy Birthday. How could you be so careless?"

"There's no way he saw that," Sinclair said.

"You think I'm making this up? Didn't you hear what I just said? He showed me the post. He took a picture of it with his damn phone. He knows about Summer Makani."

There was a brief pause.

Then Zelda said, "I told him you got fired because your boss sexually harassed you."

"Why would you say that?"

"Because he found out where you work in Chicago."

"That wouldn't be hard to do. It's on the web."

"Yeah, and so is the fact that it's not that great of an ad agency. I'm sorry, but it's not. He put two and two together. He knows you didn't leave New York for a dream job."

"Moving isn't a crime."

"I know that, but he's trying to figure out why you moved. He thinks it has something to do with Tiffany's murder."

"He can't possibly know that. He's just grasping at straws. He won't find anything, at least nothing that's important."

"He even guessed why I slept with Kurt," Zelda said.

"Honey, I'm sure you're not the first charter guest to have sex with a member of the crew. It means nothing."

"It's only a matter of time before he speaks with Angela."

"He's already met with her. He didn't learn a thing."

"I don't trust her. You don't know what she'll do."

The bed squeaked loudly again as Sinclair stood.

"Don't lose your nerve. Now is not the time. They can't pin anything on either of us. We have to stick together."

"I can't wait until we get off this damn boat. I just want to leave," Zelda said.

"You need to stay calm, and then we can walk down that gangway like nothing ever happened. They already think Reese did this. It makes perfect sense. Cops are lazy, and they want to close this case. Believe me. They want to be done with this, just like we do."

They spoke for several more minutes but nothing more was revealed. We heard the cabin door open again, and we thought we heard someone leave the cabin. The bed squeaked again, probably when Sinclair plopped back on it. Several more minutes went by, and there was a knock on the cabin. We heard footsteps across the floor, and the cabin door opened.

"The captain wants to see everyone on the main deck in five minutes," Hani said.

"Do you know why?" Sinclair asked.

"Something to do with the search for Reese."

"Okay. I'll be right up."

Foxx stopped the recording.

"Looks like your hunch was right again," he told me.

"They did it. They killed Tiffany and made everyone think my brother did it," Trenholme said. "Wait until I get my hands on them."

"No. You can't do anything," Alana said.

"Are you joking? You heard what they said."

"I did, and you heard it, too. Did they admit to murdering Tiffany? Did they say they pushed Reese overboard? Did they talk about a murder weapon or disposing of one? No. They didn't. Their comments indicate they know way more than they're willing to admit, but it's not enough to arrest them," Alana said.

"What do we do now?" Trenholme asked.

"Time for part five," I said.

Chapter 30
I Didn't Know

It took some convincing to keep Trenholme and Artemis from being involved in my next stage. I wanted to have a one-on-one conversation with Catherine. I told Trenholme while we were all still in my cabin. He was confused at first, as all I was willing to tell him at that moment was that I thought his mother might inadvertently hold a piece of information that could break this thing wide open. I thought I knew what had happened, but I still wasn't one hundred percent sure.

Furthermore, what I thought and what I could prove were often two different things. That was very much the case here. Alana would need more than my hunches. She would need a confession, especially since the damning physical evidence was at the bottom of the ocean.

I made it clear to Trenholme that I wasn't going to accuse his mother of anything wrong. She was innocent in all of this. That wasn't entirely true. I thought her quite guilty of many things, but none of which would land her in jail. Of course, I would gain nothing by telling him that.

He finally acquiesced and led us to his parents' cabin, even though we already knew which one it was. Artemis was still furious with me. I can't say I didn't blame him. I'd broken his nose, after all. I won't even bother writing what he said to me when he opened the door and saw me standing outside his cabin. I think I would give everyone a heart attack after hearing the foul language that came out of his mouth. I suspect the only reason he didn't lunge at me was because he was confused as to why Trenholme was standing beside me.

To Trenholme's credit, he was the one who got his father to agree to me meeting alone with Catherine. I think Trenholme finally saw the logic in what we were trying to do and realized this was the only way his brother would be cleared of murdering his fiancée.

My plans for a one-on-one also didn't fly with Alana. She was determined to be a part of it, despite my objections about her current state of wellbeing. She swore that she was fine and that her presence at the interview was important if anything crucial were to be revealed. It was hard to argue with that logic, so I said yes despite not really having a say in the matter. But we men always have to try to save face, don't we?

Alana and I conducted our discussion with Catherine in her cabin after Artemis finally agreed to leave. I saw Catherine's eyes move to the huge bump on Alana's head. The swelling had gotten so bad that the eye on the same side of her head was starting to shut. What a pair Alana and I were. We only had two good eyes between the two of us.

I expected Catherine to apologize for her husband's attack on Alana. She didn't. Was I surprised? Yeah, a little. I knew the lady wasn't the nicest person on the planet, but I thought she might have the slightest bit of empathy and concern for another human being, especially another woman. Apparently, not.

"I think something has been lost in all of this," I said.

"Really? And what would that be?" Catherine said, making no attempt to hide her disdain from us.

"Tiffany and Reese really cared for each other. You don't stay together ten years without having some affection for the other person."

"Of course, they loved each other. They were getting married."

"Yes, but then there was talk about Reese's affair with Sinclair and the possibility that he murdered Tiffany in a fit of rage," I said.

"He didn't kill her."

"You've been pretty consistent about that. If it wasn't your son, then who was it?" Alana asked.

"I don't know. I've thought about that for hours. I don't see who would want her dead."

"Not just Tiffany. Both of them. If Reese didn't kill her, then there was no reason he'd have committed suicide," Alana said.

"Don't you think I know that? Someone on this yacht killed them. Maybe we'll never know."

"I think we will. I think you already know who it is. What I can't figure out is why you aren't saying anything," I said.

"Me? I know who did it? I wish I did. I'd come right to you."

"I don't think so. Did you know it was her?" I asked.

"What are you talking about?"

"We all know Tiffany hired Hani to be her wedding planner, but did she go over any of the plans with you? Did she ask for your opinion?" I asked.

"Of course. The poor girl had no mother. She asked my advice on a number of things."

"Like what?"

"What does it matter?"

"Indulge me, please," I said.

"We went over the guest list. She showed me the different resorts Hani offered. We spoke about the food and the cake for the wedding reception. I went shopping with her for her dress."

"You did? I would have thought Zelda would have done that," I said.

"Zelda is very busy. She's an attorney, like Tiffany was."

"Did she show you the different yachts that Hani offered?" I asked.

"No. She'd already picked this one."

"Do you know why she did?" Alana asked.

"No, but I just assumed it was the nicest one. Tiffany had great taste. I certainly wasn't going to question her decisions."

I found that hard to believe, but I let it slide.

"Did she ever mention Angela?" I asked.

"The head stewardess?"

"Yes. You know who she is," I said.

"Why would she mention her?"

"Sinclair discovered that Angela lived on Maui and worked on this yacht. She and Zelda told Tiffany that, which was her main reason to charter this vessel. They wanted to torment Angela. They, particularly Tiffany, wanted to show her how much better their lives had turned out," I said.

"That's absurd. Why would they care what she thinks? The girl's a waitress on a boat. Tiffany had already won."

"I can see you don't have a high opinion of Angela," Alana said.

"Why would I?"

"I'll ask you this again. Did you know it was her?" I asked.

"I still don't know what you're talking about."

"Of course, you do. We're talking about Angela. Did you know it was her or did Reese tell you?" I asked.

Catherine didn't respond. She looked down to the floor. Remember what I said about the art of lying?

"Did he tell you on the first night or the second, or did he tell you that day on the beach?" I asked.

"I know nothing about that woman," Catherine said.

"Maybe you didn't know her name. Maybe you did. Maybe the name Angela is such a common one that you didn't think much of it when you heard it spoken on the first day of this cruise. In fact, there are two Angelas here on the same yacht. Maybe you hadn't even met her when your son was in college. Maybe you had. Ten years isn't a long time, but people can still change. They can gain or lose weight. They can change their hair color. For example, they can dye it metallic gray."

"I didn't know."

"Your son's not here to defend himself. Do you want people thinking he killed his fiancée?" Alana asked.

"People will think what they want. I can't change that, even if what they think is a lie."

"Did he come to you and your husband after Tiffany died? Did he tell you who he thought did it?" I asked.

"No. He said nothing."

"Let's go back to an earlier question. When did he tell you that the Angela on this yacht was the same Angela from Harvard?" I asked.

"He didn't have to. I could tell Tiffany and the other girls knew her. Everyone could tell that."

"You know that's not what we're talking about," Alana said.

"I want to show you something," I said.

I tapped the photo button on my phone and pulled up a shot I'd taken of Angela's Facebook page. It was one of the birthday photos where Angela was standing behind her son, who was about to blow out the candles on his cake.

"The reason I wanted to talk to you and not Artemis is because you're the mother. Guys are bad about these things, but mothers can always tell. They can see things that we guys...well, most guys, just miss."

I handed her the phone. She took one look at the photo and then put my phone down beside her on the bed. She'd looked at the photo for one second, maybe two.

"Is it that much of a resemblance? I recognized the blonde hair and the blue eyes, but I've seen Reese as a six-foot-four-inch man. I'm sure you remember exactly what he looked like at nine years old. You probably have a photo just like that one. Substitute you for Angela. I bet that's the only difference."

Catherine looked up at me, and I saw tears forming in her eyes.

"You didn't know, did you?" I asked.

She shook her head.

"What's your guess? Did he keep it from you and Artemis, or did Reese not know?" I asked.

"I have no idea."

"Let's say he didn't know, which I suspect is the case. Why wouldn't she tell him? What are the circumstances that a mother wouldn't want the father of her child to know what's going on? There's also child support. Why wouldn't she want that? Instead, she picked about as far a place as she could go without leaving the country. I don't think that was an accident. I think she wanted to make sure she never ran into him. She told me she had a love of traveling. Kind of hard to travel, though, when you're broke and have a baby to care for. I think this job was a brilliant compromise. She got to see things she'd never get to see, and she could make money to provide for her son. You mock her and call her nothing more than a waitress on a boat. I think she's done a hell of a lot more than you have. She's a survivor. What have you ever done?" I asked.

"It's so easy for you to stand there and judge us," Catherine said.

"Like you judged me? What was it you said to me after my photoshoot with you and your husband? We were talking about my mother, and you said, 'My, how the Allertons have fallen.' That was what you said, wasn't it?"

"What would you like me to do? Has Angela put you up to this? Is she going to demand we support her and her child next?"

"Really? That's where your mind went, right to some financial matter?" Alana asked.

"What would you like me to do?" Catherine repeated.

"We'd like to know the truth. What happened between the two of them? Help us clear your son's name. Help us find who really killed Tiffany. If we figure that out, then we find out who killed your son. I'm assuming Tiffany never really mattered that much to you, but your son had to. You've got to care who killed him."

"I don't know that anyone killed him."

"What happened between them, Mrs. Lockwood?" Alana asked.

"You want me to restore his name? Is that what you said earlier? I can't do that. What difference does it make if we substitute one crime for another? Right now, no one can say for sure what happened to Reese. Maybe it's better if I leave it like that. Either way, he's gone. He's not coming back."

"You've got to care. Tell us what happened," I said.

Catherine looked at Alana's head again.

"Are you going to arrest my husband when we get to the marina?"

Alana hesitated.

Then Catherine said, "I'll make a deal with you. I'll tell you what I know, but you have to promise me you won't arrest Artemis. We all know it was an accident. You grabbed him from behind when he was fighting Raymond. He was just trying to shrug you off."

"That's what you think?" Alana asked.

"Do I have your word? No arrest and I tell you what happened ten years ago."

"Agreed," Alana said.

My, how the Lockwoods have fallen. That's what I really wanted to say it, but I didn't.

"Now tell us what happened between Reese and Angela," I said.

Catherine did.

Chapter 31
Counter Moves

I revised my six-part plan to include a seventh part. The original part six was to go directly from Catherine's cabin to speak with Angela. The new part six was much more dramatic.

Alana walked directly to the main deck and found Kimi, who'd been her intended target. Alana asked her if the crew had any restraints onboard that they could potentially use on unruly guests. Kimi said she'd have to speak to the captain, which was the first response we thought she'd give.

Captain Piadelia was predictably concerned after Kimi went to him, and he left the bridge to speak with Alana on the main deck. Alana informed him that she was placing Zelda and Sinclair under arrest and wanted to know if the captain could provide handcuffs or zip ties or something to keep the two women from potentially hurting other guests. The captain naturally asked why Alana thought Zelda and Sinclair were dangerous, and Alana said, more loudly than she needed to, that they were being charged with the murders of Tiffany Calloway and Reese Lockwood.

I say "more loudly than she needed to," but I don't want to give the impression that she yelled it. It was an impressive performance on her part, just loud enough for the lurking Kimi to hear. I don't mean to imply that we thought Kimi was guilty of anything beyond being a busybody and a loyal friend to Angela.

I wish I could adequately describe the reaction on the captain's face as all of this went down. It was a bizarre combination of shock, concern, and excitement. His face morphed quickly between those reactions as his brain processed what was going on. It wasn't the kind of excitement you get while riding a roller coaster or some other thrilling event, but the kind that happens when you see two people verbally going at it and you know it's about to get good.

The captain returned several minutes later with a pair of plastic zip ties. Alana asked him to accompany her to the guests' cabin area where she proceeded to read a stunned Zelda and Sinclair their rights. All of this occurred while Captain Piadelia zipped the plastic ties around the women's wrists, which were pulled behind their backs.

I know all of this because I was watching from the hallway just outside their cabin, as were the Lockwoods and a few of the yacht's crew. Alana set her phone to record. Then she walked over to the cabin door and shut it, cutting us all off from the action but not before we heard her say to the two women, "I know what you did and I have a recording to back it up."

I turned to leave and saw that Kimi was one of the nearby crew members watching, as were Kurt and Baakir. Both men had huge grins on their faces. Karma is a bitch, isn't it? I'm sure that's what they were thinking.

I left the cabin area and went back to the main lounge. I had a seat on the sofa by the bar and waited for stage seven to begin. It came about thirty minutes later, which was about twice as long as I'd predicted. I'd been tempted to make myself a Manhattan as I waited for Angela to appear, but I knew I apparently wasn't very good at making the drink myself, nor did I want my head unclear for the mental game of chess I was sure was about to occur.

"Can I talk to you?" she asked.

"Of course."

Angela sat down beside me, and she winced as she did so. Why? I didn't know.

"I heard about Zelda and Sinclair."

"I'm sure you did. I'm sure everyone heard."

"Is it true? Did they really murder Tiffany and Reese?" she asked.

I didn't answer her. Instead, I pulled out Foxx's phone and pressed play on the recorder app. I'd set the recording to the exact point I wanted her to hear.

Zelda: It's only a matter of time before he speaks with Angela.

Sinclair: He's already met with her. He didn't learn a thing.

Zelda: I don't trust her. You don't know what she'll do.

I stopped the recorder and put the phone between us on the sofa.

"You're a smart woman. You know what they'll do. They'll turn on you. They did it before. They'll do it again," I said.

"It's their word against mine."

"Maybe, but something tells me they'll have more than that to offer."

"Only a fool would have kept the murder weapon onboard. What other proof can they possibly have?"

I looked over to Tiffany's body on the other side of the lounge.

"There's a dead girl over there, and it was murder. There's no denying that. All the proof they need is their word. Who is going to look guiltier? The two women who were part of the wedding or the woman who moved six thousand miles to get away from the man who abused her?"

"Is that all rape is? Abuse?"

"I'm sorry for what happened to you."

"That's funny. That's what everyone said. They were sorry, but no one was willing to do a damn thing to help me."

"Why wasn't Reese arrested?" I asked.

"What did Catherine tell you, or was it Artemis? I doubt Trenholme knew, but I could be wrong."

"She said you claimed you'd been raped. She said that Reese called them one morning and said he thought he was going to be charged. He told them that you'd made the whole thing up because you were jealous that he'd left you for Tiffany."

"I had no idea what he told them. I just saw what they did. They swooped in and made the whole thing go away with both the campus police and the local cops. I never had a chance. It wasn't just his word against mine, though. There was Tiffany's word."

"What do you mean?" I asked.

"I filed a police report the morning after he raped me. It was the night of the party where he met Tiffany. We got into an argument that night. I'll admit I was jealous of her. She always wanted what everyone else had. She saw him. She knew he was with me, and she wanted him. Reese and I argued about it. He said it was nothing. He said he wanted to be with me. I told him no. I told him to leave. He started touching me, groping me. I told him no again. It didn't matter. He wouldn't stop. I tried to fight him, but I never had a chance. You know how much bigger he was than me."

"You said it was Tiffany's word, too. What exactly did she do?" I asked.

"I don't know exactly what he told her, but they came to some sort of agreement. She told the police that she witnessed Reese and I break up at the party. She said that he went home with her and was with her all night. Therefore, he couldn't have raped me."

"What about the physical evidence?" I asked.

"We'd had sex a few times that week. Reese said that I liked it a little rough. The bastard lied about everything."

"And Zelda and Sinclair? Did they say anything? They must have known Reese didn't leave with Tiffany?"

"I talked to them about it. They said they knew he didn't go with her, but then they changed their stories when they were interviewed by the police. They chose Tiffany over me. I wasn't surprised."

"You left school because you found out you were pregnant?"

"No. I left before that. I couldn't go anywhere on campus without seeing one of them. I couldn't deal with it. I found out I was pregnant a few weeks after leaving. I didn't want the child, but I couldn't get rid of it, either."

"Did Reese know?"

"No. I never told him. I hadn't seen him again until the day he set foot on this yacht."

"How did Sinclair find out you were on Maui?" I asked.

"There was a giant flaw in my plan. I tried to get away from them, far away, but then I went and picked a place that people like to come to. I ran into a friend from high school in a bar in Kihei. I remembered really liking this girl, and she wasn't part of the same crowd. I didn't think she'd have any contact with Tiffany, Zelda, or Sinclair. I told her about Summer Makani and asked her not to say anything to anyone. Obviously, that didn't happen."

"Why do you think Sinclair reached out to you?"

"Because she knew what Reese had done to me. Yeah, she had no sympathy for me then, but then the same thing happened to her, and all of a sudden, she needed a shoulder to cry on."

"Reese raped her, too?" I asked.

"She told me how she would meet Zelda and Tiffany for drinks. Sometimes Reese would come. Tiffany wasn't there one Friday. She was out of town for work. Reese invited Sinclair back to his apartment for drinks. She didn't think much about it. They'd been friends for years. There was nothing between them. He was drunk. He put the moves on her, and she said no, just like I had. He reacted the same way he did with me."

"Did she tell Tiffany?"

"No. She probably knew Tiffany would jump to his defense again and try to destroy her. Her life fell apart, just like mine had. She got fired from her job because her work suffered. She started showing up late. She couldn't concentrate on anything. She couldn't sleep. She couldn't stop picturing the attack in her head. I'm sure she could have gotten another job, but it wouldn't change the fact that she'd keep seeing them. So she did what I did. She fled."

"That's when she got in touch with you?"

"I don't know how long she'd been in Chicago when she contacted me online. She told me how sorry she was. She said she'd been young and foolish. I didn't want anything to do with her, but I could almost hear the pain in her writing. I knew what she was going through, and I eventually wanted to help. I was a sucker."

"Why would she agree to be in Tiffany's wedding?" I asked.

"She told me about it when she got the invitation. She hadn't spoken to Tiffany in weeks. She wasn't going to do it. Then Reese showed up in Chicago. He said he was there on business, but I'm not sure she believed him. He told her not to accept the wedding invitation. He said that he didn't want her anywhere near Tiffany. They got into an argument, and he threatened to kill her if she said anything about the rape. Sinclair told me all of this, and then she made this comment that she should go to the wedding. I should, too, and we should find a way to get rid of them both for what they had done to us. She was drunk when she said it. I knew she was, and I also figured she probably didn't really mean it. So I said yeah, we should do that. The next day she calls me again and asks if I was serious. I ask her what she's talking about. That's when she tells me her plan to suggest to Tiffany that she charter this yacht, and then she and I can carry out our plan. She said she'd told Zelda about the rape and that she'd gotten in touch with me. She said Zelda felt guilty too for how she'd sided with Tiffany. She said Zelda would help us."

"So that's it then. You three murdered Tiffany and Reese," I said.

"No. That's not it. I couldn't follow through with it. I looked at my son when I was leaving to drive to the marina for this charter. I wanted Reese and Tiffany dead. I'll admit that, but I couldn't risk going to prison for the rest of my life. I couldn't risk my son growing up without me."

"You're saying they killed Reese and Tiffany and you had nothing to do with it?"

"Tiffany had no idea about my son. I really think her entire intent for this trip was to mock me, to let me know that she had won after all of these years. The night she died, everyone had gone to bed but her. She was mad at Reese. Zelda had let it slip to Reese's brother that Reese and Sinclair had slept together. Of course, she didn't say it had been a rape. Tiffany was furious. I left the galley after cleaning up. It was my night to clean. We each take turns. Tiffany called out to me as I was walking through the lounge to get to my cabin. She demanded that I make her a cocktail. I refused. I told her to go to hell. She really lit into me. We argued. She admitted to what she'd done to help Reese avoid jail after raping me. She said that Reese was all hers now. That I had nothing. I don't know why, but I showed her a photo of my son. I told her Reese was the father. She snapped. She went crazy with rage. She grabbed a knife that had been left on the dining table. I thought Banks had cleared away all the silverware, but she hadn't. Tiffany attacked me with the knife. I defended myself."

"You killed her in self-defense?"

"Yes, I did."

Angela lifted her shirt to just below her bra. She had a bandage on her stomach. She peeled the bandage back, and I saw two long cuts that ran the width of her stomach. They didn't look that deep, but they were more than superficial.

"She did this to me before I could grab the knife from her. I stabbed her once to get her away from me."

"You didn't appear hurt when we spoke with you before. In fact, you haven't seemed hurt in the last several hours as you've made your way around the yacht."

"It's been hard not to let anyone notice, but I didn't want anyone to figure out what I'd done, even though it wasn't my fault."

"And Reese?" I asked.

"I hated Reese. I've already admitted that, but I'm not going to kill the father of my son. How could I ever face my son again if I did that?"

"You're saying Zelda and Sinclair killed him on their own?"

"They told me they found him at the stern. He was drunk. Sinclair grabbed a knife from the galley. She stabbed him to incapacitate him. Then she and Zelda pushed him over the railing."

"They told you this or you saw it?"

"They told me later that night. You should have seen Sinclair. It was like a crushing weight had been lifted. She was so happy. I couldn't believe it. She made me sick. I told them I didn't want anything more to do with them. I told them to stay away from me. They both threatened me. They said they would turn on me if I went to Detective Hu."

I looked at the two cuts on her stomach again.

"I know you just cut yourself. I suspect you did that after Kimi told you that Alana had arrested Zelda and Sinclair."

"If you say so, but it happened exactly as I said it did. I killed Tiffany to protect my own life. I'll admit to that. I'm sure I already did. I'm guessing you're recording this conversation."

She was right. I'd put Foxx's phone on the sofa after turning off the recording we'd made between Zelda and Sinclair, but I'd left my phone in my pocket on record mode.

"Your insurance policy," I said.

"I don't need insurance. I know the truth."

"I thought I had you, but now I see you have me in checkmate."

Angela didn't respond. She just smiled. The audio recorder, of course, didn't pick that up.

Chapter 32
The Real Epiphany

The yacht docked at the Maui marina around midnight. There were several police cars, an ambulance, and a forensics van waiting for us. Angela, Zelda, and Sinclair were taken into custody. Tiffany's body was removed and placed into the back of the ambulance. The forensics team started in the main lobby and the back deck, as directed by Alana.

The remaining guests were driven to a nearby hotel. Their IDs were taken from them so they couldn't board a flight off the island. I had no idea how long they were going to be forced to stay on Maui, nor did I understand the protocol for such a thing.

Foxx and Hani were allowed to go home, as were the members of the crew. A skeleton crew remained on the yacht while the police and forensics team conducted their investigation.

Alana stayed on the yacht as well for a few more hours. She insisted on leading her team. I finally convinced her to leave around three in the morning. Despite her objections, we took a taxi to the emergency room to have her head injury examined. She said that it was a waste of time since we already knew she had a concussion and all she needed was rest. She was in no condition to drive, however, so I pretty much kidnapped her and took her to the hospital instead.

We were in the emergency room for five hours, and the various test results confirmed her concussion. The doctor's prescription? Go home and rest. I thought Alana was going to grab his stethoscope from him and wrap it around my neck to choke me. Sometimes you try to do the right thing for your loved ones, and you lose anyway.

Alana missed the next week and a half of work while she rested and allowed the swelling to go down. I stayed around the house and took care of her. We both spent most of our time out by the pool in our backyard. She stayed under the large umbrella to shade herself and read a book. She couldn't read for more than ten minutes or so before her head would start to hurt, so she eventually put the book aside and spent her time watching Maui run around the yard chasing imaginary squirrels or rabbits. The pooch either had an overactive imagination like I did, or he was simply intent on putting on a show for us, demonstrating that he was doing his due diligence in guarding every inch of the property.

What did I do? I pretty much slept for the first two days. I was exhausted after the flight back from Italy and then pretty much staying up straight for forty-eight hours on that yacht. After I got my energy back, I alternated my time between wading in the pool and sitting beside Alana under that patio umbrella while I wrote down my notes for this tale.

The big news for me, in terms of my health, came when I went to the eye doctor to have my patch removed. He examined my eye and proclaimed that I would be as good as new in a few more days. He gave me more eye drops to use, but I didn't have to wear that dreaded patch anymore. I felt such tremendous relief that I wasn't going to lose my eyesight. Of course, that didn't mean that I'd changed my feelings about selfies and those damn sticks. I still hated everything about them.

Alana got a call a few days after we departed the yacht from Piper Lane, who was one of the prosecutors at the District Attorney's office. I somewhat shivered when I heard her voice on the speaker phone since Ms. Lane was the one who tried to put me behind bars for a lifetime sentence when she thought I'd murdered a young woman on the island. Piper is not one to trifle with, and I knew our three yacht ladies were in trouble. I was somewhat disappointed to hear that I might have been terribly overconfident, though, as we listened to Piper update Alana on the case.

Piper said they were close to striking a plea deal with Angela, who had stuck with her story that it was self-defense, using the two cuts on her stomach as her proof of Tiffany's attack. Piper texted Alana a photo that Angela had taken of herself. The photo was a selfie that showed Angela standing in front of the mirror in her cabin. She was holding up her shirt and showing the two cuts. The data on the phone indicated she'd taken the photo the same night that Tiffany was killed, not the second night after Kimi had witnessed Alana arresting Zelda and Sinclair.

It went a long way in supporting her claim of self-defense. Alana and I both still believed that Angela had done it to herself. Piper claimed that the angle of the cuts indicated that they'd been made by a right-handed person. Tiffany had been right-handed. I knew Angela was a highly intelligent woman. She could have easily used her left hand to imitate being attacked by a right-handed person. Simple enough.

Piper pointed out that Tiffany had only been stabbed once, not multiple times, which is almost always the case when someone is intentionally murdered. Angela told her, as she'd told me, that she stabbed Tiffany once and then fled the lounge. She didn't realize Tiffany was actually dead until she came back when everyone else was already there. Piper asked her why she didn't go for help, and Angela told her that she didn't think anyone would believe her story, just like they didn't believe her when she claimed Reese had raped her years ago.

What did Zelda and Sinclair say? They told Piper they would testify that Angela bragged about killing Tiffany. I thought that would be enough to tip the scales, but apparently they were refusing to accept any responsibility in the murder plot, which we knew wasn't true based on the recording on Foxx's cell phone.

Piper felt they didn't come across as believable or sympathetic witnesses, especially in comparison to the woman who'd been raped in college and had raised a young boy on her own. She'd gotten a job that often took her away from her child, and then she had the indignity of the Lockwood and Calloway wedding party chartering her yacht in order to humiliate her. She said jurors would easily see themselves in her position. I couldn't disagree with that.

I told Piper that Angela had done a magnificent job of manipulating the entire thing. She knew that Zelda and Sinclair would probably betray her, so she concocted this tale of self-defense in advance and let her two former friends do the rest.

Piper agreed with us, but she said that she would be asking a jury to accept the fact that this was a highly planned event. Most jurors, according to her, wanted things simple. There was more than enough reasonable doubt, especially since there were no witnesses.

The result: Piper was going to offer Angela a deal. Plead guilty to involuntary manslaughter and serve six months in a minimum security prison. She said she was confident that Angela would accept the deal. I wasn't so sure. I thought Angela might be confident enough in her plan to roll the dice and go for a full acquittal.

Things were even more uncertain with Zelda and Sinclair. As you know, they didn't admit to killing anyone or witnessing anyone being killed in the audio recording. Alana had gotten nothing out of them after she'd arrested them and confined them to their cabin. They'd both immediately demanded to see a lawyer and had said nothing more beyond that while they were on the yacht.

They told Piper that there was no murder plot and that Angela was lying about killing Tiffany after getting into an argument with her. They claimed they certainly didn't murder Reese, and they had no idea who might have done it, outside of Angela.

Piper asked Sinclair if she'd been raped by Reese, as Angela had claimed. She denied it and only admitted to a brief consensual relationship with him. Piper brought up my question as to why Sinclair would leave a great job in New York for a not-so-great job in Chicago. Sinclair gave her the quick excuse that Zelda had crafted for me: Sinclair was the victim of a serial sexual harasser at her New York workplace, and he blackballed her in the industry, which forced her to move. It was another believable story, even though I thought it was most likely untrue.

There was really no hard evidence against Zelda and Sinclair, outside of Angela's claims that they told her they'd stabbed Reese and tossed him over the railing. Yes, I know what you're thinking. What about the bloody fingerprints under the railing? Forensics determined they did belong to Reese when they compared fingerprints on some of the items in his cabin with the prints on the railing. However, that wasn't proof that he'd sustained the injury when being murdered by Zelda and Sinclair.

Piper didn't say as much, but Alana and I could figure it out. She didn't like to lose, and she probably saw the odds of trying a successful case to be against her. Bottom line: The murder charges might get dropped. It was a depressing thought.

Although I felt like we'd more than likely brought the truth to the light, it didn't seem to matter in the end. There were really two sets of guilty people. Reese had committed rape at least twice, maybe more. Tiffany had lied to help cover it up. They both paid for those crimes with their lives. Was that sentence the correct one? I didn't think it was my place to judge, and I'm sure you'll come to your own conclusion on the matter.

Angela, Zelda, and Sinclair were also guilty. They'd all committed murder in my opinion. Would justice ever come to them? I didn't know. Maybe it wouldn't happen today, but years from now? Possibly. Either way, I didn't want to be there when karma came knocking at their doors.

There was one mystery that I solved completely, and it was because I got a confession. After staying at home for more than a week, I drove Alana up to Harry's so we could visit Foxx and also have lunch. Both Alana and I had burgers and beers. I chose a Negra Modelo, while Alana had a Corona.

A familiar face walked through our doors while we were there. It was Banks, our friendly third stew. She asked Foxx and me if we would be willing to give her temporary work at the bar as they refitted the yacht. They were changing some of the interior décor and also the name of the yacht because of all the bad publicity.

The case of the Lockwood and Calloway murders had gotten national attention, as Foxx and I had predicted. Our favorite bosun, Kurt Parrot, had leaked the story, along with several photos he'd taken of the murder scene and some of the guests. He even talked about his passionate one night stand with one of the guests and he named her, including a shot he'd taken of her without her consent, as she was getting dressed. The guy was an even bigger scumbag than we gave him credit for. Captain Piadelia finally fired him for good. I doubted Kurt really cared since I was sure the money he got for the media story was the equivalent of a full season of charters, maybe even more.

Speaking of publicity, Hani jumped on that band wagon without thinking twice. She contacted the media and informed them that she'd been the wedding planner. She also included a few photographs I'd taken of her on the yacht, as well as on the beach on the Big Island. Hani is a gorgeous woman, and the media was more than happy to showcase her photos and her inside story on what had really happened.

It was a shameless plug for herself and her business but damned if it didn't work. She got flooded with calls from brides-to-be who wanted to get married on Maui. I'm not sure why someone would specifically want a wedding planner who had inadvertently been part of the Death Cruise from Hell, but apparently they did. Hani was booked up for several months. I thought about asking her for a cut of the new business since I had been so involved on uncovering the plot, but I didn't. By the way, she never paid me a cent for my two days of photography on the yacht before people starting showing up dead. Rule number one: Never do business with family.

I asked Banks what the new name of the yacht would be. She said she didn't know but that it would be at least six months before it was ready for the next set of guests. Foxx told her that we could give her a few shifts per week, and she seemed pretty grateful for it.

As she was leaving, I asked her about the liquid laxative we found in Kurt's and Baakir's cabin. She hesitated and then said that she was the one who dumped the laxative into the guests' drinks. I asked her if it was in retaliation for Catherine's racial insult to Baakir. She said no. Her intention was to frame Kurt for the crime. Apparently, they had a romantic thing, and she was furious with Kurt when she saw him heavily flirting with Zelda. She knew what the inevitable conclusion would be, so she sprang her plot of diarrhea into action.

She laughed and said she hoped that wouldn't give Foxx and me second thoughts about hiring her. I gave her a nervous smile and replied, "Of course, not." Foxx turned to me a second after she left the bar and said there was zero chance he was ever going to call her.

Oh, I almost forgot to tell you this. Alana's new police captain came by the house to check on her recovery and congratulate her detective work on the yacht. He took one look at the large lump on her head and her swollen eye and asked her what had happened. Alana told him about the fight on the yacht and that she had to give Catherine Lockwood her word that she wouldn't press charges against Artemis in exchange for Catherine telling us what happened between Reese and Angela at Harvard.

The captain stated that although she might have made that deal with Catherine, it didn't mean that he had to honor it. We watched as he called in the arrest warrant for Artemis Lockwood. Alana and I weren't at the hotel when the Maui Police Department arrived, but it didn't take much imagination to know what Artemis' and Catherine's reactions would be.

I didn't know if Artemis would be able to get a plea deal to avoid jail time. It didn't really matter. His name and the name of all the Lockwoods were prominently mentioned in all of the media attention. The Lockwoods were done. Their good name was ruined, if it had ever been good at any point in their family's history. My, how the Lockwoods have fallen, as I like to say.

After lunch at Harry's, we returned to the house, and I went for a swim in the pool. I got out of the pool, dried off, and climbed into my shorts, t-shirt, and running shoes. I took a long, well, long for me, four-mile jog around the neighborhood.

As I ran, I thought about the case. The one thing that jumped out at me was the name of the yacht: The Epiphany. I thought it the perfect word for everything that had happened. I realized as I ran that I'd had my own epiphany of sorts.

I finally accepted the fact that I loved the thrill of the hunt. These investigations made me feel alive, even though they were always filled with death. I know that sounds weird, and maybe I don't completely understand it myself. I'd tried to escape the realization that I wanted to do these cases after Alana had been attacked in our home. I couldn't stop doing them, though. They had become a part of who I was now. For better or for worse. That was the truth of the matter. I might as well embrace it.

I finished my run and walked into my backyard. Alana was back in her chair under the umbrella, attempting to read her novel again. Maui was also back to his normal activity. He was barking at the waves and running around the yard like a mad man.

"Did you have a good run?" Alana asked.

"Yes. It was a good one, but I'm exhausted."

"Those are the best ones."

"How are you feeling?" I asked.

"Good. I feel much better."

She smiled at me. I smiled back.

Alana was good. I was good. The dog was playing. The sun was shining. What else could a guy ask for?

Did you like this book?
You can make a difference.

Reviews are the most powerful tools an author can have. As an independent author, I don't have the same financial resources as New York publishers.

Honest reviews of my books help bring them to the attention of other readers, though.

If you've enjoyed this book, I would be grateful if you could write a review.

Thank you.

Acknowledgements

Thanks to you readers for investing your time in reading my story. I hope you enjoyed it. Poe, Alana, Foxx, and Maui the dog will return.

About the Author

Robert W Stephens is the author of the **Murder on Maui** series, the **Alex Penfield** novels, and the standalone thrillers **The Drayton Diaries** and **Nature of Evil**.

You can find more about the author at www.robertwstephens.com.

Visit him on Facebook at www.facebook.com/robertwaynestephens

Also by Robert W. Stephens

Murder on Maui Mysteries

Aloha Means Goodbye (Poe Book 1)

It's Poe's first visit to Maui after numerous invitations from his best friend, Doug Foxx. The vacation quickly becomes a disaster, though, as Foxx is arrested for murdering his girlfriend, a wealthy and world-renowned artist. Can Poe prove his friend's innocence, and can he win the heart of the beautiful detective who arrested Foxx?

Wedding Day Dead (Poe Book 2)

Poe's life couldn't be better. He's just relocated to Maui, and he's dating the sexy detective, Alana Hu. Things take a turn for the worse, however, when Alana's ex-lover returns to the island. Soon, Poe's relationship with Alana falls apart, and he's dragged into another murder investigation where he's also one of the prime suspects.

Blood like the Setting Sun (Poe Book 3)

Poe now works as an unlicensed private investigator. His first client is the eighty-year-old owner of the Chambers Hotel. She's convinced someone is trying to kill her. Her main suspects? Her adult children. Poe thinks she's a bit senile, but then the lady shows up dead. Poe is thrust deep into the Chamber's family history, and it's much darker than he could have possibly imagined.

Hot Sun Cold Killer (Poe Book 4)

Poe is hired by Zoe James to discover the truth about her mother's death a decade ago. The police ruled it a suicide, but was it murder? As Poe conducts this cold case investigation, the bodies soon pile up until the killer has his sights trained on Poe. Can Poe uncover the truth before he ends up dead?

Choice to Kill (Poe Book 5)

Poe helps Alana with a case that is deeply personal to her: the murder of a childhood friend. At first, the case seems fairly straightforward. Soon, though, Poe realizes that things are not always as they seem. He's up against his most ruthless adversary to date, and he'll have to face his worst fear.

Sunset Dead (Poe Book 6)

A murdered mistress. A wrongful arrest. Can Poe and Alana take down a killer from both sides of the law? Poe can't stand to take another case after his last one nearly killed his wife. When he's accused of murdering his supposed mistress, he's forced back into a familiar role to prove his innocence. But can he do it from behind bars?

Ocean of Guilt (Poe Book 7)

A murdered bride. A suspicious groom. Can Poe catch the killer before the anchor drops? Edgar Allan "Poe" Rutherford is ready to dive back into his work as Maui's top private investigator. But before he can unpack his suitcase, his sister-in-law begs him to photograph her client's extravagant nautical wedding. Poe is confident he can handle the wedding party from hell, until he finds the bride's dead body on the top deck.

Alex Penfield Novels

Ruckman Road (Penfield Book 1)

A jogger has spotted a body on the shores of the Chesapeake Bay at Fort Monroe, but the body has vanished by the time the police arrive. The jogger tells Detective Alex Penfield that she recognized the man as Joseph Talbot, a neighbor who lived inside the stone walls of the old Army fort. Penfield goes to Talbot's house, only to discover he's placed video cameras in every room. Penfield learns the cameras were placed to capture strange occurrences in the house that Penfield eventually sees, too. Are there logical reasons for these mysterious events and the disappearance of Joseph Talbot, or is Penfield losing his mind from the trauma of a recent shooting and other dark events in his past?

Dead Rise (Penfield Book 2)

Detective Alex Penfield has to solve a murder case before it happens. His own. Retirement never suited Penfield, but there's nothing like a death omen to get you back in the saddle. A psychic colleague warns the detective that his own murder is coming. When a local death bears an eerie resemblance to the psychic's vision, he can't help but get involved. As the body count rises, the case only gets more unfathomable. Witnesses report ghastly encounters with a man sporting half a face. And the only living survivor from a deadly boat ride claims he knows who's to blame. There's only one problem: the suspect's been dead for 20 years.

Standalone Dark Thrillers

Nature of Evil

Rome, 1948. Italy reels in the aftermath of World War II. Twenty women are brutally murdered, their throats slit and their faces removed with surgical precision. Then the murders stop as abruptly as they started, and the horrifying crimes and their victims are lost to history. Now over sixty years later, the killings have begun again. This time in America. It's up to homicide detectives Marcus Carter and Angela Darden to stop the crimes, but how can they catch a serial killer who leaves no traces of evidence and no apparent motive other than the unquenchable thirst for murder?

The Drayton Diaries

He can heal people with the touch of his hand, so why does a mysterious group want Jon Drayton dead? A voice from the past sends Drayton on a desperate journey to the ruins of King's Shadow, a 17th century plantation house in Virginia that was once the home of Henry King, the wealthiest and most powerful man in North America and who has now been lost to time. There, Drayton meets the beautiful archaeologist Laura Girard, who has discovered a 400-year-old manuscript in the ruins. For Drayton, this partial journal written by a slave may somehow hold the answers to his life's mysteries.

Made in the USA
San Bernardino, CA
28 August 2018